The Truth about Eggs

Delphine Richards

ISBN 978-0-9955317-0-3
Copyright ©2016 Delphine Richards

A CIP record for this book is available from the British Library

This work is a work of fiction. Names and characters are the product
of the author's imagination and any resemblance to actual persons,
living or dead is entirely coincidental. Contains content and themes
of an adult nature.

Published by
Llyfrau Cambria Books, Wales, United Kingdom.
Cambria Books is a division of
The Cambria Publishing Co-operative Ltd

Discover our other books at: www.cambriabooks.co.uk

Dedication

To Hedd, who showed me the 'real' Devil Tree!

Acknowledgements

I owe a huge debt of gratitude to those who guided me through the sensitive topics of mental health issues, eating disorders and rape. You remain un-named here for obvious reasons, but your input has been greatly valued. Any errors in this respect will be mine alone (or, possibly, artistic licence!).

Thanks also to the friends who spurred me on to complete this book when technology tried its best to throw a spanner in the works!'

This is a prequel to 'Blessed Are The Cracked' also by Delphine Richards and contains many of the same characters, and available from Cambria Books. ISBN: 978-0-9574894-3-1

CHAPTERS

The Devil Tree Myth.

The Devil Tree that grew on the outskirts of Llanefa was a legend based on false pretences. If it had grown on almost any other piece of farmland in the area, no-one would have noticed it and the fable would never have been created.

The tree was a stunted oak growing on a hedge opposite a public footpath that linked two lanes and gave access to a riverbank for fishermen. The regular walkers who took the path had very little to look at as they passed through. The only objects to claim their attention were the fields that ran alongside the path, the horses (and sometimes sheep) that grazed on those fields, and the lone tree that struggled to survive despite being covered in ivy.

No-one remembers who had first said, 'That tree looks a bit like the shape of a devil, don't you think?' but it was probably a throw-away remark in the same way as people say 'Doesn't he look a bit like Brad Pitt?' when they see a face in the crowd.

It was true that the tree had two up-raised arm-like branches, while a third one hung down like a tail. The top of the tree was formed by a rounded cluster of small branches that were entwined in ivy – with two small, pronged branches that emerged like horns from the parasitic plant.

But Llanefa was an area with little to offer in terms of industry. Farming and its related works were the heartbeat of the community; tourism was easily the second most profitable form of income in the area. The castle ruins on one hill and standing stones on the opposite one were genuine historical features and were much visited during the spring and summer months. Unfortunately, while the visitors flocked to see the castle and standing stones, their location did not necessarily entice people into the small town to sit in the coffee shop, Mair's Cafe (10% OFF ON TUESDAY'S – a faded sign outside proclaimed), or pubs. Instead, they continued on their route towards more populated areas that have more to offer.

The Devil Tree was a different matter. Its location was nearer to the town and, as visitors had to make their way to and from it by going through the main streets and two smaller roads, many stopped for refreshments before leaving the area. So, local people decreed that the Devil Tree was a 'must see' for tourists.

The subsequent tales told by Llanefa residents in order to enthral visitors were varied and inventive. It was generally accepted that tourists should wave to the Devil Tree to avoid bad luck. Another stroke of genius was to tell people that during the month of August (the period of Lammas in particular) – it was essential to have a photograph taken with Devil Tree in the background. This would prove that the person had paid homage to the Tree and would appease the evil spirits of Lammas. This final piece of advice was a great source of amusement to those who were enjoying the combined effects of alcohol and company after a day of solitary work on the land. The men would gather together in the Red Lion, the White Horse or the Poacher's Rest and, once they had put to rights the price of milk and the upcoming rugby fixtures, they would relate amusing stories about tourists who had gone the extra mile while attempting to please the evil spirits of Lammas. Owen Bell, the landlord of the Poacher's Rest had even managed to include a Devil Tree shaped symbol on his menus and on a wooden plaque behind the bar. This had originally pissed off the proprietors of the other pubs, but Owen had said, with accuracy, that he was a relative newcomer to the area and that if no-one else had used the symbol prior to his arrival, it had to be assumed that they didn't want to. On the rare occasion that Owen was in his cups, he could be heard telling visitors that the tree had once been used to hang thieves who had been convicted of rustling cattle on the olden droves. This, he said, was the reason it had become so wizened – it had absorbed the negative vibes of so many executions!

Even more hilarious than Owen's storytelling (to those who knew better), was that the 'legend' had extended to a small un-verified feature on Wikipedia – one of several that came under the heading of 'Devil Tree'.

Someone had once asked (during a particularly lively evening to celebrate Dai the Fish's sixtieth birthday at the Red Lion) what Llanefa would do when the tree eventually became strangled by ivy and would need to be cut down. A silence had followed as everyone present had considered what other natural feature could be adapted as a Llanefa legend.

No-one considered trying to save the tree.

After all, there were no such things as evil spirits!

1. Manon.

Stealth is paramount, Manon tells herself as she shuts the front door gently for two reasons; she does not want to wake the baby and, more importantly, she does not want to disturb the people next door. She has managed to park the car quietly outside the house; it would be a shame to draw attention to herself at this stage. She corrects herself; it would not be a shame - it would be a disaster!

It is very early; the sky is still streaked with the remains of the night. It is a good time of day to travel when you want to avoid being noticed. She knows the pattern of the police shifts here. Six o'clock in the morning is the time when the shifts change over. A car carrying precious cargo, as hers has done, was less likely to be seen or stopped; officers are winding down, thinking about ending the shift and going home. She congratulates herself on her timing.

Most of Llanefa is still asleep, though she can hear the occasional car moving on the by-pass. The August Bank Holiday traffic has already started. It is an unfamiliar sound to her ears. She has not yet acclimatised to the by-pass, though it has been there for a few months. There are many things she hasn't gotten used to: living here in the Housing Association bungalow that was a council owned property when she was a child; being without a job; being without a husband. Though, if she's entirely accurate, that last part isn't true. He is still her husband; she will *never* sign the divorce papers. Let him wait, she thinks, him and his tart!

She hears the door click as she closes it. It sounds like a gun in the quiet gloominess of the hallway and she quickly glances at the baby. She is still asleep. She twitches slightly as if aware of being watched.

It's just not fair, Manon thinks. Why should careless mothers have it all when they obviously did not deserve to. I wouldn't have let this baby out of my sight if she had been mine, she thinks. But she *is* mine now!

I'm going to call her Gwenllian, she decides. She is not a fan of the modern trend of naming babies after the Kylies and Harpers and Taylors of the world. Why would anyone name a little girl after a common celebrity when they could name her after an ancient princess who defended her people against all-comers?

She pushes the buggy along the narrow hallway. It is an expensive buggy. Everything about this baby smacks of money, success, a happy marriage. There is a fluffy pink toy lying next to her – a rabbit with *'Daddy's Little Princess'* embroidered on the front of its tee-shirt. There is a small carrier at the front of the buggy. She checks inside it for the umpteenth time. It contains the sort of items mothers need to have with them when they take their babies out for the day. Anything else she needs is right here in the house. She has planned ahead.

She parks the buggy in the room she thinks of as the 'nursery'. Everything is perfect for a baby. She imagines that this house has waited for a baby. *She* has certainly waited for a baby! She feels a little thrill of pleasure. This house feels like home for the first time since she returned to Llanefa. She yawns. It has been a long journey and she has not had her quota of sleep – excitement and anxiety have eaten into her resting time. The baby is still sleeping so she decides to let her rest in the buggy while she makes the most of the opportunity by catching a nap herself.

She goes into her bedroom and changes into lightweight pyjamas – it is too hot to wear anything, but it doesn't *feel* right to sleep naked while she has a baby in the house. She gets into bed but sleep suddenly deserts her.

Imagination kicks in with scenarios of child-stealing burglars, kidnappers – she realises how easily it could happen.

She gets out of bed and goes to the nursery. She watches the baby for another moment. Gwenllian makes sucking movements with her mouth before settling into a sulky-looking pout. I'm going to have trouble with you when you're older, she thinks. She smiles. Teenage years will be a challenge, but one she is already relishing. She pushes the buggy out through the nursery doorway, carefully avoiding the door frame, and glides it into her own bedroom. She parks it once more. She glances down at Gwenllian. She is breathing with easy little breaths, a picture of contentment.

She gets back into her own bed. She can still hear the comforting rhythm of Gwenllian's breathing. It acts like a sedative and she drifts into sleep where she dreams of sitting on a blanket in the park while the baby crawls beside her.

2. Tegwyn.

As he pulled his black suit out of the wardrobe, it occurred to DCI Tegwyn Prydderch that he had been to too many funerals – many of them for people he had never even met. It was expected of senior police officers to attend the funerals of murder victims or those who had been killed as a result of a natural disaster that had been subject to a police enquiry. Though, this present one fitted into neither of those categories.

He allowed his attention to wander and gazed out through his bedroom window. Tegwyn could see his neighbour's caravan being towed out onto the roadway. He grabbed his black tie from the depths of the wardrobe and held his breath as, in his peripheral vision, he caught sight the caravan's white side panels barely miss the stone pillars of the gateway. He continued to watch while Edgar painfully manoeuvred the caravan into what he must have believed was a roadside position, though the rear end jutted out over the centre of the road. It was just as well they lived in a cul-de-sac with only residents' traffic, thought Tegwyn. He hoped he would have enough room to drive by if the caravan was still there in half an hour. He watched while Edgar got out of the car and carefully straightened the trouser-legs of a dark suit. It dawned on Tegwyn that Edgar must also be going to the funeral, though he was unaware that Edgar had known Tommy Elfyn well enough to want to pay his respects.

Tegwyn returned to the full length mirror as he knotted his tie and picked up his black jacket. He glanced at his shoes; they shone wetly and reflected the sunshine coming in through the bedroom window.

He ran a hand over his head, flattening his hair into submission once again.

Downstairs, the doorbell rang and he heard Gwenda's voice as she opened the door. Marg, Edgar's wife, replied to her though Tegwyn could not make out what she was saying.

He went downstairs and saw both women in the kitchen.

'Marg was just asking if the caravan would be in your way for an hour or so,' Gwenda said, 'but it'll be fine there, won't it?'

'We've got it ready to go and Edgar thought we could save time if we brought it out now so that when he comes back from the funeral, we can head straight off,' Marg said.

'But you'll have to unhitch the car!' said Gwenda. She looked at Tegwyn, 'Wouldn't it be easier if he went with you? Save a lot of trouble.'

Tegwyn winced.

'That is so kind of you, Mr Prydderch,' said Marg, looking at Tegwyn (even though he had not said a word!), 'It would be easier.'

Tegwyn flinched at the habitual use of the formal 'Mr Prydderch'.

'As long as Edgar doesn't mind that I have to pop into the police station on the way,' said Tegwyn in a desperate attempt to dissuade her.

'I'll go and tell him,' Marg said, 'and I can get the rest of the stuff ready. Oh, and Watkin needs a tidy-up and I need to put his food in...'

Tegwyn looked at Gwenda with a subtle quizzical lift of his eyebrows.

'New puppy,' she mouthed back at him.

By the time Tegwyn had started the car engine, Edgar appeared, looking awkward in his suit.

He opened the car door without further invitation.

9

'Don't know why I didn't think about you going as well,' he said as he thumped into the passenger seat.

'Didn't realise you knew Tommy,' Tegwyn said.

'Bowls club,' Edgar replied, 'Poor soul. Not even sixty. That's no age these days. Very sudden, wasn't it?'

Tegwyn made a noise which suggested agreement. He felt unwilling to be drawn into meaningful conversation. Since Edgar and Marg had moved into the cul-de-sac three years previously, they had been ideal neighbours, but Tegwyn had always felt that they tried too hard to integrate into the community. He had the impression that they were permanently on their best behaviour with him. Their constant use of 'Mr Prydderch' as a greeting irritated him immensely.

'Was he a personal friend of yours?' asked Edgar.

'Not really. He helped out a lot with the charitable fund raising we did from time to time.'

'Aah,', said Edgar, as if a great question had been answered wisely.

'Unusual, this Gentlemen Only funeral,' Tegwyn suggested, 'Quite an old fashioned way of doing things.'

Edgar opened his mouth to say something then closed it again.

Tegwyn guessed he had been about to say 'Even in Llanefa,' but good manners had intervened. That was the thing with Edgar and Marg – they never seemed to drop their guard. Tegwyn had a secret wish to be walking past Edgar's garden at the very moment he hit his thumb with a hammer or stood on the lawn rake. He knew that he would take great delight in hearing Edgar yell out, 'Fucking *bastard* thing!' He half smiled to himself and turned it into a clearing of the throat.

'Where are you off to in the caravan?' he asked. (He hated the 'Are you going anywhere nice?' nonsense. What did the questioner expect - 'No, we're going somewhere *really* foul?).

10

'Tenby,' said Edgar, 'Same place every year. We even get pretty close to the same pitch every year.'

Tegwyn felt a wave of panic engulf him. He couldn't imagine anything as boring as going to the same holiday destination year after year. And in a caravan! Tegwyn hated caravans. He could not understand why people like Edgar, who had a large, four-bedroomed house, would want to spend a fortnight in a metal box!

Tegwyn turned the car into the street where the police station was situated. He kept a look out for traffic coming the wrong way. The new by-pass was confusing to those who had been long-term Llanefa residents; he fully expected to see someone driving the wrong way down the one-way system that filtered traffic passed the station.

Llanefa police station was a relatively small building that housed some twenty-five uniformed officers and a handful of CID detectives who were generally under-worked. He turned into the police station car-park, noting that DS Alun James's car was in the space reserved for senior officers. He could see a small flurry of activity through the window at the front desk. Someone had obviously spotted him driving in. Llanefa was not Tegwyn's regular station. He had his main office in the West Wales Constabulary headquarters at Carmarthen.

He parked the car.

'I won't be long,' he told Edgar as he got out.

'That's fine,' he said 'take as long as you need.'

Tegwyn walked away and entered the building. He walked down the narrow hallway and past the glass hatch that served as a contact point for the public. He had a key that would have let him into the back of the building – a common practice for him if he had been called out during the night – but, that route took him past the block of three cells and their interminable smell of liquor, farts and piss despite the best attempts of the two station cleaners.

'Morning, sir,' PC Gareth Davies called out from behind the front desk, 'Off to the funeral?'

'Yes, in a few minutes,' he replied, 'Just having a look at what's been happening before I head off.'

He walked through into the CID Office where DS Alun James and Jamie Bowen were drinking tea. Jamie leapt to his feet.

'Tea, sir?'

'Not for me, thanks. Don't let me stop you though!'

Jamie's pale complexion coloured a little.

Alun James reached out to some recently printed out bulletin papers on his desk, 'Not much to concern us here, boss. Just the usual stuff from Headquarters about the theft of scrap metal... No mention of them thinking of closing down Llanefa CID office...'

'I'm sure they'll let us all know if it's going to happen,' replied Tegwyn, reluctant to pursue this particular topic. He knew what the general feeling was at Headquarters. As Detective Chief Inspector he had been included in meetings where it had been discussed. Tegwyn also knew that it was a choice between closing Llanefa CID or that of one of the other small towns within the Force area, but he knew better than to discuss it with Alun James.

'I'm on call all weekend,' Tegwyn said, 'Anything I need to know about?'

'Just a shoplifter this morning. Took a bottle of vodka from CutCost. She's been processed and bailed. Usual stuff. Jamie's been dealing with it.'

'Good,' he picked up the bulletin, 'I see they've sent us a bulletin about that missing baby in Herefordshire. I heard it on Sky News this morning...'

He read the details while Alun demonstrated his vigilance by adding what he knew.

'Six-month old baby girl. Believed taken by her father. Doesn't have any connections with Llanefa, it's just a general bulletin. Uniform boys are doing plenty of routine car stops, but I think it says that he's probably gone abroad... I saw it on Sky News, too. Some lucky Herefordshire CID officer will probably be sent to the father's last known address in Spain!'

'Hmm,' Tegwyn read, 'Seems he's never been allowed access to the child... they'd broken up before the baby was born. Well, pass it on to the next shift at two o'clock. Can't be too complacent.'

Tegwyn turned to Jamie, 'How's the studying for the sergeant's exam coming along?'

Jamie blushed again. Tegwyn marvelled at the fact that he was so easily embarrassed when he was such a good copper.

Before Jamie could answer, Sergeant Dai Morris came in with a folder in his hand.

'Until they start doing the sergeant's exam in primary school question form, we won't hold our breath for Jamie! What's this I hear that they're closing down Llanefa CID, sir?'

Dai Morris was close to retirement, a fairly embittered character who believed that the world owed him a favour and was extremely opposed to any change that would upset his comfortable routine. His delight at the thought of CID officers' inconvenience was obvious.

'Well, maybe not *just* CID...' Tegwyn said, a streak of devilment taking over. 'You never know, even *you* could be moved to Outer Pengolau by the end of the year!'

Dai went pale. He handed over the folder to Alun.

'Right, things to do,' said Dai, 'Got to sort out traffic control for Tommy Elfyn's funeral. Then there's the Young Farmers Club show and the bloody travelling funfair. Some of us have got work to do. You know the truth about eggs!'

Tegwyn rolled his eyes at Alun. Dai and his sayings were legendary in Llanefa police station – mainly because they never made any sense! His usual ploy was to trot out

13

some nonsensical saying until someone asked him what it meant. Only after he had publicly humiliated the questioner did he move on to another phrase. This particular gem had been Dai's favourite for about two weeks. Tegwyn had an inkling that it was a phrase he had read in connection with an anti-battery farming campaign, but he was certain that Dai's take on it would have a far crueller or basic slant. Luckily, so far, no-one had taken the bait.

Jamie's facial expression began to take on the shape of a question being formed.

Don't ask him what it means, Tegwyn thought, just don't! Some telepathic force must have intervened because Jamie's face relaxed again.

Tegwyn continued to read briefly through some more reports until he remembered Edgar waiting in his car. He put the documents down.

'See you later – or, hopefully, not!' he said to Alun before following Dai's route.

Passing through the narrow passageway that linked the offices, Tegwyn could hear Dai ranting to Gareth Davies.

'Looks like the fucking Donkeys are staying for a bit longer,' he said. Dai always referred to the CID as 'Donkeys' – an apt description in his opinion – as well as the opportunity to use the letter D to the detriment of the Department, 'Wonder what we've done to deserve them sticking in here like shit to a blanket!'

Gareth muttered some non-committal reply.

'There's only one thing worse than a CI Donkey and that's several Donkeys,' he continued, 'Still, I suppose a high ranking Donkey or a bloody Donk-ess would be even worse than...'

Gareth broke into a volley of artificial coughing and Tegwyn knew he had been spotted through the glass hatch.

He decided to let it go. Dai's vitriol was well known and his list of Most Hated was a long and eclectic one. How Dai's wife had ever put up with him was a miracle, Tegwyn thought. Every time he heard of a domestic assault where the husband had been seriously injured, he always expected to hear that it had been Dai Morris's wife who had finally had enough. Dai's daughters had long flown the nest as soon as an opportunity had arisen and Tegwyn had often wondered how long it would be before Mrs Morris followed suit.

Tegwyn went back out to the car where Edgar was waiting patiently with the car door open – it was already too hot for comfort.

'Lot of cars gone by with people wearing black ties,' he informed Tegwyn.

'Be a big funeral, I expect. He was quite involved in so many things.'

'I'm surprised that the Young Farmers show is still going on. With Tommy's connections, I thought they would have cancelled it as a mark of respect,' Edgar remarked.

'They're starting the show later than scheduled. Then the men can go on there after the funeral. There's a bar so I suppose it will be like some kind of wake.' Tegwyn said.

Tegwyn felt some sympathy for those who would be on duty throughout the day; the combination of alcohol and stories about the departed would provide plenty of activity for the uniformed officers.

He pictured the scene; elderly farmers propping up the bar while the youngsters tried to out-do them, alcohol fuelled friendships re-affirmed while others fell apart; he sighed with relief that his career was at a stage where he would not need to be involved with sorting it out.

Edgar's voice broke into his thoughts.

'Salt of the earth that man. Help anyone. Strong too. I've seen him helping to move furniture for someone.'

Tegwyn glanced across and saw that he was looking at the roadside where a thickset man carrying a backpack was walking with a strange, hurried gait. A lurcher loped along beside him.

Tegwyn had a moment's surprise. Those who had always lived in Llanefa called Bara a 'boy', though he was now about forty years old, Tegwyn thought. But Edgar was right. Bara was a man and a powerfully built one at that. He was striding along the roadway with his head and neck jutted out while the dog trotted alongside. It was obvious to anyone who saw him that Bara had learning difficulties – most Llanefa people had known him since he had been a small child and those same people regarded him with a cautious fondness.

'Just as well there's no harm in him, though, is there? No-one would want to tangle with him!' said Edgar.

'Hmm,' said Tegwyn. He was never convinced that anyone was 'harmless'. He had seen too many people acting out of character during his career. Even Bara, in recent times, seemed to have developed an edge to his character. Tegwyn couldn't put his finger on it, but something had changed. He dreaded to think what would happen when Bara's elderly parents died and he would need a different regime of care.

'Funny name – Bah-rah,' said Edgar, 'A Welsh name, I suppose?'

'Nickname,' replied Tegwyn. He had no intention of explaining that the unkind name was the Welsh word for 'bread' and that Bara had been given it as a shortened version of 'in with the bread, out with the buns' to explain his mental shortcomings.

As they passed Bara, Tegwyn was aware of two teenage girls who walked ahead of him. One was wearing tight-fitting jodhpurs and carried a bag and riding hat; the other was taller – dressed in baggy jeans and oversized T-shirt. She also carried a large leather bag slung over her shoulder. Tegwyn felt a small pulse of alarm as one of the girls glanced nervously back over her shoulder at Bara. He checked the driver's mirror as they left the walkers behind.

Edgar loosened his tie slightly - a combination of the heat and his unfamiliarity with such an item of clothing. Tegwyn turned the air conditioning up. Over the years, he had discovered the fact that rain was the best policeman. Blazing sunshine was a public hazard, he thought. He recalled plenty of instances, even before he joined the police force, where high weather temperatures had accompanied serious assaults. He was no scientist, but in his opinion, heat did strange things to a person's mind.

He carried on driving in the direction of the funeral; he had no way of knowing the gravity of the incidents that awaited him within the next twenty-four hours, but his internal 'policeman's radar' had started to beep an alarm.

3. Natalie.

In her seventeen and a half years, Natalie had never had to keep such a big secret. Or as many smaller ones – which were linked to the main one. As a child and even as a younger teenager, secrets had been fun – meant to be shared with friends – but the present one was like a large bag of sand pressing on her head. She had to keep it to herself but it was not easy; there seemed to be people always on the lookout for clues. She considered sharing one of the smaller secrets with a friend, but she could see that it would lead to more questions until the whole thing was out in the open. Natalie could not even bear to think of her shame if that happened!

As they walked along the road towards Llanefa YFC Show, Natalie and her best friend, Llinos, strode out in silence. Relationships were like some fucked-up game of Tetris, Llinos thought as she glanced quickly at Natalie. You thought you knew what was coming and how to deal with it, but that was the moment you discovered that you had no idea where the shapes were going. Growing up had been an eventful journey in itself, but the jungle of relationships had left her as clueless as a sleepwalker. She walked in time to Natalie's step. Each footfall matched her thoughts, 'Why, why, why?' Another noise from behind made her pay attention.

'That weirdo is still behind us,' Llinos said, looking over her shoulder at a man and a dog who appeared to be following them.

Natalie pretended to sweep her hair back and turned her head.

'He's probably just walking to the show. Like us,' she replied. (Natalie could always be expected to provide logical responses, though she stepped up her pace a little).

'He gives me the creeps. And that poor dog looks as if it's suffering in the heat.' Llinos always noticed animal related issues – it was one of the reasons she wanted to become a vet.

'He does look weird, but I think he's ok as long as we leave him alone. It's just a medical thing, the way he looks...' Natalie said kindly.

'Oh lush!' said Llinos. 'You'll be dealing with people like that when you're a doctor!'

The opportunity to tease Natalie was a welcome respite from the constant wondering what was wrong.

Natalie grinned, 'While you'll be tending to shitty calves and dogs with worms! Actually, you'll have dog owners like him coming to your surgery. Looking down your shirt when you're examining the dog! I will be *so* happy for you!'

'Bitch!' Llinos said, laughing. 'Anyway, we might both mess up A Levels this year and we'll end up selling the Big Issue in Cardiff and living in a shop doorway!'

The sound of panting made them look around. Bara was walking quickly and had caught them up. There were beads of sweat on his face and the dog's mouth was open and its tongue was showing as it panted slightly.

The girls drew together to one side of the road. Bara strode past without a glance. The smell of fresh sweat made them wrinkle their noses. They saw that he carried a backpack as usual. Bara was the unofficial 'pest controller' for Llanefa farmers. The rumour around school was that he cut off the body parts of the rabbits and rats he killed and kept them in the backpack. Both girls knew that this was scaremongering on the part of the sixth form boys, but nevertheless, they both peered intently at the backpack. All that could be seen was a bottle of perfumed anti-bacterial hand gel and the tines of a dismantled fishing rod.

Llinos swapped the carrier bag and riding hat into her other hand, 'I bet there's something minging in that backpack,' she said.

'Like what you've got in there, you mean?' Natalie teased, 'Give me the bag to carry.'

'But you've already got your own bag to carry,' Llinos protested.

'No problem. I haven't got to save my energy today like you have,' Natalie said with a mischievous grin.

Llinos handed the bag over. It contained clean jodhpurs, jacket and boots ready for the show. Just then, a single beep from Natalie's pocket signalled a mobile phone message. She dug it out, gave it a disgusted glance, then pressed 'Delete' before putting it back in her jeans pocket.

'Jack?' Llinos asked.

'Hit-the-road-Jack. That's his new name,' she said with finality. The conversation was over.

Llinos thought about new ways she could ask about what had happened between them, but all her mind offered her had already been asked – and no answer had resulted from it.

The girls had been friends throughout secondary school and had shared the most intimate details of each other's lives – from the mysterious and worrying developments of their bodies as they went through puberty right through the ritual of boyfriends and loss of virginity. But Llinos was perplexed by this present silence. Natalie and Jack had been an item for nearly a year – a real love-job, they had all called it in school. Then, a few months ago – it was suddenly all over and Natalie refused to talk about it.

'Maybe you should change your mobile number,' Llinos suggested, 'if he's being a pain in the arse.'

'Or maybe he should change where he lives,' Natalie retorted, 'like Jupiter or somewhere.'

'So, what has he done, Nat?' Llinos almost wailed in frustration. 'Why won't you talk to me about it?'

'He's not worth wasting the conversation,' Natalie said. 'It's over. I'm happy with that. I just want the wanker to leave me alone!'

They continued to walk along. Llinos noticed that Natalie's pace had increased – a sure sign of temper in someone who was normally so placid. Llinos was certain that Jack had not been messing about with anyone else. She would have heard. School gossip would have floated such a fact to the surface – even though it was the summer holidays. They all met up regularly and there had been an even bigger gathering at the recent AS exam results. And yet, it was unusual that no snippets of information had appeared. Everyone else seemed to accept that Jack and Natalie had split up – a simple fact of teenage life, but Llinos was convinced that there was more to it than that. The fact that Natalie was seething with rage was obvious; that made the situation more than just a simple parting of the ways. It was also obvious that Natalie had dumped Jack and not the other way around. Llinos remembered other boyfriends who had dumped Nat, as well as the opposite scenario. Both instances had been discussed and dissected by the girls. Whatever had happened in the past had been talked about – even the really embarrassing stuff. What possible action could Jack have taken to result in the present shut-down of information?

Meanwhile, Natalie's pace was getting ever faster.

'God! Slow down!' Llinos complained. 'I've got to ride three horses today. My legs will be wrecked before we even get there!'

Natalie grinned, her temper dissolved, 'And you've got an evening of partying as well! What a hard life! I feel so sorry for you!'

'Now I bet you're sorry you swapped the babysitting with me!'

'No probs. It's not as if I was doing anything else tonight. Anyway, I'd probably be too weak to party because of laughing after I watch you fall off later!'

'Yeah, thanks for that,' Llinos said drily. 'Especially as it's your fault that I got volunteered in the first place...'

A car pulled up beside them.

'Trish!' exclaimed Llinos, as she realised it was her mother's best friend, 'Are you going to the show?'

'No way, babes! What do I want to see cows and sheep and farmers for? I see enough of them every day around here. Your mother's still working and she sent me a text to see if I could give you a lift. I went to the house but you'd obviously left! Get in! I'll drop you off quickly at the show field.'

As the girls climbed into the car, another beep came from Natalie's phone. They exchanged quick glances before Natalie repeated her earlier action.

Natalie sat in the back watching the hedgerows flow past. Jack was pissing her off, she thought. Big time! His constant texting was getting to her. She had dumped him months ago; why couldn't he accept it? His pretending to not know why she had dumped him was even more annoying. What if he really didn't know the reason, an inner, doubting voice asked? The thought produced a blush. She couldn't bring herself to tell him even if the stupid arse had not realised what he had done wrong, she admitted privately. She made herself angry again; it was the only way she knew to avoid tears of humiliation.

'I might come over with your mother to watch you later,' Trish said to them, 'They've delayed the start of the show because of the funeral of that ex-councillor, so I won't miss anything.'

Llinos rolled her eyes.

'You really don't have to. It's no biggie. I'll probably fall off and make an idiot of myself anyway. They only asked me because there was no-one else that could do it...'

Trish looked worried. 'Just be careful.'

'Yeah, whatever.'

Trish looked in the driver's mirror, 'I thought you were the competitive horse-rider, Natalie?' she asked.

'No thanks! Horse-riding was a passing phase. I don't feel safe anymore. That's why I swapped with Llinos. Instead, I get to look after four-year old twins tonight and for two whole days! Good deal, eh?'

'As far as I'm concerned, looking after a dozen pythons would be a better deal than riding a horse! Dangerous animals with no brain!' Trish said with a shudder.

'You should try riding again, Nat. Build up your confidence,' said Llinos, 'Mike and Sarah said I could go and ride their horses anytime. Sarah won't ride at all while she's pregnant and she said they could do with some exercise. You could come with me. It'll be fun.'

'Uh-uh – I just know I'll fall off! Horses just scare me now. No more riding for me.'

Llinos had half turned around in her seat and was perplexed to see that Natalie's face had gone red. She sighed. It was no use trying to change her mind. In the great scheme of things, Llinos didn't really mind, but she harboured the hope that Natalie would have a change of heart so that she would be spared days like today. Llinos was not a natural in the saddle.

The thing that Llinos had failed to understand was that Natalie had loved horse-riding and had easily been the better rider of the two of them. A loss of confidence was common – usually after a fall or near-fall – but Llinos was unaware that either of those incidents had happened. But, suddenly, before the start of the summer holidays, Natalie had said that she would not be riding anymore; that it scared her. It was the sort of thing that happened,

Llinos knew, but her instinct told her there was something not right in Natalie's decision. But, the way Natalie had come straight out and told Sarah that she would not be able to ride her horses at any shows as she had lost her confidence was very much out of character.

The car slowed down.

'If I drop you off here, I won't have to pay to go into the show field,' Trish said, steering the car to the side of the road.

They stopped and the girls got out.

With further safety commands from Trish, they slammed the doors and went into the showground.

Llanefa YFC Show was held on the grounds of a hosting farm. The usual routine was to rotate the hosting farm in a three year cycle – a means of sharing the inconvenience of lost grazing due to the show field being trampled by visitors and cars. A travelling fun-fair that spent a week at the show venue also added to the amount of land that could not be used until the ground had recovered. This time it was the turn of Cwm Isaf Farm, conveniently situated at the edge of the town and although not close to the by-pass, the road to it was straight and wide – an ideal venue for visitors who could locate it easily.

The field was a scene of great activity with horse trailers and livestock carriers moving carefully to their chosen parking place. Even though the start of the show had been delayed until after the funeral, there was plenty to do beforehand. Exhibitors had animals to unload and place in pens; some of the volunteer stewards were already there and directing people to the right location. The drivers of the ice-cream and hot-dog vans were waiting for instruction as to where they could be parked. In two large marquees, the bar and food areas were being prepared. A man was wheeling plastic containers of ice into the bar tent. At the other side of the field, a lorry was unhitching the last of the two porta-toilet trailers. The fairground at the far end of the field was sat in silence and no obvious movement could be seen.

'Oh shit! Why did I let myself be talked into this?' wailed Llinos, 'I need a pee. Do you have some tissue in your bag? Just in case they don't have it in the porta-loo...'

Natalie opened her bag and dug around for a new packet of tissues while Llinos looked on in disbelief. The usual scrunched up foil chocolate wrappers glinted as the sunlight penetrated the innards of the bag – Natalie was a constant provider (and eater!) of sweets and chocolates. But next to it were the strangest items Llinos had ever seen in anyone's bag!

'You've got a jar of peanut butter in your bag!' she said.

Natalie half closed her bag and gave the tissue to Llinos.

'And a spoon,' she added incredulously.

'Yeah,' Natalie said, too casually, 'I love peanut butter.'

Llinos turned away and said no more, but her brain once again confirmed that she was right to worry about Natalie.

4. Anna.

The morning before Anna was raped started so well for her.

She had the house to herself for the Bank Holiday weekend; her parents had just driven away to make their annual visit to a great-uncle who lived in North Wales. As a child, she had always accompanied them, but now she sighed with relief as she shut the gate to the driveway.

She was still wearing her dressing gown and pyjamas. It felt as though she was on holiday, though nothing could be further from the truth. She made a mental note of her timetable for the day. She intended to have a long shower, coffee and a read of her 'Film-maker' magazine before she started her working day. It was to be a particularly long working day; firstly, a woman was bringing her dog for a minor trim and nail clipping at the temporary grooming salon in the garden; then she had the Llanefa YFC Show to attend, where she was serving in the Bar and Refreshments tent.

She had some foot therapy cream in her dressing table drawer. If she had time after trimming the dog and having a second shower, she thought, maybe she would use it and also paint her toenails before getting ready for the show. The fact that it was going to be a long day did not worry her - show days always dragged on. But, looking on the bright side, they were always profitable and Anna was saving up. She had told her parents that she was saving for a car. She told them that she had no objection to borrowing her father's car (and it was freely available on most occasions) but she felt that the time had come to be more independent. By degrees, she was acclimatising her parents to the thought that she needed to be less under their control. She felt a twinge of guilt. It wasn't just her parents. Llanefa stifled her too; she wanted to be somewhere else. She had been spending two days a week at a college in Carmarthen during the past academic year, although it meant she had to come home every night – her mother would not hear of her staying away for one night a week when there was a regular bus to Llanefa every evening. She was training to be a Canine Beautician. This career had been chosen for her by her mother. While her school classmates had gone on to various universities and careers after their A Levels, Anna's parents had baulked at the prospect of her moving away and had persuaded her that clipping and bathing pet dogs was a profitable career. Even more convenient, they said, was the fact that she could use a large outbuilding in the garden to carry out the work. Her father had renovated and adapted the building so that she had everything she needed in readiness for her completed training. It would be good practice for her, they had suggested, to take in friends' dogs for clipping in the meantime. Then, when she was fully trained, they would apply to the council for planning permission to use the building as an official grooming parlour. Her future had been mapped out for her; it was obvious to Anna that they depended far too much on her.

Since her earliest memories, Anna had always known that she was cherished. Her parents were old-fashioned in a sweet kind of way, but their perception of her was straight out of the 1950s. She had once seen a television programme about people who lived as though they were still in an earlier decade – no electricity, old fashioned clothes, some kind of stew for dinner every evening; she thought that her parents were only a few degrees away from that image. She had heard them lamenting the fact that they couldn't get 'the top of the milk' or Green Shield Stamps anymore to their nearest neighbour, who was in

27

his eighties. Anna had no idea what the 'top of the milk' was – and had no desire to know, but had been certain that it would be something that had no useful purpose in modern-day living.

She couldn't begin to remember how many times she had been paraded in front of her parents' friends as a young child.

'So this is Anna,' the friends would say, 'hasn't she grown. Before you know it, she'll be planning her wedding.'

Her mother's face would collapse slightly.

'Anna's going to stay at home to look after us when we're old,' Anna's mother would say, 'All this time we wanted a little girl.'

Anna was their fifth child, a cause for celebration after four robust boys. It wasn't fair, Anna thought, that the boys had grown up with her parents' attitude making allowances for them.

When David had been caught trying to climb in through a distant neighbour's window late one night and had been arrested, their mother had dismissed it as the actions of a foolish youth who'd had too much to drink. It had been an accurate assessment, but Anna dreaded to think what would have happened if it had been *her* who had been arrested! When Steven had crashed his car into the fence around the Garden Centre, they had naturally been relieved that he was generally unhurt, but the facts surrounding his excessive speed had been overlooked by their mother.

'Oh, you know what boys are like!' she would say with a wave of her hand, 'Full of mischief!' and that would be the end of the subject. Anna could not believe that her mother, who was, for God's sake, only the same age as Madonna, could be so old fashioned about what was acceptable for boys but not for girls!

But, while her brothers had their own distractions, Anna was fascinated by the world of film and theatre. All aspects of that magical territory attracted her – from theatre make-up to stage equipment and sound effects. She had a brief period of wanting to be an actor before deciding that being a director or producer held more appeal for her. Despite her secretly chosen path, Anna could have been a talented actor. She always kept her feelings to herself and reacted to people in the way she thought they wanted. In reality, she felt superior to many of those she saw on a daily basis, gauging them shallow and somewhat stupid. The people she had grown up with in Llanefa had closed minds, in her estimation. Hardly any of them had heard of Oscar nominated directors and were completely ignorant of locations that had been film-sets for famous productions. The few school friends that had shown any interest in such matters had moved away to study or work, leaving Anna in a quagmire of frustration and disdain.

Anna had attempted to go out with some of her new college friends on the occasional weekend, but her mother had reacted with a smooth dominance.

'Whatever do you want to go out with them tonight for? You'll be seeing them again on Monday! Anyway, you knew I wanted help to change all the curtains ready to go to the cleaners. The arthritis in my hands...'

Anna had tried to feel anger at her parents but was never able to make it last. The truth was that they were happy to provide her with anything she wanted – as long as it kept her in their house. The list of wants had been a long one and Anna was surrounded by the latest model laptop computers, iPad, mobile phone, Sky television and anything else that could be kept at home. It had even been half-suggested that if Anna ever *did* want to get married (this was voiced in the same way as if it was a suggestion that there *was* human life on other planets), there was plenty of room in their house for the couple to live in – a suggestion that had made Anna's heart race in panic.

The new car was another source of debate. Her mother could not understand, she said, why Anna needed a car of her own when she could use her father's any time she wanted. Why go to all the expense? Not only would her father lend her his car, but she could also call upon any of her brothers who, despite having homes of their own, would always help out if she needed to be driven somewhere. But Anna had been making an effort to be seen reading the car advertisements in the Llanefa Guardian. She told her mother that she knew the sort of price she would have to pay for the kind of car she wanted. It was the goal she was aiming for, she said, while trying to quash her misgivings for lying to them. Her secret goal (that she dared not tell them about yet) was going to take a while to save the necessary amount. The real aim was the possibility of moving to Newport – nearly two hours away – where the chance of working at a studio that made theatre and television props was a real possibility. A girl in college with her had told her about it - her uncle held a senior post there. It was also no coincidence that a renowned School of Film was situated in Newport and Anna had an even greater hope that she would eventually gain a place there.

The girl in college with Anna had told her that she could arrange for her to have an interview at any time if she was interested in a studio job and Anna found herself in the terrifying position of trying to find a way to tell her parents she intended moving away. She frequently brought up the topic of how interesting she found background images and props in film and on television. Her parents had done no more than acknowledge her comments before resuming their perusal of the Lakeland catalogue and the sports page of the daily paper respectively.

30

Meanwhile, she worked at various casual jobs in Llanefa whenever possible so that she had a financial cushion ready if, as she suspected, her parents refused to help. Today's job at Llanefa YFC Show was part of that fund raising attempt. The bar at Llanefa YFC Show was run by Owen Bell. His team of helpers included students and casual staff who needed extra pocket money. He had been happy to have Anna on the team as she had been a regular help in the food tent on previous years and had coped well with the long day. Since she had been old enough to work in an environment that sold alcohol, he had also hired her in the Poacher's when weddings or special celebrations warranted additional staff. He had offered the girl a more regular job at the Poacher's but her father had mentioned to him that they would prefer if Anna only helped out at special occasions. Owen thought this an unhealthy view as it was obvious that they disapproved of her making too many close friendships with other staff. There was no chance of chatting and making new friends at the YFC show, he thought, the place would be positively throbbing with activity. The prospect of the full till at the end of the day gave him a small jolt of happiness. And with an attractive girl like Anna behind the bar, he reasoned, he would never be short of customers. As well as being pretty and with a nice figure, (Owen admitted to himself that he had noticed), she was an approachable character who was able to react in exactly the right way to each punter. He found it hard to believe that she had not left Llanefa to go away to college. He had even mentioned it to her once, but she had just shrugged and grinned, leaving Owen with no answer at all. He gave it no further thought. As far as he was concerned, it was his good fortune that she was available for occasional work.

Anna's parents lived at the edge of Llanefa in what had originally been a farm labourer's cottage. It was surrounded by fields with some similar scattered properties out of sight. Their house was the last one before the country lane wound into narrow bends and whose adjoining fields were inhabited by animals only. About two hundred yards along was a lay-by parking area and the public footpath which ran past the Devil Tree; the lay-by and path were used mainly by fishermen as it accessed a favoured fishing spot. For those who did not want to go fishing, the path continued on until it reached another minor road and a junction, where nothing of note could be seen apart from another farm labourer's cottage and a bus-stop before the larger road opened up into a straight stretch that passed the entrance to the show field.

The most logical route for Anna to take was via the public footpath; it saved a mile of walking around the roadway and, with her parents on their way to visit a relative, the possibility of a lift from her father was out of the question. Anna was familiar with the public footpath. She had played there when she was younger and had used the path regularly in the past year when she had gone to the bus stop to catch the bus to college. Prior to that, she had used the same route daily to catch the bus to school.

As the fields were inhabited by horses and, occasionally, sheep, the land owner had erected a small fence to separate them from anyone who passed through. The sheep ignored all walkers, apart from shying away in great panic if they were grazing close to the fence when someone walked by. The horses were far more curious and would usually amble up to see if the passer-by had anything edible for them. Of the six or so horses present, most were dark coloured with white facial markings but one was white all over. He was a smaller pony and was always the one who followed walkers along the fence even though he was rarely rewarded for it. Anna was one of few people who *did* give the pony something to eat. She would stoop and pull a handful of grass from the side of the path and offer it to the animal – who usually munched at it as though he had not been fed for weeks!

It was in the second of the two fields that the Devil Tree grew; its stunted appearance gave no shelter from rain or sun for the horses. Whether it was the ivy that prevented it from growing further or whether it was some lack of nutrition in the soil on the hedge that stunted it was a question that that no-one had ever asked; in truth, no local person paid it the slightest attention. Its only purpose in life was to boost the tourism industry – albeit by deceit.

When the weather was windy, the tree swung wildly with its 'arms' and 'tail' lashing from side to side as if its anger had almost reached breaking point. On milder days, it would do no more than wave gently in the breeze.

To Anna, as she walked through the path later that day on her way to the show, it was like passing an old friend in the street, except that on this warm, still day, the old friend did not wave at her as she went by.

5. Manon.

Manon is dreaming again. Her over-active mind refuses to let her rest. Visions of driving her car through the early morning light intrude into the refuge of her sleep. A digital display of numbers shows on the dashboard – green at first, then changing to purple before becoming a row of letters.

'*TURN ON THE RADIO*' the letters read.

She glances at the baby on the passenger seat. When did the baby move her position from her securely held cradle to this vulnerable place? The baby kicks her legs; her eyes are open. What if putting the radio on upsets her?

'Go to sleep, Gwenllian,' she tells her gently.

The car is travelling around the bends, making the baby roll from one side of the seat to the other. It frightens Manon and she puts out her hand to steady the little body. Gwenllian reacts with an irritated grunt.

Meanwhile the dashboard light flashes its instructions and Gwenllian continues to make discontented sounds.

Maybe the radio will soothe her, she thinks.

She looks for a straight stretch of road before removing her hand from the baby's tummy. She grips the dial of the radio and turns it clockwise. The resulting sound is a mixture of white noise and faraway broken voices. While she attempts to tune it by turning another button, Gwenllian's protests grow louder.

She turns the button repeatedly but the noise it makes is strange and becomes louder. She tries to switch it off, but the noise remains. She slaps at it with the palm of her hand, but the car horn sounds instead. She lets go of the steering wheel and pushes at the dial with both hands.

Then, the car plunges slowly down a grass bank. The baby begins rolling forward out of the seat.

The car rolls over and they both tumble out through the open top of the car that has now developed in her dream. She cartwheels down through the long grass; she is aware of Gwenllian tumbling away from her.

They come to a halt but the baby is nowhere to be seen. Instead, there are broken parts of a doll scattered on the grassy bank.

'*GWENLLIAN?*' she shouts and looks about wildly.

A man stands on the bank above them - a vague silhouette.

'There is no baby,' he says. 'You imagined it.'

She knows this cannot be right and rummages wildly through the long grass while the man continues to watch. All she finds are small cards decorated with gold writing.

'Help me find her!' she calls to the man, but he ignores her.

She hears Gwenllian cry. The wail gets louder and louder. She starts to dig at the earth and finds a toy rabbit. The discovery creates more panic and she digs harder, feeling her nails filling with soil. Still Gwenllian cries – louder and more distressed.

At the loudest wail, Manon sits up in bed, her heart hammering and sweat on her skin.

Next to the bed, Gwenllian is crying the insistent sound of a baby who has needs.

Manon leaps out of bed, her hands still clawed from the remnants of her nightmare.

She runs to the buggy and lifts the baby out.

'It's all right, it's all right,' she repeats while rocking the baby from side to side. She is soothing herself as much as the baby.

She is aware that the child felt wet. The bedside clock shows her that she has slept longer than intended. Her nightmare fear is replaced by shame; she has a baby to care for. She feels the need to chastise herself.

She weighs up the options – what to do first? Then, maternal forces kick in and she transfers the baby to one arm while taking out a clean nappy from the bag. Gwenllian is slightly calmer though still unhappy.

'Let's get you changed. Then you can have some breakfast,' she murmurs in a soothing voice.

She looks over her shoulder towards the window. Her car is still parked outside - undamaged. She is finally free from the nightmare.

'It was just a bad dream, little one,' she says. 'I will always keep you safe.'

6. Tegwyn.

The inside of Penybryn Chapel had transformed from gloomy coolness to stuffy and muggy. The close proximity of men dressed in unfamiliar suits with their necks confined by buttoned up collars and further enclosed by ties had set off a chain reaction of sweating that could be detected as far back as the porch.

While the doors had been closed prior to the arrival of the mourners, the inside had stayed cool; the thick walls regulated the temperature and the prospect of entering the building was a pleasant one as the external heat increased. Since then, the double doors had been left open and the stocky workmanlike bodies of those who attended the funeral (many of whom did not believe in the use of deodorant) had gone into overdrive.

Tegwyn was acutely aware of the overwhelming scent. He could feel his own armpits adding to the blend and he tilted his head very slightly sideways to check that his antiperspirant was still the dominant odour. Another tilt of the head to his right gave him grateful confirmation that Edgar was also sweet-smelling.

The chapel was filled to capacity. From the back, where he sat, Tegwyn could see an ocean of male heads – bald patches and utilitarian haircuts marking out the older members of the farming community while other hair styles and attire belonged to the Youth Club, Llanefa Council and all the other organisations that Tommy Elfyn had been involved with.

Tegwyn had let his mind drift. A surreptitious glance at his companion showed him that Edgar was also in 'another place'. Meanwhile, the Minister preached on.

Tegwyn was aware that they had reached the part of the service where much of Tommy's background and achievements were being listed. The Minister swung from Welsh to English and back again in an attempt to please everyone.

'... should have had time to enjoy his recent retirement, but when the Lord calls....'

Tegwyn had a brief vision of his own retirement in a few years' time. He pictured himself on a Spanish golf course with Gwenda, cruising around Alaska or driving the length of New Zealand.

'...and although they are old fashioned phrases not heard so much these days, Tommy Elfyn was what we called Salt of the Earth, A Good Egg and, in his mother tongue, *Boi Bach Ffein...*'

Salt of the earth, thought Tegwyn. It was what everyone said of Bara with his willingness to help the local farmers with any difficult task that required muscle and a blatant disregard for safety.

Tegwyn drifted off once more; his plans for the weekend, dismantling the greenhouse and preparing the ground for a summerhouse, were taking priority.

'... Treasurer of the Bowls Club and a talented player in the past. But we must not forget the most important part of Tommy's life – outside of his family, of course - was his charitable work...'

Tegwyn began to think again of Bara and the girls he had seen walking ahead of him on the way to the show field. A small shaft of coldness was working deep in his gut. Another word jolted him back to the present.

'... together with Llanefa Police, raised a huge amount of money for...'

Next came the long list of other projects that Tommy had assisted with. In the front row, Tegwyn could see Tommy's widow bow her head further and a small sob could be heard. One of Tommy's two daughters turned towards her and murmured some comforting words. Both sons-in-law sat near the end of the row where their presence as bearers would be needed. Tommy's widow and daughters were the only female mourners in the chapel and the obvious signs of grief were met with an uncomfortable shuffle from the men who sat behind them.

Eventually, the last hymn was sung and the mourners gathered in the chapel graveyard as Tommy's coffin was lowered into the grave. Many people stepped forward to bid a private farewell, but Tegwyn was not one of them. His presence was a duty rather than a sincere mourning. Edgar glanced towards the graveside but followed Tegwyn's lead in not stepping forward. The steady stream of men headed for their cars and the journey to Llanefa Showground where the wake was to be held.

'Did you want to go on to the showground?' Tegwyn asked him. 'Or did you want to get off sooner with the caravan?'

Edgar's face showed the battle he had with answering the question; obviously trying to work out if Tegwyn was attempting to save him some time or whether he did not want to go to the wake.

'Well, just for a quick cuppa, I thought,' he said, watching Tegwyn's reaction to see if he had gauged it correctly.

With neither knowing what the other wanted, the two of them climbed into Tegwyn's car - the heat of the interior setting off another bout of sweating.

The quick drive to the showground was soon complete and dark-suited men once again gathered inside a Refreshments Tent where the staff waited with tea, coffee and cold drinks. On a trestle table were plates of covered sandwiches and cakes. Next to the Refreshments Tent was the Bar. Many of the mourners headed into the bar area with murmured words of 'taking a little one' to send Tommy on his way.

'I don't suppose you'll want to go in for a small drink?' Edgar asked, looking slightly worried.

Tegwyn shook his head, 'Or you?' he said.

Edgar's negative answer came threefold; he shook his head, made a distasteful expression and made a driving gesture with his hands.

'I don't drink anyway. Well, hardly ever,' he added, 'Doesn't agree with me.'

Tegwyn nodded; he was not entirely surprised. Edgar seemed such an innocent that it was a miracle he'd had any children.

A few people stepped forward to talk to Tegwyn – the usual complaints about illegal parking, noisy teenagers and stray dogs. He was used to it. The people of Llanefa did not seem to grasp that he was not the one who dealt with such matters, but nevertheless he nodded and said he would pass the information on to the uniformed branch.

Edgar looked on in awe while drinking his tea and eating a Welsh Cake. As soon as the last complainant had turned away, Tegwyn got to his feet. Edgar gulped down the last of his cup of tea and hurried out of his chair.

The air in the tent was getting warmer, not that the men in the Beer Tent seemed to notice. Tegwyn could hear loud exclamations and even laughter as someone related a funny story about Tommy. The three women sat together in the Tea Tent, sipping from small cups and acknowledging condolences from various attendees.

Tegwyn nodded to them as he went past.

'Thank you for coming,' Tommy's youngest daughter said – Tegwyn could not remember her name.

'Wanted to pay my respects,' he said, aware of how hypocritical that sounded, 'Let me know if you need any help when you're sorting out everything...'

Edgar said something suitably respectful and they both left the tent.

Outside, the sun had risen higher and there was a great deal of activity on the showground. Tegwyn glanced towards the Fairground but little movement could be seen there. Although the Show was a one-day event, the Fun Fair was to spend a whole week at Cwm Isaf Farm; their main profits began after the show day.

On their way to the car, he saw Bara again; he was standing near a scruffy van and was staring at it.

Tegwyn peered in the direction of the interior of the van but no-one could be seen inside.

He kept walking to his car, aware that Edgar was saying something but not listening. Edgar repeated his question.

'Do you like dogs, Mr Prydderch?'

'Not particularly. I don't mind them but I would never want one,' he replied.

'That van,' said Edgar, 'it's owned by that dog breeder up in Pooly Code. Terrible conditions. Marg and I went there when we were looking for a new puppy. Marg would have bought them all – she felt so sorry for them, but I talked her out of getting one from there.'

Tegwyn knew who he meant and that his poor pronunciation was an attempt at saying Pwll y Coed – he had some vague memory that Bara had worked there at one point.

Tegwyn looked again. Bara was still motionless; probably waiting for the van's owner to come back. If Tegwyn had to make a guess, he would have thought that Bara had not been paid and was waiting for a chance to see his one-time boss again. He kept on walking but a female laugh caught his attention. He looked again at Bara and beyond the van that he appeared to be staring at. Was it the van he was watching or the two girls across the field – he thought they were the same ones he had passed on his way to the funeral. He kept his gaze on the girls and Bara until one of the Bar Staff from the Beer Tent walked across his vision and broke the contact - Tegwyn recognised her as Anna who often worked in the Poacher's Rest. But, once Anna had gone, Bara continued to stare at the same spot as if transfixed. The object of his attention was not obvious – and that fact bothered Tegwyn a great deal.

7. Natalie.

Llinos dismounted from the third horse she had been schooling in readiness for her competition. She felt prickly droplets of sweat running down her back.

Mike and Sarah, who owned the horses, were standing watching with Natalie.

'They're looking well,' Sarah remarked, 'I just hope they behave.'

'I'm sure they'll be fine,' replied Natalie, 'and we'll give them a once over with the grooming stuff later on.'

'Feels very strange to me - not riding!' Sarah added, 'But it will be nice to see them from the judge's point of view.'

'Oh God!' said Llinos, 'I hope I don't make a bollocks of it!'

'You'll be fine,' said Sarah, 'I'm just grateful that you could do it. I just can't take the risk at the moment. Precious cargo!' She patted her pregnant tummy to emphasize her words.

'In a few years' time, you might have a ready-made jockey!' Natalie joked.

Mike joined in, 'Yes, one who eats flapjacks and Marmite! I've heard of pregnant women getting daft cravings but that one has to be right up there in the Top Twenty of Weird Cravings!'

The girls laughed while Sarah protested, 'I don't eat them *together!* I've just got to have one after the other!'

Llinos had unsaddled Minstrel, the cob she had been riding, and threw a sweat rug over him.

'I'll take him back to the lorry,' she said, 'he can have a munch from his hay-net until we're ready to tack him up again.'

Relieved of his burden of rider and saddle, Minstrel swung around eagerly to face the direction of the lorry.

'Whoa! Steady!' said Llinos, and attempted to pull him back towards her.

Sarah stepped out of the way while Mike strode forward to help. Minstrel threw his head around and swung his hindquarters in the opposite direction. His rear end pushed against Natalie, who put both her hands against his rump to move him back.

'Get over!' she said sternly, showing no signs of the fear she had supposedly developed of horses.

Minstrel came to a halt and swished his tail angrily.

Llinos collected a better grip on the lead rope and stood beside his shoulder.

'Tie him up on the opposite side of the lorry to Seren,' Sarah said, 'they fight over the hay-net otherwise. Mike will come with you to make sure...'

'OK. C'mon, boy.'

As soon as she started to move, Minstrel swung around impatiently again, this time catching Natalie unaware and almost knocked her over. She took two rapid giant strides sideways to stop herself from losing her balance.

'Naughty boy!' Sarah admonished before turning to Natalie, 'Didn't step on you, did he?'

Natalie did not answer the question. Instead, she stared at them all – looking through them with a faraway expression.

'Nat? You ok?'

'Going...' Natalie said in a weak voice before her knees buckled and she fell on to the grass.

Sarah and Mike immediately went to her aid while Llinos anxiously looked on with Minstrel still walking around her in impatient circles.

Almost instantly, Natalie sat up with one arm on the ground to support herself. Her face was a greyish white.

'Whoo! Just went woozy. It's so hot,' she said in a shaky voice.

'Are you all right?' Sarah asked.

The colour was coming back into Natalie's face.

'Really. I'm fine. Just... I'm fine.'

'I'm taking Minstrel to the lorry then I'll be straight back,' Llinos said, 'just wait there for me.'

Llinos and Mike walked away but not before Llinos heard Natalie reply 'Bad period,' in answer to Sarah's worried questioning.

Llinos was unable to say for certain, but she had an idea that Natalie was lying.

***

Two hours later, after Llinos had finished competing in her first two classes, Natalie sat on the grass by the refreshments marquee and watched Llinos disappearing through the canvas opening.

After a minute, she stuck her head out.

'They've got vegetarian pasties there. Do you want one?'

'Ugh!' Natalie said, 'They're disgusting! Have you ever tasted them?'

'They look foul, actually,' Llinos agreed, 'but I can get you something else...'

'I'm fine. I had an ice cream when you were taking the last pony back to the lorry. Sorry, I couldn't wait any longer! And they had the ones with double Flake and caramel sauce,' Natalie grinned apologetically.

Llinos shrugged and went back in to join the queue. The vegetarian fad was another change in her friend that she failed to understand. Natalie had always been a meat eater; had never even gone off lamb after seeing those same animals playing in the field (it was a phase that Llinos had gone through briefly).

She moved slowly up the queue – it gave her time to think about Natalie. Her mind switched back to the contents of Nat's bag. Natalie was renowned for carrying almost everything imaginable in the enormous leather and canvas bag she took everywhere with her. The bag was split into several compartments with zips to keep them secure. Natalie rarely closed the zips fully and the contents often tipped out into the body of the bag where, locating an item was a case of rummaging and stirring everything until the right one came to the surface. It was a standing joke between them that Natalie's bag had been a skip in a previous life. But, in the carnage that lay in the bag that morning, Llinos was certain that no sanitary items were present.

Llinos paid for her beef roll and can of coke before coming out of the tent. The short time spent in the confines of the tent had created lines of perspiration on the back of her shirt. It made her feel uncomfortable and self-conscious. Maybe, she thought, just maybe Natalie had simply been a victim of the heat and had, for some unknown reason, been too embarrassed to admit it...

She sat on the grass beside her friend. They watched the steady procession of men wearing black ties coming out of the bar area where the last part of Tommy Elfyn's funeral had taken place. Some of the men blinked as they emerged into sunlight and one or two walked with a slightly less than sure step. The 'wake' should have been over long before. The anxious show committee had gone ahead and started the classes at the arranged later time, though some had been heard to mutter that it demonstrated a great lack of respect to run the show while the mourners still remained in the bar area.

Someone must have given the nod to the fairground staff as their loud music had also signalled that the fair was open for business. Exceeding that noise, a loud speaker announcement gave the order of the next classes and in which ring. Llinos's hunger suddenly gave way to feeling sick. Why had she agreed to riding Minstrel for Sarah? The other two cobs had been well behaved and she had gained a respectable third place with one of them. But Minstrel was a strong willed animal who knew that he could dispose of any rider if he had a mind to do so. Was there any way she could back out of it? She wanted to be fit and able to attend at the YFC Disco on the show field that night. She would look such a fool if she fell off and injured herself – and, more to the point, she felt that leaving her new boyfriend to his own devices at such an event was asking for trouble! It was a thought that she dared not say out loud. The subject had almost caused an argument between her and Natalie. Natalie had been the chosen rider all along; Llinos had arranged to babysit for the local vet's twin children while the parents went away to an event in Berkshire. Then, not long after Jack and Nat had split up, Natalie had announced her loss of confidence and suggested to Sarah that Llinos could probably ride instead. It had resulted in a swapping of roles for them.

She chewed half-heartedly at her beef roll; her mind lurched into several scenarios – all of them worrying her in one way or another. She jumped as Natalie's elbow nudged her.

'There's that nutter again,' Natalie said.

Llinos looked up from her roll to see Bara staring towards them.

Both girls looked away quickly.

'Oh fuck, he's still staring,' Llinos muttered, 'what's wrong with him?'

After another furtive look, she said, 'He's staring at you, Nat!'

'Come on, let's move from here,' Natalie said and got up.

They walked away towards the Stock Judging section where YFC Members were being tested on their knowledge of sheep. After a few minutes of half watching, they turned around to move to another ring only to find

Bara and his lurcher standing behind them. He stared unashamedly with his usual stance of head and neck jutted forward and one hand clenched by his side. His other hand was in his pocket.

He stared at Natalie's chest.

'Woof,' he said.

Natalie blushed a deep crimson before Llinos said, 'Yes, it's a picture of a wolf on her T-shirt. Do you have a problem with that?'

'Wolf,' he said, more clearly the second time. He scratched at his groin with the hand in his pocket. His face was red and covered in shiny spots of sweat.

He stared for a few more seconds, then, alarmed by Llinos's challenging look, turned his head away. The three of them stood there for a few seconds before a nearby shout alerted them.

'Bara! Come and help us with these sheep pens.' It was one of the show organisers.

Bara turned away and the girls hurried off.

'I think I'll head off home now. I'm just too hot,' said Natalie, 'and I want to get my stuff sorted for tonight's babysitting.'

'I'll come with you,' offered Llinos, whilst the beginnings of a plan to get out of riding Minstrel formulated in her mind.

'No, it's ok. You'll need to stay here for the presentation of the prizes and stuff...'

'If you're sure...'

'Yeah, yeah. And you've got to ride Minstrel in the last class. I'll head off now. I *might* even get myself another ice-cream on the way! Have a great time tonight. Don't get ratted!'

She grinned and began to walk away. Llinos heard Natalie's mobile phone beeping the arrival of a text message as she increased the distance between them. The response was instant and Llinos watched Natalie take the

48

phone out of her pocket and, almost automatically, press a key. Llinos felt a moment's pity for Jack.

She wiped the grease from the beef roll off her hands and headed towards a litter bin. She dropped the tissue in and turned around to walk towards the horse lorry. She caught sight of Natalie across the showground. She grinned to herself. What was Natalie eating *now?* She hadn't even got as far as the ice-cream van.

Something metallic glinted in the sun. Was it a lollipop, Llinos pondered? She immediately remembered the peanut butter jar and spoon she had seen in Natalie's bag. A new thought formed. Surely, Natalie couldn't be *pregnant?* The horror of it began to make sense in her mind. The reluctance to get on a horse, the change in eating habits; now, a craving for peanut butter! Was that why she had split with Jack? Did she intend to keep the baby and Jack was pushing her to have an abortion? Everyone knew that Natalie loved children. She decided she needed to speak with Natalie when she was home from babysitting. Getting pregnant now was going to change her life in the worst way, Llinos thought. It was something that they both assumed would happen one day, but with university, careers and fun times to be had first. It was time to have a Girl Talk.

***

Llinos made her way over to the lorry where the horses were tethered. She was deep in thought about Natalie. The music from the fairground screamed on. Every so often a voice would break into the music, '*Leeeeean to the left, pretty lady!*' as the Loop-de-Loop gathered momentum and whirled its passengers around.

She sat down on the lorry ramp and tried to think of a solution. She was concentrating so hard that she did not notice the approach of two young men until they called her a second time with a loud 'Oy!'

She looked up. They were strangers to her but obviously part of a Young Farmers group; their T-shirts, bearing the slogan 'Young Farmers Do It By Sowing Seeds' gave it away.

'Well, do you fancy having a go?' said one, laughing, 'You can pretend you're my girlfriend.'

'What?' Llinos said in a shocked tone.

'The Girlfriend Carrying Race,' he repeated, 'There's twenty quid for the winner! I'll give you five if I win!'

'Get out of it,' laughed Llinos, 'You're not carrying me!'

'What about the tall thin girl, then?' he said.

'What tall thin girl?' she asked and, at the same time, wondering if they were drunk.

'She was with you earlier. She'll be easy to carry.'

Llinos searched mentally through her list of friends to try to understand who they meant. Not Sarah, surely...?

'With a wolf on her tee-shirt...'

'Natalie?' Llinos said, 'She's not...'

She thought a moment about what she had been about to say.

'She's not here. She's gone home.'

The boys turned away, disappointed and headed towards another group of girls.

Llinos felt ashamed. She had been about to say, *'She's not thin!'*

What kind of friend am I, she thought?

Poor Natalie – always eating something. Now, pregnant and going to eat even more! She was going to have to watch what she said, Llinos realised, or she would end up offending Natalie.

***

Natalie walked along the roadway outside the showground. She made herself take longer, faster paces. The harder she walked, the less time her mind dwelt on unpleasant things. Her stomach growled. She stopped and took a bottle of water out of her bag and swigged at it. Her

50

stomach rumbled even more. She replaced the water bottle and opened the jar of peanut butter before dipping the teaspoon into it. She put the spoon in her mouth and resisted the urge to chew. Just let it dissolve, she told herself. Her mouth produced more saliva and her stomach rumbled again. The peanut butter worked loose from the spoon and its sticky residue clung to her teeth. Again, her jaw wanted to chomp at it, swallow it and dig into the jar for more. She breathed slowly, trying to delay her gastric response. With great restraint, she let the solution melt away in her mouth until it had all slipped down her gullet. She waited a minute for the nutrition to reach her stomach; to tell her brain that she was full. Peanut butter contained a lot of protein, she was sure.

She checked the clock on her phone. One hour from now. Then she would be allowed another teaspoon of peanut butter.

8. Manon.

Manon gently wipes the remains of the rice pudding from Gwenllian's mouth. The baby protests slightly, waves her arms and gives a yell. 'There you are! Nice and clean!' Manon says.

Gwenllian sweeps her hand over the high chair tray, almost sending the bowl flying.

'Oops a daisy! Are you fed up now?' Manon coos at her.

She removes the bowl and spoon away and places them on the table, before lifting Gwenllian out of the chair and putting her into the safety of a playpen. Manon wipes down the high-chair and folds it up to make more room. The high chair had been a bargain, she remembers. She had seen it in Mothercare; the price had been reduced due to an order that had been cancelled too late. Manon did not like to think too much about *why* the order had been cancelled. The possibilities were too upsetting. She had told Matthew that she had won it in a work raffle that had been held to raise money for disadvantaged children in Africa. She began to believe this scenario herself. It was better than worrying about the cancelled order and accepting a possibility that the poor child had died or had been taken into care. The few times she had let her mind investigate these possibilities, she had broken down into a marathon of sobbing. Things had already been shaky between her and Matthew by then and the mystery of his wife's despair had long passed the sympathetic stage. By that time, their relationship had been travelling at speed towards a figurative derailment.

'So, do you want a little sleep now?' she asks Gwenllian.

The baby is sitting up with her fat fists clinging to the stretchy side of the playpen. While Manon speaks, Gwenllian leans forward and tries to chew the supporting bar.

'Oh, don't do that, bach,' she says in concern, 'You're going to make Mam nervous!'

The baby shuffles around on her bottom, looking for another item to grasp. Manon regrets that she did not buy more toys when she had the chance. Though, the only toys that Gwenllian wants are the ones that were in her buggy. For some unfathomable reason, this troubles Manon.

'I know, let's put the telly on! You can watch the CBeebies!'

At this word, Gwenllian turns her head and gives a huge, open-mouthed smile and laughs out loud.

'Do you like CBeebies? Do you? Do you like them, sweetie?' Manon is well into her role of repetitive baby-talk. She recognises it as such and remembers that she always vowed that she would never talk this way to her babies. Another spasm of sadness goes through her. Babies. Plural.

And I didn't even get one, she thinks. But it's different now. She has Gwenllian.

As if reminding her of this fact, Gwenllian makes another squealing noise before breaking into another wide smile.

'You are so beautiful,' Manon whispers, 'This is my reward for waiting.'

She leans forward and picks the child up, fitting her neatly on to one hip. She marvels at the weight and warmth of her. In her yearnings, she has always imagined a young new-born baby – much smaller than Gwenllian - but nevertheless, she delights in the feel and smell of her. She inhales the unique baby-smell and is overcome by the need to cry; tears run down over her face. She hugs the baby tight and Gwenllian gives a cry of discomfort.

'It's all right, little one,' she says, 'Don't cry. I will always look after you. Mam's only crying because she's happy, that's all. Don't you worry. Mam's not sad. She's just a silly, happy Mam who's pleased that you are here.'

She rocks from side to side, singing a silly little song while Gwenllian brings her brows together and listens.

Manon leans forward to pick up the television remote and switches it on. She flicks through the buttons until she finds the CBeebies channel. At the familiar sound of the characters, Gwenllian looks around with surprise. From Manon's perspective it looks as if she is saying, 'You have CBeebies *here?*'

'Yes, we do. We do have CBeebies here!' she croons at the baby, 'We have CBeebies here all day long if you want.'

She dances around the small living room, carefully avoiding the playpen and the sofa. At the end of each circuit, she swings around in a quick circle and goes back the opposite way. Gwenllian laughs her endearing chuckle, her eyes becoming large at each new circuit. CBeebies plays on though neither of them is watching. At the fifth circuit, Gwenllian gives a hiccup then burps out a quantity of rice pudding onto Manon's shoulder.

'Oh!' she says, 'Silly Mam has made you sick! Let's get you cleaned up and then we'll have a rest.'

She puts Gwenllian down and uses the Baby Wipes to clean her shoulder and everything else that bears traces of regurgitated rice pudding.

Gwenllian's eyes are beginning to look glazed and her good natured expression is waning.

'Are you tired? Do you want a little sleepy-bye now? I think you should have a sleepy-bye. Then you'll feel better when you wake up.'

She puts her in the buggy and wheels her into the bedroom. Gwenllian scrunches up her face and cries, displaying her gums and the back of her tongue.

'Ssh, ssh. You need to go to byes now. Ssh, bach.'

Gwenllian cries until Manon gives in and picks her up again. She rocks her gently and tries to put her back in the buggy, but the baby whimpers each time. She takes the buggy back into the living room and attempts to calm her. Eventually, the child falls asleep on her shoulder and Manon eases her back into the buggy; her breathing deepens and Manon sighs with relief. Realising that the television is still on, she picks up the remote control and turns it off. On cue, Gwenllian begins to cry until Manon turns the TV on once more. The music from the CBeebies channel is too loud so Manon switches it to another channel where a family feel-good film is playing. She glances at Gwenllian, who is still sleeping.

Manon sits beside her, watching her breathe and sees her fingers twitch as she dreams of CBeebies and rice pudding and, she supposes, the other activities she has been involved in today.

Manon feels her own eyes grow heavy. The sight of the sleeping baby has an almost hypnotic effect on her. A loud knock on her front door makes her jump. She leaps to her feet and runs towards it, while turning her head so that she could see if Gwenllian has been disturbed.

Through the frosted glass of the front door, she can make out the shape of a woman. The woman's hand comes up to knock on the door again. Manon flies at it to prevent that sound becoming reality for a second time.

The woman on the doorstep smiles at her. She has a familiar face though Manon does not know or remember her name.

'Shw mai, bach,' she said, 'sorry to bother you but I'm selling raffle tickets for the Ysgol Feithrin. Lovely prizes. And it's a good cause. We need repairs done on the building and the council can only give so much towards it, you know.'

Manon nods. She knows of the Ysgol Feithrin or Nursery School; she has become accustomed to planning all the schools that her children would go to. Not that she has ever lived in Llanefa with Matthew, but since returning here, the old habit has come with her and she has glanced at the schools as she walks by. Now, she realises, she has a future candidate for the Ysgol Feithrin, (though not Llanefa's Ysgol Feithrin, she reminds herself). She is, at last, part of that exclusive club that she has been denied membership of for so long. The feeling makes her want to hug this half-familiar woman.

'Yes, of course,' she says, 'Not sure if I've got much cash on me but let me just check.'

She grabs her handbag from the coat hooks behind the door of the bungalow. She rummages through it, bringing out her purse.

'A pound a book,' the woman says, 'Lovely today, isn't it? Thought I'd take advantage and catch everyone who hasn't gone to the show.'

Manon nods in agreement though she is not sure what show the woman is talking about. She counts through her loose change.

Unexpectedly, there is a wail from the living room. Manon freezes and holds her breath. No other sound follows it up.

'Sounds as if your cat needs attention!' the woman says, 'Worse than children, some of them.'

Manon stumbles over her words in relief, 'Not mine. On the TV,' she says, while thanking good fortune that she has not left the CBeebies channel on – that would have attracted suspicion.

She hands over the money and takes the tickets. The woman looks ready to chat but Manon cuts her short.

'I don't mean to be rude, but I've got something on the cooker hob,' she says quickly.

'Lovely. Thank you, bach,' the woman says, turning around towards the garden gate before swinging back towards Manon one more time, 'Nice to see you back here. See you again!'

I doubt it, Manon thinks, I don't intend to be here long.

9. Natalie.

Natalie's route from the showground to her parents' house should have been a simple one. Although that morning she had walked first to meet Llinos, now, on her way home, the logical route was to go directly to her own parents' house. Instead, she veered up the public footpath that passed the Devil Tree. Halfway along the path, she felt the familiar faintness she was experiencing more regularly now. She stopped and took a swig of her water – trying to ignore the jar of peanut butter that tempted her. She opened her bag again, placed the water bottle inside and stared at the jar. Her stomach rumbled. In a flash of frustration, she pulled the jar out and threw it as far as she could. She saw the sunlight flashing off its plastic surface as it travelled against a background of blue sky and then trees.

She turned away and began to walk up the path, forcing her legs to go faster until her breathing started to sound like snoring. In the distance she could see a fisherman coming towards her. The sunlight flashed off the fibre-glass rod and net that protruded from his backpack. A further flash of sunshine reflected off his glasses and she assumed it was Dai the Fish (who wore the thickest lensed glasses she had ever seen). A thought came to her: what if he saw the jar lying on the ground? So what, her mind replied, doesn't have to mean you threw it, does it? But, all the same, it bothered her that it was there... There was always the possibility that he would mention it to his drinking pals and that it would get back to her mother. Questions would be asked...

She spun around and ran down the hill until she reached where she thought the jar had landed. She could hear her heartbeat and feel it vibrating throughout her upper body, neck and head. The pulse in her ears became louder and she felt the faintness coming again. She knelt on the grassy floor with her head between her knees until the world came back into focus once more. Like an answered prayer, she saw the jar of peanut butter lying in a clump of brambles nearby, though its lid was missing. She leaped forward and grabbed it, scratching the back of her hand in the process. She glanced around. There was no sign of Dai the Fish; he had probably climbed the stile and made his way towards the riverbank. Natalie peered into the jar before digging two fingers down into the soft peanut butter. She jammed her fingers into her mouth and sucked the paste from them before plunging them back into the jar for more. Her knuckles got in the way so she licked her fingers clean and opened her bag to get her spoon.

That's enough, she told herself, fat, disgusting pig! That's enough! She dismissed the thought and dug in with the spoon. Her mouth was full of peanut butter, its thickness slowing down her ability to swallow it. It clung to her teeth and the roof of her mouth. She continued to try to chomp and swallow. A small, choking cough forced its way through her mouth.

That's enough, her anguished mind cried out. No more! Woof, woof! Who looks like Mrs Jenkins's bulldog?

That image finally stopped her eating. She spat out the remains of the peanut butter and looked at the disgusting lump it made on the ground. Woof, woof, she reminded herself, that's what it looks like inside your greedy stomach.

She wiped her hands on the grass then got to her feet and stored the jar in her bag. She took another gulp of water from her bottle. It made a gurgling noise as it worked its way down her gullet. Her stomach relaxed its hunger cramps and Natalie realised that she felt better.

She drank more water in an attempt to fool her stomach into thinking it was full.

Her breathing slowed and she turned around in the intended direction of her home. She saw some brood mares in the field alongside the path. Their brown distended bellies shone in the sunlight. That's what you look like; she told herself, remember that the next time you want to pig-out. She walked steadily to the end of the public footpath. Her pace had slowed somewhat and she felt slightly sick.

Natalie knew that it would be easy to make herself sick while she felt this way but she always stopped short of doing so. It was not just the dislike of vomiting that stopped her, but vanity and her self-image. Despite her self-loathing, Natalie had one physical attribute that she was satisfied with - her teeth. Like all her immediate family, Natalie had square, even teeth of a natural brilliant whiteness. Someone in school had even asked her where she'd had her teeth bleached.

Natalie had read that constant vomiting produced stomach acid that eventually destroyed the protective tooth surface. And, while the present hatred of her appearance dictated almost everything she did, she was unwilling to sacrifice the one attractive feature she believed she possessed. She had occasionally taken laxatives, but that was not an easy option for a teenage girl. It would have been difficult to use the school toilets while the obvious sounds of diarrhoea would have given her away to anyone in the proximity. Sometimes, at home, she would time the taking of her chocolate laxatives (they were easier to keep secret – the presence of foil-wrapped chocolate in her bag had been a normal sight before this current... *problem* had arisen) to times that she knew her parents would be out. It was hard to hide a bout of diarrhoea from her mother, so the laxative method was used sparingly.

The only way left to her was starvation. After the first few days, it had been difficult; she had always had a good appetite. But as the weeks wore on, she found it easier to avoid eating and was able (so far) to fool her mother. Immediately after she had split up with Jack (and all the self-loathing had consumed her), she had tried to cut down what she ate. Her mother chivvied her along and said that no boyfriend was worth missing meals for and that she would get over him. Natalie was relieved that her mother had put the lack of appetite down to being heartbroken. She had originally told her mother that it was she, Natalie, who had dumped Jack and not the other way around, but her devious mind had already appreciated the way that it was easy to lead her mother to think otherwise. It was a good excuse for not eating as much as she used to.

Someone had let slip that Natalie did not eat school dinners so her mother had insisted that she took sandwiches if she did not like what was on offer at the school canteen. As an excuse, Natalie explained that she felt unable to eat meat or to watch others eat it and was going to be a vegetarian. She would sit in the sixth-formers' room with the others who brought sandwiches and picked at a fraction of her salad roll, chewing slowly and thoroughly until everyone else had started packing away their lunch carriers and she could follow suit. On the way home, she would tip the remains of the box into a litter bin that she passed once she was alone. She had, a few times, thrown the bread roll to Mrs Jenkins's bulldog, who paraded up and down the garden when Llanefa School pupils arrived or left school – the proximity of the garden to Llanefa School meant that the dog felt driven to patrol its territory twice a day. But, most of the time, Natalie could not even look at the bulldog – it brought back too many bad memories.

To quell her hunger, she ate apples and drank water or Diet Coke (which she deceitfully poured into a regular Coke bottle). To her friends, it seemed that Natalie was always eating! They sometimes teased her about it, but in a kind way and Natalie went along with their teasing - grabbing another opportunity to hide her true eating habits.

Natalie stopped for a breather at the end of the public footpath; the faintness was often present and she was determined not to attract attention to herself by constantly fainting. A quick glance to her right, where the road lay-by and parking place was situated, spurred her on. The scene of the crime, she thought, while humiliating images flashed through her mind. This was accompanied by some sadness too. She had loved Jack. And she thought that he had loved her, too. They had talked of going to universities where they would be together despite the difference in their chosen courses. And then he had let her down by... She felt tears building up and a hard feeling pressed inside her chest.

Forget it! Move on, she told herself. Walk! Take big energetic steps – use the calories. She walked, striding out like an athlete in training, past Anna's house, past another house – she ticked them off as she covered the distance. Sweat formed and ran down her back – still she kept going, faster and faster to keep her thoughts at bay.

Eventually, she turned into the more built-up area and reached the road where she lived. Her legs felt weak and her vision blurred as the sweat ran into her eyes. She went through the gateway and opened the back door of her parents' house. Her mother was in the kitchen, cleaning down the worktops.

'Good grief, Natalie, what have you been doing?' her mother said, 'you're covered in sweat!'

'Hot out there,' she answered, 'got to have a wee...'

Natalie kept up her fast pace and continued through the house, up the stairs and into her bedroom. She dropped her bag on the floor and went to the bathroom, kicking off her trainers and pulling off her jeans as she got there. She sat on the toilet and urinated. After flushing and washing her hands, she also took off her baggy tee-shirt. She stood still for a moment to listen if anyone was coming upstairs – nothing. She could hear the television – her father was watching some sporting event. There were faint clunking noises still coming from the kitchen. She leaned down and carefully slid the weighing scales out of its corner. It often made a noise as it caught the side of the bath. Equally carefully, she tipped it on to its base and checked where the pin was facing. Slightly under the zero, she noted, before adjusting it to its accurate position. She leaned on it a few times to check that it still went back to zero. She listened once more for any movements coming up the stairs or on the landing. The door was locked but she didn't want anyone to hear the telltale noise the scales made whenever she stood on them – a type of click that sounded as loud as gunshot to Natalie's over-sensitive ears.

With the coast clear, she stepped on to the small platform, holding her breath as she waited for the pin to stop as it swung back and forth between numbers.

She stared at the reading. Her face showed disbelief. Just under forty-nine kilos! How could that be? She had been slightly over forty-eight kilos that morning! She got off and tried again, shuffling her feet until she felt that she was standing central to the platform. The pin nudged downwards slightly. Ok, she told herself, I'm not standing in the same position every time. That's all it is. Don't panic!

But she still got on three more times and checked the result.

She carefully put the scales back in their storage position and put her clothes on. Ideally, she would have liked a digital weigh scale, but it would be difficult to find a reason to tell her mother *why* she wanted one. She had considered finding some way of damaging the present scales when her parents were out, but the thought of her mother not even bothering to get a new one, frightened her. A non-digital scale was better than no scales at all.

Her mother called up the stairs.

'What time is Ben picking you up later?'

'About four o'clock,' she called back, 'they have to go to some dinner thing tonight and it will take a couple of hours travelling to get there.'

'Shall I make you something to eat now?'

'God, no! I've eaten constantly all day!' she called back to her mother, 'I couldn't even eat a slice of cucumber at the moment!'

10. Natalie.

Natalie lay in the bath. Her head pounded due to the heat of the water. She pulled the plug to let some water out, then turned on the hot tap once more. She let her mind wander to the next two days. She quite enjoyed babysitting for Ben and Rachel; she loved children - particularly when they were at an age when they were apt to say funny things. She often looked after the children when Llinos was not available. Ben was one of the Llanefa veterinary surgeons and Llinos's interest in pursuing that career meant she often volunteered to babysit for them (as she had originally done for this weekend) as she liked to hear what advice he had to offer. But the incident that had put a stop to Natalie's horse-riding days (woof-woof, here comes Mrs Jenkins's dog, she played that thought in her mind several times a day) had seen them swap duties for the weekend.

Natalie smiled to herself. It had been a stroke of luck for Llinos, she thought. There was a new boyfriend on the scene and Llinos had been determined not to leave him unaccompanied at the YFC Disco after the show. A brief image of Jack dampened her mood. How disloyal some people could be! She wished she could suffer some kind of amnesia so that the whole sorry episode would be wiped from her mind. As far as she was concerned, it was the only way she could possibly forget the humiliation she had suffered.

'Are you still in the bath?' her mother's voice carried up the stairs.

'Just getting out,' she called back, though she continued to lie there while the steam clouded everything in her sight. She had heard that jockeys used the same method to lose weight. She did not know how long it took for the body to shed weight due to heat but every little was certain to help.

She sat up and began to get out of the bath. Her head pounded harder and her vision doubled for a second. With effort, she got out and reached for a towel to wrap around her. She picked up another towel to rub her hair roughly. Her eyes drew to the weigh scales – a faint metallic glint showing through the steam in the room. She resisted the temptation. It was best to dry her hair completely first. Wet hair would only add weight.

She opened the bathroom window, feeling light-headed as she reached up to the metal catch. With the bath emptied and walls wiped down to disguise the amount of steam that had accumulated, she went into her own bedroom and took her hairdryer from its shelf. Meticulously, she dried her hair, ensuring that no dampness remained. Similarly, she dried her skin equally thoroughly, turning the hairdryer on to her body where she felt that she had not dried properly. Finally, she went back into the bathroom and locked the door. She sat on the toilet, attempting to squeeze out a trickle of urine. Then, with the same practised stealth, she slid the scales out of its corner.

'Aren't you out yet? He'll be here before long!' her mother shouted up.

'Yes, ok. Just having a wee,' she called back, 'I've put all my stuff ready.'

Her heart thumped with anxiety. Where exactly was her mother? On the stairs? Natalie carefully checked the scales and reset the pin on zero. She stopped for a few seconds to check if she could hear her mother. Nothing. Cautiously, she stepped on the platform once more. Her heart gave an extra hard beat! Yes, she thought! The pin was definitely a shade lower than before. She got off and then back on again. Was it lower? Was she standing centrally? She shuffled around slightly. Yes, it was lower. If only they had a digital weighing scale, she thought for the thousandth time, it would be far more accurate.

She put the scales back where they lived and hurried into her bedroom to get dressed. Somewhere outside she heard a dog bark. A sob worked its way to her throat before she could stop it. The heat from the bathroom had weakened her and she felt the tears spill over her eye rims and down her cheeks. The image of Mrs Jenkins's bulldog waddling up and down its garden with its fat bulging and swinging side to side was very clear. She dressed quickly, trying hard not to catch sight of her reflection in the mirror; her perceived image of her pink bloated body and its trapped layers of fat would be too much to bear. Nevertheless, she saw it in her mind's eye and that kept the tears flowing for another few minutes.

She picked up her overnight bag; she had packed it earlier. After a moment's thought, she added an extra book and a magazine. The magazine's cover had the magic words 'The New Way To Count Calories' on the bottom corner while a sun-kissed model adorned the main part. Natalie turned the magazine so that the calorie heading could not be seen. Instead, the words 'Star Interview' faced outwards from the side pocket of the bag. She checked her other bag – the peanut butter and spoon were still there but the water bottle needed renewing. She sometimes refilled a used lemonade bottle with fizzy water so that it looked like calorific lemonade to anyone who saw her drinking from it.

Was there anything else she needed? Remembering Sarah's concerned questioning earlier that day, she added a box of tampons, though she had no idea when her period was due. She could not remember when she had last had one, but it was always best to be prepared.

She made her way downstairs. The smell of fresh bread rose to meet her and her stomach rumbled in appreciation.

'What's the matter? Have you been crying?' her mother asked in great concern.

Natalie laughed shakily.

'Got shampoo in my eyes! Stings like mad!'

'Oh, thought something had upset you. Do you want to take some fresh bread with you? It's just come out of the bread-maker.'

'No thanks,' she said, though her brain screamed, *Take it! Eat it all!*

Her mother was looking at her in a curious way.

'You've done something different to your hair...' she said while she kept on looking.

It unnerved Natalie, the way she stared at her. She shrugged and turned away.

'And how you can bear that big shirt in this heat...' she continued.

'Keeps me cool,' Natalie said, 'Circulating air and stuff.'

'What have you had to eat today?'

The question came out of the blue. Natalie could feel her face heating up.

She blew out a sigh.

'Where do you want me to start? Ice cream, roll, coke, more ice cream, chocolate, blah, blah... And I'll get a big supper when the twins eat. Rachel always leaves a lasagne or something for us.'

Her mother continued to stare.

'What? Why are you staring? What are all the questions for? God's sake!'

'Just make sure you eat properly,' she said, 'just because you won't eat meat, doesn't mean you can fill yourself on junk.'

'Whatever!'

'And don't be flippant with me! You look a bit peaky. I think maybe you need iron or something...'

'Yeah, well...' Natalie shrugged and see-sawed her hand.

'You're not still hankering after *that boy*?' her mother said. She had stopped calling him by his name – an unreasonable dislike of him had found its way into her mind.

'Who? Jack? Waste of space!'

Where the conversation would have led was nobody's guess but to Natalie's relief, the doorbell rang.

'Ben's here!' she said and went to answer the door.

Ben and Rachel lived in a remote farmhouse on the far side of Pwll y Coed. They had bought the property in an almost derelict state and had restored it to its present remarkable condition. The decor and general style was a mystery to those who were brought up in Llanefa - the shabby-chic design with plenty of 'distressed' furniture was reminiscent of their own poor upbringing. Despite this, visitors to the property felt compelled to wipe feet and brush down clothes before entering the farmhouse. Rachel grew all her own herbs for cooking and several pots stood in serried ranks next to a Belfast sink in what would be called a utility room in another house, but regaled in the title of 'herbery' here. A further boot-room stood next to it with an antique metal rack for keeping shoes. Matching coat hooks on the wall above gave defining style to the room.

In an earlier generation, they would have been described as Bohemian, but their easy lifestyle and laid back attitude to life gained them more friends than most and they were treated with fond indulgence. Before moving to Llanefa to take up work in the Efa Veterinary Practice, they had lived in Kent. Ben's overburdened workload of small animals and household pets had left him with a hankering for a country practice and a less frenetic lifestyle. When the farmhouse in Llanefa had come up for sale, they both felt that their prayers had been answered. Ben had spent three months working as a temporary vet at Llanefa until a permanent position became available.

Rachel's childhood had been spent with horses and the ownership of some acreage with their farmhouse gave her the opportunity to rekindle her interest. She bought some Arabian horses and began to breed them – achieving a high standard of animal and an enviable reputation throughout that particular field. She became a member of the Arab Horse Association and, eventually, a committee member. Before the twins were born, she was asked to judge at Arab horse events throughout the UK. Once the organisers had discovered that Ben was a vet, it became convenient to ask him to examine the exhibits (as the rules dictated) before they were allowed to take part in some of the competitions.

August Bank Holiday was the pinnacle of the Arab Horse Association calendar; their annual International Show was held at Newbury showground over two days. The Annual Dinner Dance was held on the Saturday night, while a lesser competition took place on the Sunday, with the main event going ahead on Bank Holiday Monday. On this particular Bank Holiday, Ben was to be the official vet but Rachel had volunteered to help with the show organisation during the two day exhibition. It was to cover this time that they had wanted a babysitter to look after the twins. Rachel had realised that it would not be practical to take the children with her. They were both used to having Llinos or Natalie to look after the twins and were happy that they were in capable hands. However, Rachel left copious notes of instructions to the girls so that almost every eventuality was covered.

When Ben and Natalie arrived back at the farmhouse, the twins were in a high state of excitement at seeing 'Nattee' and almost climbed over each other in their eagerness to show her their drawings.

'Good luck!' Ben said, 'Give me a wild Charolais cow any day! These two are enough to put you off having children forever!'

Natalie squatted down to their level and responded with appropriate amazement as the girls chatted away in partial baby-talk.

'Leave Natalie alone!' Rachel's voice interrupted the melee.

Natalie looked up and saw that Rachel was dressed in a black cocktail dress that showed off her enviable figure. Her hair had been pinned back and her face was made up. Natalie felt a pulse of jealousy in the pit of her stomach.

'You look lovely,' she said, and meant it.

'Thank you, Natalie,' she replied, 'Trying to make an effort! Makes a change! I've spent the last four years covered in Weetabix or horse hair! I just hope I don't look too crumpled by the time we get there! I didn't want to leave here too early and change when I got there...'

She continued to look at Natalie.

'You look different, too,' she said, 'have you lost weight? Or have you done something different to your hair?'

'Just the hair, I think,' she replied, 'but I may have lost a pound or two. I don't really know. I haven't weighed myself for ages.'

Rachel turned around and moved on to another subject.

'Here's the notebook with all the stuff for you. Caitlin has been a bit funny with her food – she had a nasty cold a few weeks ago and it dragged on into some kind of hay-fever. I don't think her taste is quite the same. Funnily enough, Ffion didn't catch it.'

Natalie looked up at where the notebook was kept and nodded her head.

'And I've made a lasagne for tonight – with veggie mince. I remembered you don't eat meat any more. There's loads more stuff in the freezer – come and see.'

Natalie followed her and noted all that she said. She read through the notebook and double checked with Rachel where necessary.

'They've had a bath earlier today so just make sure they have a wash and brush teeth before bed,' Rachel said, 'It won't hurt them to go without having a bath while we're away! I just get twitchy about them going in the bathwater when I'm not with them! I know they're four years old but I suppose I'll be just as bad when they're eighteen!'

She quickly disappeared through the doorway to shout at Ben to hurry up.

Ben came down the stairs with the overnight bags and Natalie saw that he, too, was looking very smart; the combination of black trousers and white shirt with his white-blonde hair transformed him into a celebrity lookalike.

'Wow! You look just like the bloke on TV... on that adventure travel programme...? What's his name...?'

Ben pulled a mock disappointed face, 'Not like Jacob from Twilight then? I'd rather be dark and handsome than look like an albino.'

Rachel gave him a glare.

Natalie winced inwardly. She was certain that Jack was the only Jacob lookalike that Ben knew.

'People who look like Jacob are just overrated,' she said before turning away and studying one of the twins' drawings.

Ben continued out to the car with the bags while Rachel followed behind him.

'What?' Natalie heard him ask incredulously.

'Oh, never mind, mouth-of-the-south!' she replied.

11. Natalie.

When she was certain that Ben and Rachel's car had time to reach the top of the drive, Natalie began to make her way up the stairs. She had already taken her overnight bag up to the bedroom she used as soon as she had arrived, but that had been different - the difference that two observant adults could make to someone with Natalie's careful character.

Now, a cry alerted her before she got to the halfway point.

'Ffion takin' my Peppa Pig!'

Natalie turned around and went back down to see Caitlin standing in the living room with her fists tight against her eyes while Ffion stood guiltily to one side clutching a Peppa Pig toy. Natalie sighed – bloody kids! Why couldn't they have waited ten minutes to have an argument! She thought about the quickest way to resolve it.

'No!' Caitlin screamed, 'Mine!'

'Come here,' Natalie said to Caitlin, 'You and me only. We'll have a look through your Naughty Penguins book.'

'And me!' screeched Ffion.

'No,' said Natalie firmly, 'Caitlin is a good girl who doesn't take other people's toys. We're going to look at the Penguins book together.'

Caitlin took Natalie's hand and they began to leave the room.

Ffion stood in bemused silence.

'Are you a good girl too, Ffion? Do you want to say sorry and give Peppa Pig back to Caitlin? Then we can all go and read the Penguins book together.'

Natalie was wise to their moods and mentally counted to five. Just in case it hadn't worked, she began searching her mind for another solution – desperation was creeping into her thoughts.

After a moment, Ffion ran at her sister and threw her arms around her.

'I'm sorry Cay-tin. I love you!'

Caitlin took her Peppa Pig back and let her sister hug her.

Natalie sighed with relief – at last she would be able to sneak back upstairs.

'What special girls you are!' praised Natalie, though her mind was only half on the scene in front of her, 'Let's sit down and get the book, shall we?'

They sat either side of Natalie and she began to read the story of the two naughty penguins, stopping every few sentences to ask the girls what they thought would happen next. They shouted their replies at her, each wanting to be the first to give the correct answer. They had heard the story so many times that Natalie was surprised that they didn't recite it with her!

After a few pages, the important thing pressing on Natalie's mind provided her with a plan.

'I know! Before we read the next bit, why don't you both draw me a picture of the naughty penguins sliding down the sea-lion's back?'

The girls squealed in excitement and ran to get their colouring pens and some paper from the stack that Rachel kept on the windowsill – presumably for situations when she needed some space from the girls.

'I'm just going to go for a wee now. You do the drawing and it will be a big surprise for me when I get back,' she told them.

They bent over their sheets of paper and sat close together while they began to draw. Natalie glanced around automatically to see if there was anything hazardous within reach before beginning her second attempt to go upstairs.

She had half an answer ready if the girls asked why she was going upstairs when there was a toilet and shower room downstairs, but they were too young and too absorbed in their drawing to notice.

Once in the bathroom, she locked the door and hunted around for the weighing scales. It was a huge bathroom and the scales never seemed to be in the same place each time. She had thought about sneaking up here while Ben and Rachel were loading the car, but they probably *would* have noticed and pointed out that the downstairs toilet (which had *no* weigh scales) was far more accessible, so she had patiently waited until they had left. The agony of waiting was gnawing at Natalie's insides – the longer she waited the more weight she imagined she was gaining. She stripped off her clothes and then sat on the toilet to urinate, though she only managed to force a tiny amount from her bladder. It was an automatic gesture to try to ensure that her body contained no extra fluids which would add to the weight.

She stood on the platform and saw the reading settle at forty-seven-point-six-four kilos. She breathed a sigh of relief. She had been certain that she had not gained weight. She felt her spirits lifting as she quickly got dressed and put the weigh scales back before going downstairs to see how the art work was progressing. She stopped in the kitchen and helped herself to a spoonful of peanut butter from the jar in her bag. She followed it up with a few gulps of water to add volume to the contents of her stomach. As was becoming the norm, her stomach rumbled hungrily in response.

The two girls were still side by side – Natalie never failed to be touched by their need to be together – and offering each other encouragement and ideas as they drew. Their communication was by means of the 'twin talk' that they used. Rachel knew exactly what they were saying but it took others a little longer to understand the code and abbreviated language they used.

Natalie picked up the notebook again. Rachel's instructions went on for several pages and contained the most exact of details. Ben was more laid back about his own directives. Today's instructions had included telling her that a neighbour had borrowed some veterinary equipment to use at the YFC Show as part of the quiz that the Young Farmers Teams took part in; it was possible, he had added, that the neighbour would bring the implement back later that evening but that he would not disturb Natalie and would place the item in the herbery. His usual mantra was only to say, 'Use the phone as much as you want, but try not to phone Australia!' Even the twins would join in on this phrase while Rachel would roll her eyes.

Coed y Bryn Farmhouse was in an area known as a 'Not Spot'. There was no Broadband or mobile phone signal and the computer that Rachel used at home had an old dial-up access to the internet and would take ages to download an email. Much of the area around the property was included in the 'Not Spot' and, at regular intervals letters would be written to the newspaper and to various official bodies to complain about the lack of technology that most other people took for granted.

To Natalie, though she had found the lack of mobile signal a disadvantage in the past, in her present situation she accepted it as a blessing. She had received five text messages from Jack that day – (all of which she had deleted without even reading – she knew they all said the same kind of thing) and the prospect of having two whole days without his constant harassment was another reason to lift her spirits. She was also looking forward to the relative peace from prying adult eyes that watched what she ate; and to the simple pleasures that looking after the twins brought.

At the back of her mind was the added bonus that she hoped to be able to cut her weight by yet another kilo by the time she went home.

12. Natalie.

The twins and Natalie sat around the kitchen table with the re-heated lasagne in front of them. There were glasses of water and a salad bowl also on the table. Natalie had given small portions of lasagne to the twins, but neither wanted salad.

'That means I have to eat your share of the salad too!' she told them. For some reason this made them laugh.

She piled the salad leaves on to her plate and said, 'Now there's no room for lasagne!' which made the twins laugh even more. However, Natalie had developed a cunning since her anorexia had taken hold. She always considered what might be reported in innocence to another person – and the possibility of it getting back to her mother. So, she took a very small helping of lasagne and put it on her plate. The salad leaves stood several inches deep and hid the pasta.

Ffion, with her mouth full of food, looked at the pile of salad and said, 'Your belly gonna be *this* big like a elephant!' and drew a rounded shape in the air to demonstrate.

Natalie's stomach clenched and she fought the impulse to push the plate away. The green leaves that had promised to do no harm to her weight suddenly took on a *calorie-laden* look to Natalie. She began to pick at the thinnest leaves and minute crumbs of pasta.

'Hippo got a bigger belly than a elephant!' Caitlin declared.

'Not!' Ffion argued while waving her fork around.

'That's enough. Eat your food nicely,' Natalie reprimanded them.

They gave each other challenging glances. Probably continuing the argument telepathically, Natalie thought.

She ate more green leaves and then took a piece of lasagne. Rachel was a talented cook and the flavour caused her gastric juices to go into overdrive. Natalie's mouth watered as she chewed into the veggie mince and pasta. The desire to bolt it down and eat more was almost uncontrollable. She disciplined herself to chew a hundred times until the food had almost dissolved completely. She took more salad and did the same with that, drinking half a glass of water on top of it.

The twins compared pieces of pasta to familiar shapes they saw every day.

'This is my sipper,' Caitlin said, holding a vaguely shoe-shaped pasta layer on the end of her fork.

'Not sippers! Wellies!' Ffion corrected.

'Don't play with it. Eat it properly!' Natalie said, aware of what a hypocrite she was. She pushed a huge forkful of lasagne into her mouth. Her mind warned her of the number of calories it contained – the number seemed to be displayed in bright lights on her retinas and visible wherever she looked.

She suddenly got to her feet.

'Got to blow my nose,' she said and walked briskly into back hallway and through the door of the downstairs shower room. She leaned over the toilet and spat out the lasagne. It floated partially. Natalie imagined that she could see globules of fat on the surface of the water. She flushed the cistern and took some toilet paper from the holder. She made a great show of blowing her nose before returning to the kitchen.

'You got a cold,' Ffion announced. 'Cait-in had cold. Atishoo, atishoo, all day!'

'Atishoo-atishoo!' Caitlin agreed.

'Mam said my nose was red like a clown!' she added proudly. Natalie noted inwardly that, since they had been in nursery school, they had abandoned the more English 'mum' for the Welsh 'mam' as their peers did.

'I don't want a nose like a clown! I want a nose like a giraffe,' Natalie said, in reference to a story she had read to them on a previous occasion. Once again, they giggled and began a 'twin talk' debate while eating their supper. Natalie let them be. Her mind was on the remains of the food on her plate. How much of the salad could she eat? The small chunk of lasagne that remained on her plate was easy to deal with – she pushed it under the salad leaves where she and the twins could not see it.

'No more. Full up,' Caitlin said, putting her fork down.

Natalie glanced at her plate. 'Can't you eat a little, teeny bit more?' she wheedled.

Caitlin shook her head and folded her arms. Natalie could see that the subject had been broached before.

'Ok. So you don't want jelly and ice cream if you're full up...' she said.

Caitlin's eyes lit up.

'Yes I do!' she almost shouted.

Remembering what Rachel had said, Natalie decided that it was better for the little girl to eat something even if it was not the most nutritious food.

'Don't shout! It's rude,' she said, 'you can have some jelly and ice cream when we're all ready.'

The thought of jelly and ice cream made Natalie's head spin. She wondered how she would ever serve it to the twins without gorging herself on it. The salad heap on her plate was diminishing faster than she would have preferred and she was conscious of the lasagne hiding underneath.

Eventually, Ffion put her fork down and said, 'Finished!'

Aware that there was a small piece of pasta left on her plate, Natalie was almost overcome with the need to grab it and shove it into her own mouth. Woof, woof, she reminded herself, but that did nothing to her while she was in such a state of hunger.

In the end, it was Caitlin who saved her by looking at her sister and saying, 'Your belly gonna be like a hippo!'

They both burst into laughter and Natalie realised that the image of her own belly had stopped her from weakening. She began to gather up the plates and very quickly scraped the left-over food into a recycling bin before the image could leave her.

She stacked the plates in the dishwasher then went to get the ice cream and jelly. She put small amounts in front of the girls and an even smaller portion in her own bowl. Then she sat at the table and began the battle once more.

13. Manon.

Manon can't remember when she has enjoyed a day as much. She feels as though she has been cleaning up or entertaining Gwenllian all day. She knows that there is one more thing she must do, but her courage is fading and the sanctuary of her home is too tempting for her to leave. Today is not safe, unless she makes special arrangements - maybe tomorrow...

She half wants to take Gwenllian out in the buggy. The dream of pushing her baby along in a buggy has always been a fantasy of hers. She used to imagine how strangers would speak to her or simply give an indulgent smile as they saw the precious bundle asleep in amongst a cluster of teddy bears.

She remembers giving strangers that same indulgent smile as she witnessed other proud mothers taking their babies to the park when she had lived in the other place with Matthew (she consciously tries not to even give a name to the other place – the memories are too painful). She had felt great annoyance when she saw irresponsible mothers smoking or talking on mobile phones while their babies screamed for attention.

She glances at the buggy. Perhaps a little stroll would be nice. As that woman who had been selling the raffle tickets had said, most people were at some show. It should be safe to take her out – just down the road. The people in the other bungalows beside her are elderly. There is a good chance that they won't notice... Her heart starts to thump harder as she imagines what may happen if someone *does* notice. How long would it take for the information to reach the police station?

She goes to the front door. It is such a quiet road; a nice place to bring up a child – though Manon has no intention of staying here. She looks out, up and down. There is no-one in sight. They are all probably sitting in their back gardens, she thinks. The evening is warm and full of birdsong. The distant hum of lawnmowers and strimmers has died away. A stab of pain goes through her – she recognises it as fear. She can take this kind of pain – unlike the pain of the miscarriages she has had. Perhaps it would be better to wait here – enjoy her baby one-to-one. Tomorrow, she will do that one thing that is necessary. Why spoil such a lovely day?

She goes back indoors and gazes at Gwenllian. How was it possible for anything to be so beautiful? She feels that pain of loss inside her again. How many beautiful babies like this have never reached the haven of being born? How many women who have felt her pain? She wonders how she has ever coped with it. Matthew had no understanding of the pain. Bastard, she thinks bitterly, then glances guiltily at Gwenllian. She must remember not to say such words out loud. Mothers do not swear in front of their children. (Apart from those uncaring, cigarette-smoking, mobile-phone-chatting women who, in her opinion, do not deserve children!)

Matthew had been a frequent user of swear words. Manon remembers the first time she had found out that she was pregnant. She had waited eagerly for Matthew to come home and when he did, he had accidentally pinched his finger in the front door and announced his presence with a loud declaration of 'Oh shit, shit, shit!'

'You'll have to watch those little words by the end of the year,' she had teased, 'Unless you want our son or daughter to copy your foul mouth!'

Matthew had stared at her in astonishment. Manon had thought it was stunned pleasure, but now she believes it was unpleasant shock that he had felt. For some reason that Manon cannot fathom, it has become clear that Matthew did not want children with her.

'How? When...?'

He shook his pinched finger while his ability to form sentences seemed to have deserted him.

She acknowledges that she was a tad underhanded – they had agreed to wait until finances were in a stronger situation before starting a family, but women forgot to take the pill all the time, didn't they? Most men needed a push or no-one would ever have babies!

When she told him that she was late, he was cautious.

'If you haven't had a test, how can you be sure?' he'd said.

She had patted her tummy, 'I know. All women know.'

He had slumped into a chair – his face alternating from smiling to a panicked expression and back again.

'So, how late are you?' he'd asked.

She had not answered him directly, 'Late enough.'

She felt that he would not understand. She was a day and a half late, but she *knew*!

Three days later, a pain cramped her abdomen. She went to the toilet and urinated. On the toilet paper was the unmistakable rusty-brown smear of blood. That it was a miscarriage, she was in no doubt. Her baby was leaving her body. She sat on the toilet seat and cried until Matthew came to see what was wrong. He had been sympathetic. There would be other attempts, he had said. Perhaps this wasn't the right time for a baby. Manon could not understand why he was unable to grasp the fact that her baby had died.

The next time she had believed herself to be pregnant, she had been seventeen hours late. Again, she regaled Matthew with baby-plans while he looked on with, what she realises now, was a disgruntled expression.

Their marriage had gradually crumbled. Every time they went out or had friends around to their house,

Manon's behaviour embarrassed Matthew as she told people about her miscarriages. Even the women, who had been sympathetic at first, began to look uncomfortable and check their watches. One of them had mentioned a 'friend' who was having trouble getting pregnant, ending the story with the fact that not everyone was able to conceive and the 'friend' had since focused on other positives in her life. Manon had felt the bitter taste of hatred in her mouth! How *dare* she insult her intelligence! There *was* no 'friend'!

Each month, Manon relived her anguish as the familiar cramps reminded her that she was not pregnant. She had become devious. Matthew was showing signs of reluctance to have sex with her. She pretended to put on the non-caring face and *'focus on the other positives in her life'* as suggested by the stupid woman who had been in their company. She told Matthew that she was taking the Pill again and that it would be beneficial eventually as her womb would be resting from its trauma.

He appeared to believe her and she was forced to endure her agony in secret as each period appeared on cue – each one rating as a miscarriage in her mind unless she was actually early. Meanwhile, she shopped on her way home from work and spent increasingly longer browsing the displays at Mothercare before going to buy food. The 'Sale' items she told Matthew about were items that she could not resist – though most purchases were bought and stored in secret – he rarely went into the spare bedrooms. Manon had emptied the cupboards and storage areas of their previous contents and re-filled them with a variety of baby items. Her earnings became used up almost totally by her obsession.

After a year of suffering in silence, she went to see her GP. The mystery of why she did not conceive was beyond her understanding; she had read every article on nutrition, exercise, hygiene, sleep, timing of having sex and still no pregnancy had resulted (though she believed that every time she was a day or two late and subsequently had her period, that there had been the beginnings of a baby growing in her womb).

The GP had suggested that some tests on both Matthew and Manon may have provided an answer but she had refused.

'It will happen when the time is right,' she told the doctor, though her true reason was that she could not tell Matthew and it would have been a pointless exercise for her alone to have tests. Another pain goes through her now as she remembers this – at least she has answer to the question of which one of them is not fertile. Matthew, who had been so reluctant to make her pregnant, is now the ideal expectant father with his *tart*, she thinks. Life has been unfair to her. She glances at Gwenllian. But things are looking up.

14. Natalie.

There was something about evening air that stimulated appetite in Natalie's opinion. The heat of the day had helped to keep her appetite in check, but now, she realised, the urge to eat *anything* was becoming overwhelming.

'Nattee!' a little voice called down the stairs.

Natalie jumped guiltily. She had the fridge door open and was squatting in front of it, fighting the urge to take a Mini Mars from the packet in there.

'What's the matter?' she called back.

'Want a drink of water.'

She got up from her crouched position and held on to the worktop for a moment while her vision blackened until only two small central points of sight remained. Her head pounded and felt as if her skull cavity was filling up with gas. In a few seconds, it passed and she let go of the worktop and went to get a plastic glass.

From upstairs she could hear giggling and animated conversation. She half-filled the glass and took it upstairs. The bedrooms felt uncomfortably warm and she was not surprised that the girls were reluctant to go to sleep. She glanced at the window; it was open as far as it would go. Two mischievous faces looked expectantly at her. Natalie sighed. She had been in this situation with the twins before - it was going to be a long night.

Caitlin held her hand out for the glass and then took a few sips. A coughing fit followed.

'Gone down wrong hole,' she gasped.

Ffion giggled.

'Are you ok now?' Natalie asked.

Caitlin nodded and took another sip.

'Can we have another story?' Ffion said.

'Yes! Story!' echoed her sister.

Natalie looked sternly at them.

'I'll only tell you another story if you promise to go to sleep afterwards. Ok?'

They both nodded, happy to agree to anything while their wishes were granted.

Natalie went to the bookshelf wearily.

'Which one do you want?'

A chorus of three or four suggestions came immediately.

'Only one,' she said.

Once a decision was made, Natalie sat on the chair and read to them. They both lay down with much resigned sighing and fanning of their faces to demonstrate how hot they felt (hoping, Natalie thought, that they would be granted a reprieve to come downstairs where the air was cooler and they could play). Natalie pulled the duvets off them and folded them at the bottom of the beds.

She finished the book and saw that the twins were still not ready to go to sleep. The heat was oppressive and Natalie felt sorry for them. But, more significantly, she felt the pull of the bathroom and its digital weigh-scales – just being upstairs felt like she *had* to weigh herself once more.

'Just try to go to sleep,' she said. She got up from the chair and felt the familiar blackness engulfing her sight. She quickly sat down again.

'Nother story?' Caitlin said hopefully.

'No more stories tonight. Sleep time now.'

She got up again, this time without incident, and left the bedroom door open so that the air would circulate as much as possible.

After giving in to her obsession by weighing herself again, she went downstairs. She could hear the girls chatting to each other. Oh well, she thought, they would go to sleep once they were tired enough. Like a sleepwalker, she went automatically to the fridge and opened it. She stared at the Mini Mars packet and then, as if it had a mind of its own, her hand had shot out and taken one from the already open packet. She ripped the paper off and put the whole Mars in her mouth. Salivary juices flowed over her tongue and she chomped at it, feeling the chocolate and toffee coming apart. In little more than seconds, she had swallowed it. The taste of chocolate remained in her mouth – evidence of her weakness, she thought. An image of the weigh-scales consoled her – she had not gained any weight since the previous time.

Eating one was the start of an even greater craving and soon she was gazing at the packet a second time. Woof, woof, she told herself. A brief image of Mrs Jenkins's fat dog appeared in her mind before it was replaced by the sight of the Mars packet in front of her. Just one more, she told herself, just one.

She took a second bar and slowly ripped open the paper. Then, she nibbled tiny bits off the chocolate coating, eating all around the bar; she made a rule for herself, she was only allowed to eat it if it lasted for one hundred bites. When that seemed too easy, she added another rule – she had to eat each part separately, chocolate, toffee and filling without any trace of one on the other. She sat on the kitchen floor next to the fridge and set about her challenge. She miscounted a few times and had to guess the number of bites she had already taken. The heat of the evening melted the chocolate and her hands became sticky with brown streaks. She was aware of loud thumps and excited squealing coming from upstairs but she ignored it. When she had finished, she sucked the chocolate from her fingers and licked her hands where the stickiness had worked into the creases of her palms. Once she had licked them clean, she washed them. The fat girl in her mind was encouraging her to take another one – working out the calories for her and keeping her eyes focused on the fridge door. Natalie hated the fat girl in her mind – she was the one who made her fail in her bid to escape the clutches of Mrs Jenkins's dog. She made a deliberate attempt to remember the day it had all happened. It was one certain way of not giving in to the fat girl.

She let herself re-live it. Walking to school and trying to remember how to work out the Physics calculation she had been having trouble with. Physics 'A' Level was proving to be much harder than she had expected. She had been aware of the groups of boys walking in front – boys from a younger class. She had recognised one as the brother of one of Jack's friends. Her phone had given a beep to signal an incoming text. Llinos.

'Got 2 have another adjstmnt to brace. Fuck!'

Natalie texted her back, *'Ouch! Gd Luck!'*

Llinos usually joined her as she walked to school but she'd had an appointment with the orthodontist due to her brace not putting pressure on the relevant teeth. Llinos had been complaining about it for weeks.

Natalie had her head down and kept walking while searching for another joke text someone else had sent her. She intended to send it on to Llinos to lighten the moment. Too late, she had caught up within earshot of the younger boys who all had their backs to her and were looking over Mrs Jenkins's garden wall. One of them laughed and the others joined in.

'Here, here!' one of them called over the wall. Natalie regularly saw Mrs Jenkins's bulldog strutting along the perimeter and now she heard it bark at the boys – a strange muffled bark.

She half glanced up and saw that the dog held a large cushion in its mouth (no doubt, stolen from the house) and was dragging it through the garden. While in this state of agitation, the dog stopped and, with most of the cushion underneath its body, began trying to hump it. Natalie would always remember the way its fat body jiggled and wobbled while it attempted to have sex with the cushion.

'Natalie!' one of the boys called to the dog, 'Here, Natalie!'

They had not seen Natalie behind them.

'Natalie, leave Jack alone!' another one managed to get out before collapsing into giggles.

Natalie stood still while her heart hammered faster and faster. She felt her face glowing with embarrassment and the prickling of tears at the back of her eyes.

A boy's voice asked some question – obviously unaware of the origin of the joke.

Another voice answered, 'Jack said. After they caught them at it! Woof, woof, wooooo...' the rest of the sentence ended in hysterical laughter.

Natalie turned around and walked away from the school. The boys never knew she had heard them. She walked at an increasingly fast pace - aware of her body fat moving as she did so. Her anger traded places with grief at regular intervals. She arrived home in a state of anxiety but had managed to halt the tears. Her mother was still at the house, having not yet left for her part time work at an accountant's office. Natalie walked straight through the kitchen without pausing.

'Sick,' she said and went straight to her room.

Her mother followed a few minutes later. She had asked the usual concerned questions to which Natalie gave single word answers apart from the phrase, 'Leave me alone.'

'Well just ring me at work if you get really bad or if you're in pain,' her mother had said. Natalie had nodded and lay on her bed with her back turned towards her mother.

While she lay there on her own, her phone beeped again. She looked at it, expecting it to come from Llinos. Instead, it read JACK.

A flash of hate went through her. Scumbag!

She read his message. *'Where r u?'*

She texted back *'Fuck off. U been dumped.'*

Another beep came.

'Haha! U not in school today?' Jack came to school on the bus from the opposite direction to Natalie.

She replied, *'Leave me alone.'*

And that had been the last time she had texted him.

Later that day, she weighed herself. Her sixty-one kilos was within normal range for someone of her height, though she had always attempted to lose the occasional pound when a special occasion beckoned. If she had ever looked at a chart of average height and weight ratios, she would have seen that she fitted within what was termed as 'normal'. But she had never looked at such a chart; the only numbers that concerned her now were the ones she read on the scale from one weigh-in to the next. If anyone had been asked to describe Natalie's build, they would most likely have described her as 'average'. However, like many active people, Natalie was also very well muscled which gave her an illusion of being more sturdy than people who had a greater ratio of body fat.

Jack had tried on many occasions to contact her and even called at the house, but Natalie had been adamant that she would not speak to him. In school, she would take routes that meant she was less likely to bump into him. He occasionally appeared in unexpected corridors or classrooms; as soon as he saw her, his face would show a shifting of emotions – anxiety, hope and affection – but her vicious glare at him would stop any further contact. Eventually, he became reluctant to let his humiliation be witnessed by school-friends and he limited his communication to sending her texts.

There had been a long list of girls who delighted at his new availability, but Jack was far too immersed in his misery to respond to any of them.

Natalie had gone back to school after two days, her courage almost failing her at the thought of how other people viewed her. She kept her head down when passing Mrs Jenkins's house and, from then on, deliberately looked the other way if the dog was in sight. She did not tell anyone that she had dumped Jack, but when his name had come up in conversation with Llinos, she had abruptly said, 'He's history,' and refused to say any more on the subject.

She had been miserable at first – a feeling due to shame and the fact that she missed Jack. That had taken the edge off her appetite. Then, once she set about her challenge to stop eating, she found that she had already lost some weight quite easily and this encouraged her to cut out even more food. She began to wear shapeless clothes in an effort to hide her body (which she viewed as obese) and avoided wearing anything that displayed her arms or legs. She had taken the decision to stop horse-riding as she had visions of her 'fat' bouncing up and down like the rolls of flesh on Mrs Jenkins's dog. She became obsessed with the weigh scales and used them several times a day – even if she was merely visiting at someone else's house. She blanked out the fact that she had lost a great amount of weight but focussed entirely on the pin never going higher than the last weight she had recorded. Every small gain panicked her into thinking she was out of control and getting fatter. She made constant calculations where a gain of half a pound in one day could mean an increase of fifteen pounds per month and a frighteningly large total by the end of the year. Despite her obvious intelligence in other areas, she failed to be convinced that the human body could fluctuate in its weight from day to day.

She observed others who appeared to be watching her eating and developed many ways of fooling them. She refused to acknowledge the occasional query as to whether she had lost weight – her overwhelming shame made her want people to think she had always been thinner than they had imagined. Mirrors frightened her; in the same way that her friends saw her in exactly the same way as they always had done and did not really register her weight loss, her tortured mind saw the same sturdy figure in her reflection. She turned sideways and looked at her image with her stomach muscles relaxed and was revolted by what she saw.

Now, she sat on the floor by the fridge in Ben and Rachel's farmhouse, thinking about the other mini Mars bars left in the fridge. She felt the weight of the chocolate in her stomach and hated herself. In a few more minutes, she realised that the thought of another mini Mars did not tempt her. Instead, she imagined the two inside her spreading their weight gaining properties into her body. She leaned forward with her head on her knees and sobbed. The noise of the twins playing still echoed through the floorboards but she felt too overcome with tiredness and weakness to do anything about it. She wrapped her arms around her knees and sat there while the tears eventually dried up and, in this foetal position, she drifted into an uneasy sleep.

15. Natalie.

The voices were shrieking. There were people on a roller coaster – terrified and delighted at the same time. Natalie could see them, the small carriages hurtling down the wooden rail while their occupants held their arms up in the air. The track took a sharp right turn and the screaming intensified. Two of the riders were thrown from the carriage. Natalie saw with horror that they were Ffion and Caitlin. She ran - fighting to get her legs to move – so that she could catch them before they fell. The harder she ran, the less her legs seemed able to function. She heard them shriek her name.

'Nattee! Nattee!'

The voices became real and she woke with a start. Her hip hurt from contact with the tiled floor and her thigh was numb where she had slumped to one side.

She stared up at Caitlin's animated face.

'You sleepy-byes, Nattee. We got a bisitor!' Her slightly nasal tone increased with excitement.

Ffion stood behind her, wide eyed.

'I fell asleep,' Natalie said, rubbing her eyes.

She got to her feet slowly, testing the ability of her leg to take her weight. The life started to come back into it with agonising pins-and-needles. She hobbled along the kitchen, grasping the worktop as she felt her vision going black.

The girls turned and ran towards the door.

'Back to bed,' Natalie said sternly.

Their faces fell as they looked over their shoulders at her.

'Ok, just wait there for a minute. Then I'll come upstairs with you.'

Natalie glanced around at the clock. Ten past nine! How long had she slept for? The light was fading in typical end-of-summer shades (her favourite time of day, she thought, when the shadows lengthened and projected her body-shape on to the ground as a very tall and slim silhouette). She went to the door of the herbery and opened it. She could see no-one. She stepped outside and glanced down at the stable block yard. No car in sight.

'Car gone now,' said Ffion in a slightly anxious tone.

Natalie turned around to see both girls behind her.

'Daddy said the man was coming with quipment.' Ffion said.

'Man with quipment and don't phone Oss-tralia,' Caitlin added.

Natalie remembered the last minute instructions given by Ben. She glanced around the herbery for evidence of any piece of veterinary equipment that had been left there. Maybe he left it in one of the stables or tack-room, she thought. Either way, it did not concern her any more.

'Ok, back to bed,' she told the girls again, 'you've got to stay in bed. It's very late.'

'Car gone now!' Ffion said with her voice rising higher as Caitlin joined in with the same phrase and adding, 'Why has car gone?' in a tearful tone.

'Ok, that's fine. It's fine.' Natalie replied, 'Don't worry about it. It's ok.'

With resigned sighs, they went back upstairs and allowed themselves to be put back into bed without having yet another story. Natalie was pleased to see that Caitlin was showing signs of tiredness and was a little weepy. At least, if one of them went to sleep, the other would soon get bored and do the same. It was marginally cooler in the room so Natalie was hopeful that, this time, they would stay in bed.

Before she made her way downstairs, she went into the bathroom and once again stripped off, urinated and then weighed herself. To her relief, it showed the same reading as before. She dressed and went down to the living room where she put the television on and flicked listlessly through the channels until she saw something that caught her interest. She half listened to the programme while keeping an ear open for the twins. She got up from the chair and quietly shut the living room door. After a few more seconds of listening and hearing nothing, she lay down on the carpet of the living room and put her hands behind her head. She breathed in then pulled herself into a sit-up, wincing as the hardness of the floor beneath the carpet pushed against the bones of her spine. Up. Down. Up. Down. She aimed for fifty but had to give up after forty-four. She lay back on the carpet and listened again. Nothing. She turned on to her stomach and started to do press-ups – not the women's version, where the knees are supported on the floor, but the male equivalent with only feet and hands making contact with the ground (a far more efficient way of burning calories in Natalie's opinion). To her dismay, she was unable to reach ten repetitions. Her upper arms trembled and her body skewed sideways, but still she fought to complete the exercise. A more sudden faintness hit her and she slumped down on to the floor. Exhaustion, heat and hunger all combined to keep her there. She wanted to go to sleep. More than that, she wanted to wake up as a slim person. The fat girl in her mind was already suggesting other items that she had seen in the fridge. Natalie let a little sob escape her mouth. She should drink some water, she thought, that would fool her fat, greedy stomach. But, her mind warned her that this would involve going into the kitchen for a glass. The kitchen was a dangerous place to be while the fat-girl lurked in the forefront of her mind. Left over lasagne, Mars bars, bread, yoghurt – the list was endless and it made Natalie's stomach grumble as she pictured each one in her imagination. If it wasn't for the responsible part of her brain that insisted she stayed close to the twins, she would have gone outside and walked the entire acreage of the land owned by Ben and Rachel. Walking was always a solution to beating hunger. And the exercise used up calories.

Meanwhile, she needed to sleep. Right here on the carpet. Getting up to lie on the sofa was also dangerous. She might just keep walking past the sofa, through the doorway and into the kitchen. She folded her arms under her face and closed her eyes.

The next time she woke up, it was entirely dark apart from the flickering glow from the television. Her body felt stiff and painful. She moved slowly until she could get into a sitting position. Her jaw ached where she had rested it on the knuckles of her hand. Despite this, she still felt sleepy. She grasped the television remote control and pressed the Programme Info button – the menu displayed on the screen showed that it was half-past ten. She glanced at the sofa – she needed to lie down. She looked at the programme selection but could not summon up the presence of mind to choose one. She flung the remote control down again – it bounced onto the armchair. Perhaps she should switch it off, she thought, but felt too drained of energy to walk over to the chair to pick it up again. She walked on her knees towards the sofa and clambered on to it. Her stomach clenched itself and rumbled.

She remembered the peanut butter in her bag, but that was in the kitchen and too far away in her present weakened state. She fell back on to the sofa and closed her eyes. If she slept, she wouldn't be able to eat. The television continued with its programme and Natalie was conscious of its comforting background noise. She did not think it had woken her; rather, it had been the pain from lying on the uncomfortable floor. As she started to drift off, she suddenly thought of the twins. Was that what had made her wake up? She sat up reluctantly and listened with her head tilted. There was no sound from upstairs. She began to lie down again when her subconscious 'Sensible Natalie' planted the thought that she should creep upstairs and check. Natalie was a conscientious person and, in addition, Ben and Rachel paid well; she did not want to lose the chance of babysitting for them because of negligent behaviour on her behalf.

She leant forward until her centre of gravity propelled her off the sofa and then stood up on shaky legs. She waited a few seconds for the blackness to come and go before she began to walk. The hallway was dark and she stopped herself from putting a light on in case it disturbed the girls. She walked past the kitchen door, turning her head (and her mind) away as she did so. A cooler breeze was wafting through the house – a refreshing feeling after the heat of the day. She began to wonder if she had correctly shut the door to the herbery, but dismissed the thought. Ben and Rachel's doors were always left open and anything that cooled down the oppressive heat was welcome on Natalie's sticky skin. She went slowly up the stairs, across the landing and stood in the entrance to the twins' bedroom. The faint blue glow from a night-light at knee level showed her that both girls were asleep; Ffion half on her back, arms thrown out and Caitlin on her side, laying diagonally across the small bed.

She turned quietly and tip-toed downstairs towards the sound of the television. In the hallway, the call of the fridge came to her again. She stopped. She tried to add up her calorie intake for the day – adding extra to cover any inaccuracies.

Maybe some water then, she suggested to herself, and a dry rice cake. She had seen them in the cupboard earlier. She imagined the dryness soaking up the water and filling her stomach until she felt satiated. She considered this for a minute; the rice cakes were in a cupboard that contained dry goods, cans and flour. She would not see anything else to tempt her. The gentle breeze wafted around her feet and she sighed at the feel of it. She realised that she had stopped in mid-stride – one foot ahead of the other like a long distance runner about to start a race. The leading foot was pointing in the direction of the living room; the one behind had already turned in the direction of the kitchen door. She could hear the sounds of laughter coming from the television – some kind of chat show. To her left, the sound of the kitchen clock ticked comfortingly, like an enticement to enter and eat. Natalie hovered in her decision – rice cake or no rice cake. Eat, eat, eat, ticked the clock. Maybe she should weigh herself first, she thought.

Eat, eat, eat!

Instantly making up her mind, she spun on her heel and walked into the kitchen.

She switched on the light and came face to face with two youths standing by the granite island between her and the door to the herbery.

A scream started to come out of her mouth, but she strangled it.

'Sorry I have scare you, darlin,' said the one in front, 'I call a few time. I thought you say come in.'

'What are you... who... why...' Natalie was incapable of getting her words out.

'We hear the TV on so we know you are not gone to the bed. Sorry – so late...'

'Why... Did you bring...?' Natalie's fear had been replaced with confusion.

'We come every year. We come here,' he said. Natalie thought he sounded European but there was also a trace of something else in his accent.

'We must ask your dad if we can shoot the rabbits and foxes.' The word 'foxes' came out as 'focks–eese'.

'He's not my dad. I'm looking after the children. He's away for the weekend,' as soon as the words were out of her mouth Natalie regretted saying them.

'Oh, that is ok, darlin'. He let us shoot every year. We are careful with the horses, always. Yes, Striker?' he turned to the boy behind him as he said this.

'Yeah, yeah, we're good with the horses, right enough,' the other one agreed – a definite Irish accent, Natalie noted.

'We will just visit fields by woodland,' the first one continued (the last word sounded like woot-lant).

'Well, I don't know...' Natalie said, 'I can't say if it's ok or not...'

'Oh, he knows us, so he does! We come with the fair, darlin'. Don't get much chance for huntin'. Your boss man says we do him a favour.' The younger one added this to the debate.

Natalie had no idea whether Ben had ever said this. Llinos would have known, she thought. Llinos showed an interest in matters concerning animals. But Llinos wasn't here, she told herself. She saw that they had come prepared; both carried guns and each had a canvas bag slung over their bodies from the shoulder to the opposite hip. There was a large torch protruding from one of the bags. Natalie had a feeling it was one used for 'lamping' – the term she had heard at various times by people who went hunting at night.

'Do not concern. We will not get in the way. You will not see us.'

Natalie felt outvoted. Her head thumped with fright and lack of food (though her hunger had vanished at that point).

'Well, try not to disturb the children,' she finished.

They turned around and went out through the herbery. Natalie guessed that they were about her age, maybe a year or so younger, but obviously older and wiser in the ways of the world. They wore the usual clothing of those who went hunting. Natural colours, boots, thick belts – Natalie was well used to seeing local people dressed in the same way. It reassured her.

As they walked through the patio area, Natalie switched the outside light on to assist them. Ben had stopped it from coming on automatically as the sensor picked up every owl, bat and fox that passed that way. She felt a slight misgiving as she witnessed the one who had done most of the talking, gesturing with his hips thrust forward in a sexual movement. But the feeling intensified when the movement gave away the sound of glass clinking in the canvas bag he carried, although she couldn't have explained why.

16. Anna.

Anna discreetly pulled her shirt away from her body. Despite the lateness of the hour, the heat was stifling and she wondered if there were obvious wet patches showing under her armpits.

The sides of the Beer Tent had been opened as far as possible, but little of the night air circulated throughout its area.

Her head was beginning to ache, too; a result of the fairground music she had been hearing all day and, now, by the music being played in the disco area in the next tent. Men leaned on the bar waiting to be served and chatting to their companions. The older ones tended to linger at the bar area while others made regular exits to the disco before returning to refill their glasses. It was an unspoken rule that the older men did no more than look into the disco tent from the entrance. Despite the difference in ages, they all had the look of farmers, Anna noted. Strong arms and necks that displayed the telltale sign of 'farmer's tan', where brown skin suddenly gave way to white at the edges of collars and sleeves.

She smiled at the waiting customers – a sincere smile that showed no trace of the contempt she felt for most of them. The number of customers appeared to be increasing and Anna made a concentrated effort to focus. By then, it was only her and Owen serving – it was the usual routine of show days. Gail, who had been there throughout the day, had gone home and Diane, the other helper, had left to assist Owen's wife at the Poacher's (not all of Llanefa's social drinkers wished to spend the evening at a Beer Tent in a farmer's field!).

Owen nearly bumped into her as he reached over to the crate of bottled beer under the bar.

Anna pulled back in some alarm, conscious of the possible smell of sweat on her body. Though the waft of a similar problem from Owen's body (despite the more pleasant undertone of his body-wash) reassured her that she was not the only one who was suffering.

'...and a pint of Magners?' he checked with the man he was serving.

Anna moved away to serve another customer.

'Two pints of Guinness, bach,' he said, his eyes resting on Anna's chest.

His companion leered at her, 'Or two jugs, maybe?'

They both laughed at the pathetic joke as she turned away with their glasses. She filled the glasses and put them on the bar. Money was handed over automatically – this was the fourth time she had served them.

'Puts hairs on your chest, this does,' the seedy one said, 'though maybe not on yours!'

They both laughed again and took a slurp from the frothy top of their drinks.

Anna secretly called them Pig and Piglet (according to their height difference), it was only the tip of the iceberg of nick-names she called the people of Llanefa. It was another part of the fantasy life that she had created from her discontentment at being trapped in what she regarded as a backward, inbred town. From earlier years, when the lure of film-making had captured her attention, Anna had found a simple way of amusing herself; furious at the typically Welsh habit of calling people by their first names, accompanied by their farm names or occupations, she imagined them as characters in a film she was directing. Alun Pwll-Mawr became Russell Hobbs due to his large ears and nose reminding her of a kettle! Other Llanefa residents became Butch or Bubba depending on which low-budget American film's undesirable character they resembled. It had become such an automatic part of Anna's life that she often forgot what the person's real name was.

Pig put down his glass and looked at her.

'So, where's your boyfriend tonight?'

'I expect he's here somewhere,' she said, lying smoothly. It was a question she was often tested with when she worked at events such as this.

'Saving his energy till he walks you home?' he said suggestively.

His companion, Piglet, (who, Anna noted, must have been a relation – no two people could have had such unattractive snub-nosed, round-faced features unless they were genetically linked) – snorted lecherously.

Anna smiled tightly and moved on to a cluster of younger men – some of whom she vaguely remembered from her school days. She had rarely been allowed to mix freely with boys from school. Her mother had insisted that she brought any boyfriends back to their house to watch television and have a meal.

'Can I have four cans of Fosters, Anna?' said one of them. She suddenly remembered his name – Dylan Morgan.

She got the cans and quickly totalled up as he struggled to dig money out of his pocket. She could see that he was a little drunk.

A heap of coins appeared on the bar as he went through different pockets.

'Whoo – moths!' said his friend, while the other two chuckled.

Anna counted through the coins.

'You need another sixty pence,' she said.

His friends started walking towards the disco area. Dylan's face folded into a scowl and he started digging again before producing a ten pound note instead. He scooped up the coins and pocketed them.

Anna tilled the money and turned around to give him his change.

He looked at her incredulously.

'I gave you a twenty!'

Anna's heart skipped a beat – had she made a mistake?

'I don't think so,' she mumbled.

'You fucking check!' he said in a louder voice that over-rode the music from the disco.

Owen was instantly by her side.

'Problem?' he asked.

'I gave her a twenty and she gave me change for a ten...'

Owen looked at her.

'I'm sure it was a ten,' she said, her face already blazing with embarrassment.

'You check the till!' Dylan shouted.

'Ok, no need to yell,' said Owen and opened the till.

The inside was packed full of ten and twenty pound notes – it was a futile exercise.

Anna looked worried, 'I'm certain it was a ten.'

'Oy, boys, boys! Come here!' he shouted at his friends, 'You saw me pay with a twenty, didn't you?'

They thought it was a joke.

'You? Pay with a twenty! Fuck off!'

Dylan's expression sobered them.

'I didn't see, butt. We were on our way over there.'

'I didn't have enough coins, so I pulled out a twenty. This slag says I gave her a ten!'

'Hey! That's enough!' Owen cut in.

He turned to the till and took out a ten pound note.

'Here! Take this, finish your drink and then on your way!'

Dylan stood his ground in what he thought was a challenging pose.

'Protecting your girlfriend, are you? Going to pay her in kind before she goes home! Good luck to you. I wouldn't touch her if you put a gun to my head! Snobby bitch!'

'Right! On your way! Now!' Owen commanded, while Dylan's friends tried to steer him away with encouraging words.

'Fuck you, then! I don't have to drink here. It's no odds to me!' Dylan yelled and purposefully picked up his can and started to gulp the contents as fast as he could.

The other three continued to pilot him in the direction of the tent opening and eventually they went out of sight.

An interested audience had gathered with the excuse of needing their glasses filling; an analysis of Dylan's behaviour was soon taking place.

Anna switched to auto-pilot and served drinks as they were asked for, but was aware of Owen watching her as she took money and gave change. Her previous over-heating had disappeared, leaving her cold and shaky.

A familiar face appeared at the bar.

'All right?' he said with a slightly sheepish smile.

Anna felt a noticeable increase in her heartbeat and the beginnings of a blush.

She smiled back.

'What can I get you, Gary?' she asked brightly.

'Pint of cider and an Alco-pop', he said, avoiding her eyes.

She swung around to get the drinks, half crashing into Owen in the process. His arm connected heavily with her breast. They both laughed to cover the awkward moment.

When she turned around, she saw that Gary had company. A girl with a section of turquoise hair had nestled up to him. Anna had an idea that she had seen the girl working on the fairground earlier that day. She put the drinks on the bar and saw Gary's uncomfortable expression as he gave the bottle of Alco-pop to the girl in an effort to distance himself from her embrace. The money was handed over and he quickly steered his companion away before anything else could be said.

She continued to serve drinks, moving along the bar area to get bottles, glasses or cans while snippets of conversation became a background noise.

'... a backhander to some bent bastard on the council. No way they'd have got permission to build there otherwise...'

Anna moved over to the other end of the bar to pick up a bottle of Orange Juice.

'...tyres like that on a tractor! Saw something like it in the Farmer's Weekly, but no good for the kind of land he's got over at....'

She felt as though she was playing in a doubles tennis match as she dodged Owen once more.

'That's the only alcohol-free beer we've got...'

She rummaged under the bar to pull another crate nearer to her.

'...had given him a can of lager! Shouldn't be allowed out this time of night! And I don't trust that fucking dog of his, either. Neither of them right in the head! I sent him on his way earlier...'

The music became louder and soon it was impossible to hear anyone unless voices were raised. Anna had to lean over the bar to hear what drinks were requested and, slowly, her body temperature began to rise.

At some point, she realised that she needed to pee. She ignored the feeling until she became uncomfortable. She gave someone change and then turned to Owen.

'I'll have to nip out to the loo'.

He nodded, multi-tasking by counting change and acknowledging what she had said.

She picked up an empty crate and stacked it in the makeshift store area they had beside the bar before slipping out at the side of the tent before anyone could order anything else.

The night air was cooler than inside the tent, though it still felt muggy and uncomfortable. As she walked away she could still hear traces of conversation, '... and then he said he'd put the brake fluid in there, the dozy twat...'

'No idea how to judge a Welsh Cob! A child could have done better than...'

Anna let the sound of talking and music fade away as she put more distance between herself and the beer tent.

She climbed the steps into the portaloo van and scanned the three cubicles for an empty one. Someone was peeing loudly in one, while carrying out a conversation with the occupant of the next one.

'I don't believe she ever did! Always been a liar! I'll never ask her to come again.'

Then the sound of rustling toilet paper.

'Did you see Bethan's ankle? Still a mess...'

'No, I couldn't look at it. Poor cow! She's had another X-ray...'

Two simultaneously flushing toilets drowned out the rest of the conversation. In the distance, she could hear the siren of a police car or ambulance. The sound got closer before stopping and the distant thump-thump of the music took over.

Anna felt her ears throbbing after the siren had stopped. In comparison, traces of *'Waaaa Yem CA'* pulsed through at an acceptable level. The noise from the fairground seemed to have stopped. Anna guessed that everyone on the show field was either at the bar or in the disco. She hovered uncomfortably, waiting for a toilet cubicle to open. The two occupants who had been having a conversation, continued to talk to each other through the partition; Anna wished they would hurry up. Eventually a door opened and Anna squeezed around the young woman (who was still talking) and claimed her place with relief.

She sat on the toilet seat and urinated. For a minute or two more, she continued to sit there, enjoying the relative peace; tiredness kicked in and she gave in to it, leaning sideways against the partition wall until an army of footsteps entered the van and each cubicle door was tried.

She got up and rearranged her clothes, before flushing and leaving the cubicle. A young woman burst past her, giggling.

'I'm desperate!' she said, her wine-smelling breath catching Anna full in the face as they squeezed in opposite directions in the doorway.

Anna went to the sink to wash her hands, trying to find a space between young women re-applying make-up or brushing their hair. She had another struggle getting to the paper towels to dry her hands. She gave an apologetic, but insincere smile to the two women in her way – a sign of sisterhood, a way of indicating, 'Here we all are. In it together, girls.'

'Oh hi, um...' one said, while obviously struggling to remember Anna's name.

'Back to the office!' Anna said, cheerfully binning the paper towels and leaving the women behind.

The siren started again as she descended the steps. Her head throbbed in protest until the noise receded.

The cooler air was a mildly pleasant respite and she walked slowly back towards the beer tent. She could see flickering blocks of coloured lights emitting from the disco through the partly opened tent flap. The sound of 'Come On, Eileen' had replaced 'YMCA'. They couldn't even find modern songs, thought Anna.

'Anna,' a voice said nearby.

She glanced to one side and saw one of Dylan's friends striding to catch up with her.

'Sorry about that earlier,' he said, 'he sometimes gets a bit arsey when he's been drinking.'

'Oh,' she said. She couldn't think of a more appropriate response for a few seconds.

'It's not your fault,' she said eventually.

'Yeah, but he was such a twat,' he said. Anna was aware that he, too, was more than a little drunk.

'I remember you from school,' he said, 'I left before you did. Went to work in the feed mill.'

'Yes, I remember,' she said, while trying to remember his name.

'I always thought you were pretty,' he said, 'you never took any notice of me though!'

'Ah,' she said and cursed herself, 'Well, I'd better get back to the bar before Owen sends out a search party.'

He put his hand on her arm to stop her.

'What about... you know... sometime. Sorry, have you got a boyfriend?'

'Well, it's a bit off and on...' she stammered, trying not to look at his eyes which were rolling in random directions (the nickname *Mad Eye Moody*, from the Harry Potter film suddenly presented itself in her mind). 'Look, I'll catch up with you again – you know what Owen's like!'

She followed this up with an artificial laugh.

He loosened his grip and put his hand on the back of her neck; the palm of his hand felt sticky. His face came closer and she could feel the heat of the beery fumes in her face.

'I've got to go!' she said, 'See you again.'

She rushed towards the beer tent when a shout from behind stopped her.

'Anna!'

She half turned.

'Don't forget, now!'

She raised a cheery hand and hurried away.

Fucking peasant, she fumed to herself. This was exactly what she hated about Llanefa. Drunken country-boys thinking they were all God's gift to women! She just knew that Newport would be different. The thought produced a burst of pleasure and she was smiling as she entered the tent. The music changed to 'Pretty Woman' and an even greater thrill bloomed in her chest. She had read an interview in Film-maker Magazine where a respected director had advised novices to choose a well-known production and re-set scenes, music or dialogue as a learning exercise. Anna had done this with the old Julia Roberts film, *Pretty Woman,* and her improved (in her opinion) version came to mind as she headed behind the bar. She had forgotten all about her recent encounter and did not see her new friend standing outside and watching her through the opened tent flap.

17. Anna.

While Anna had still been in school, she had rarely had an 'official' boyfriend. Her mother had encouraged her to bring any potential boyfriend home so that they could meet him and spend an evening talking and watching television.

To all fourteen and fifteen-year-olds, this was a daunting prospect and it soon became known amongst the boys of Llanefa School that going out with Anna Evans would be a waste of time. What testosterone-topped teenager wanted to date a girl in full view of her parents while discussing what he wanted to do after leaving school?

So, apart from occasional, relatively innocent, relationships within school hours, Anna was denied the opportunity of doing what her parents quaintly called 'going steady' with a boy. Her parents' unhealthy view of keeping her close to home as a safeguard for their twilight years rebounded on them as it created slyness in Anna – her character became shallow; she presented an acceptable front to all she met, while inside, she boiled with resentment.

At the school's Christmas Discos, she was able to live like a normal teenager for a few hours though she soon concluded that being taken outside the school hall with her chosen 'partner' and having to endure wet kisses and an intruding tongue in her mouth while a pair of hands crawled inside her clothes, was not as great as it was made out to be!

It was around this time that Anna's interest in film production reached an all-time high. She read avidly about all aspects of the subject and came to the conclusion

113

that the people involved in this world were her role models. Delving further into their personal stories and relationships she saw her life in Llanefa as the start of an epic film. Being surrounded by stupid and (in her view) uneducated people was the hurdle she had to overcome. Even her closest girlfriends irritated her with their plans to go away to study teaching or medicine before 'settling down' into a traditional role either in Llanefa or in some similarly parochial community.

During her two 'A' Level years at school (her mother had suggested Biology and Art – a choice that few teachers could understand) Anna had started waitressing at the Poacher's Rest. Prior to this age, she had worked in the pub kitchen only. This was an upward move in her opinion. She occasionally met visitors from different locations and who worked in industries that did not involve farming or the feed mill; more significantly, people that her family did not fraternise with. She had a secret hope that, one day, a theatre manager or TV script writer would stop for a meal at the Poacher's. She daydreamed about the outcome while she cleared away the kitchen area or walked home at the end of the night. She relished these private reflections and looked forward to elaborating on them as she walked in the dark – the lack of streetlights as she left the main road behind was a bonus to her as it made the hated surroundings disappear from her sight.

In many other ways, Anna was developing just like any other teenager and, shortly after her sixteenth birthday, it was on the way home from the Poacher's that she lost her virginity to Gary Harris.

Though two or three years older, Gary had been in Llanefa School with Anna and had left to take up a mechanic's apprenticeship at a local agricultural machinery dealer's yard. He was an occasional visitor to the Poacher's Rest and was often accompanied by a cluster of friends and girlfriends.

On a drizzly April night, Gary had discovered that his car would not start and quickly established that the problem could be resolved by returning home to get his toolbox - which contained the magic bullet he needed. One of his male friends offered to run him home to get the toolbox and bring him back to the Poacher's. By then, the other friends had become bored and had wandered off home or to another location to complete their evening out. Once he had the toolbox, Gary waved away his friend and began to correct the fault, working under the car bonnet by the security light of the Poacher's car park.

He was still working on the problem when Anna left the kitchen to walk home. She ignored him as she walked by his car and he did not even notice her as he concentrated on his task.

Before Anna had reached the section of the road where the streetlamps ended, Gary's car was on the road and heading in her direction. Recognising Anna as someone he had seen around and being deprived of female company for the night, Gary stopped to offer her a lift. With the drizzle clinging to her hair and clothes, Anna accepted.

On the way towards Anna's house (she had to give him directions as he had no idea where she lived), Gary remarked that the car was over-heating slightly. Anna never found out if this was true, but, understanding such matters (having been raised alongside four older brothers) she agreed that it was best to stop until the water had cooled down somewhat. Gary conveniently pulled in to the parking area of Llanefa Country Park and switched off the ignition.

They began talking. Firstly, out of politeness, then with genuine curiosity until Gary asked the leading question, 'Have you got a bloke?'

Slightly flattered, Anna replied that she did not 'have a bloke' at that moment.

Gary turned the car ignition on so that he could play some music on the CD player. He had a selection of discs and he asked Anna what kind of music she liked. She answered with a vague, 'Pretty well anything', while she tried to glean some information from the pile of discs Gary held in his hand. She later despised herself for this attempt to be seen as 'cool' by Gary.

He chose one at random and punched through the selection of tracks until he found one in particular.

'You'll love this one,' he said, though it was a mystery to Anna why he would think that – having only known her for about ten minutes. He smiled and glanced sideways at her; he was really quite good looking, Anna thought. The small glowing light reflected off his face and Anna was reminded of *'Grease'* – the scene at the Drive-In. Her heart stepped up its rate and she was instantly transformed into the 'other life' that she was convinced awaited her. When Gary moved in closer to kiss her, she could almost hear the background music from the film and could picture herself leaving behind a heart-broken Gary as she set off for America to her destiny in film-making.

Whether it was the fact that Gary was a very good and practised kisser or whether it was the effect of her hormones was a question she never asked herself, but once his mouth stroked over hers and fingers caressed the side of her face, she was aware that her body was reacting in an unknown way. The kissing went on for a long time – all the while Gary's expert hands tactfully explored where they would be allowed to go and found no boundaries. At some point, the passenger seat became tilted backwards and Gary's upper body leaned over her. Anna's body tingled with unexpected warmth and she felt out of breath.

Gary stopped kissing her and looked down at her.

'Are you all right?' he whispered.

'Yes,' she half nodded, half gulped – even her voice had deserted her.

She had not understood the implication of the question, but Gary resumed the kissing while slowly undoing her buttons. Anna was aware of what was happening, but had no willpower to try to stop him.

By the time she had started to panic, it was too late. Gary had pushed her black skirt up over her hips and had partly pulled down her tights and panties and was doing something wonderful with his hands – something that prevented her from telling him to stop. She could feel a deep longing inside and had an irresistible urge to push her lower body against his hand. She was aware that he had taken hold of her hand and pressed it against his groin, where a frighteningly large bulge had appeared. He unzipped his fly and undid his belt before replacing Anna's hand on the liberated penis. She hitched her breath in some alarm. Surely something that large was not meant to go... *in there*?

Gary's hand worked its practised magic between her legs and she realised that a strange and new feeling was coming over her. He increased the speed of his movement and she heard an involuntary gasp coming out of her mouth and she clung to his shoulder with one hand and to his penis with the other. Her body seemed to be stretching longer and longer, the muscles feeling as though they were doubling their length. Then a feeling of suspended animation took over completely as she felt the earthquake of her first orgasm.

She had no concept of time but was suddenly aware that Gary had taken his hand away and was climbing over to the passenger seat. He pulled her underwear down and completely off one leg while leaving the other leg with the clothes crumpled around one ankle.

'My turn' he whispered, before she heard the ripping noise of something he had taken out of his pocket.

With relief, Anna realised that it was a condom.

He expertly put it on and leaned in towards her.

'You're not a virgin, are you?' he asked.

'No... well... yes, sort of...' she said. She thought she heard him sigh.

He held under her hips with one hand while he guided himself to the right position. Anna previously relaxed pose was disappearing and she gasped with the pain as he started to push into her. He seemed to realise that he was going too fast for her and stopped pushing for a moment. Anna froze beneath him as he recommenced the pushing. Her earlier ecstasy was being replaced by pain and she could feel an uncomfortable sweat breaking out on her back and her face. She later remembered this pain, after she was raped, and realised that it had not been pain at all – just an uncomfortable feeling – like wearing new shoes for the first time. She held her breath as he rocked back and forth. Just as she thought she could bear it no longer, he increased his speed and his breathing came in short gulps before he gave two or three brutal thrusts and collapsed on top of her.

'Oh babe!' he said while Anna cringed at the phrase which was never meant to be uttered in a Llanefa accent.

Once they had disentangled and rearranged clothing, the over-heated engine had miraculously cured itself and Gary drove her home. On the way, they made small talk (while carefully avoiding the subject of their recent activity) and Anna noticed that he had engine oil stains on his hands. A feeling of disgust came over her. What was wrong with her? What had she just let this yokel do to her? Her nether regions still smarted from the experience and the feeling added fuel to her distaste.

He pulled up the car outside her parents' house and half leaned towards her as if to kiss her. Anna had already unclipped her seatbelt and leaped out of the car on unsteady legs.

'Thanks for the lift,' she said cheerily and slammed the door.

Anna's parents had gone to bed, but her mother called down to her as soon as she opened the front door.

'Are you all right? Did you get a lift?'

'Yes. It had started raining so one of the customers gave me a lift home.'

Her mother closed the bedroom door and no more was said.

This was the beginning of a new phase in Anna's life. To discover that she enjoyed sex – even if she did despise the people she had sex with – was a surprise to her. On reading her film magazine, she discovered interviews with stars and directors who spoke candidly about their personal lives. Many of them admitted to casual affairs that did no more than fulfil a basic human need – an admission that made Anna's heart sing! This was the way such people lived! She had no interest in 'settling down' into domesticity with some country bumpkin. But, if it was ok to have sex with some of them, she was happy to go along with it.

Gary became an occasional lover. If he did not have a current girlfriend, he would wait for Anna at the end of her shift and they would have sex in his car on the way home. The fact that he never wanted to go out with her and was obviously using her, never registered in her mind. The way she saw it, she was using him! If Gary was not around, there were others – although Anna acknowledged that Gary was easily the best performer of all of them. Her previous reputation as a 'waste of time' took an about-turn. Anna was now looked upon as 'up for it'. Some potential lovers were dismissed from the start – she may have been 'up for it' but she had some taste! Although all of them disgusted her when she thought of having to share her life with them, for the brief few minutes that she enjoyed with them while she satisfied her sexual needs, they were more than acceptable.

Like many women who enjoyed sex rather than relationships, Anna had a self-confident look about her that men seemed to recognise. Her friendly manner to everyone, combined with the fact that she was known as a 'go-er' attracted men to her. It was one of the reasons that she was always chosen by Owen to help out in the restaurant and, when she was old enough, in the bar. Every man still possessed of his testicles had a glimmer of hope after speaking to her – a faint awareness of 'what might have been'. Anna did not consider herself to be a slut. She was choosy as to whom she had sex with and was careful not to do anything that would cause her any personal risk. She usually chose those of a similar age to herself – with very few unfortunate exceptions; they had to be sober and she insisted that they wore a condom.

Of the men she rejected, they almost all took the rejection in their stride. After drink, some were more persistent and whining than others and some had tried their luck on more than one occasion, but once the moment had passed, they went on their way and put the experience (or lack of it!) behind them. Very few bore a grudge. There was only one who had become very agitated when she had firstly pushed him away as he groped at her in the car park of the Poacher's. On several occasions he attempted to change her mind until the last time he tried to put his arm around her and grabbed her breast. She had spun away from him, glared at him fiercely and shouted at him to 'Fuck off!'

That had made him even angrier and he had reminded her that when they had been in school together, no-one had wanted to go out with her.

His name had been Dylan Morgan and his parting shot had been to call her a 'snobby bitch'.

18. Natalie.

Natalie finished her rice cake and washed it down with a bottle of sparkling water. She convinced herself that she felt full and didn't need anything else to eat. To test this theory, she opened the fridge door and looked in at the shelves. No cravings came. She felt slightly shocked at the spaces on the fridge shelves – she had eaten far more than she had intended. A sickening clench of her stomach reminded her how greedy she was. The Mars packet lay on its side, a large gaping emptiness facing her. She pulled the packet out to see how many it should have contained, scanning the print at the side of the bag and adding up calories as she estimated her own intake. There was one Mini Mars bar left inside. Her stomach made a gurgling sound as the rice cake and water made their way through her insides. The sound disgusted her.

She thought about going to bed. There was nothing on television that she wanted to see – every programme showed at least one sickeningly slim woman either acting or presenting. The boys had been true to their word and had not disturbed them, though she had heard an occasional gunshot in the distance.

She began to turn off lights and close doors in readiness for bed. She shut the outer door of the herbery (not locking it in case Ben's friend brought the veterinary appliance back early next morning) then closed the kitchen door and bolted it. She went upstairs as quietly as possible. There had been some noises coming from the twins' bedroom and she certainly did not want to wake them again. As normal for her, she went into the bathroom, stripped off, urinated and weighed herself. Like a knife in her heart, she registered that the reading was marginally higher. Natalie felt despair pour over her. What else could she do? How would she ever lose her fat if her body kept craving food and she gave in to it? She felt the familiar self-loathing settling on her like acid rain. She saw herself eating the rice cake, her cheeks bulging like a hamster's. She felt its weight in her stomach - and the steady progression of calories to her fat reserves. She leaned sideways and pinched a handful of flesh and squeezed it. It felt like a dishcloth to her. She wished she could squeeze it hard enough to force the fat out, reducing the weight it carried. She put her clothes back on, hiding the hated bulges that she saw clearly in her mind.

She prepared to leave the bathroom when a loud yell and cry came from the twins' bedroom. It was followed by a scream.

Natalie leapt at the bathroom door, fumbling with the lock in her haste.

'It's all right. I'm coming,' she shouted.

The shout had frightened her and her heart raced in response. The crying continued and before she had reached the bedroom, Natalie could tell that both girls were crying.

She ran into the bedroom. Both twins were huddled together on one bed, arms clutched around each other, staring at the window.

They ran at Natalie, throwing their arms around her legs and hips. Natalie winced at their touch; she hated anyone touching her fat.

'There's a man looking...!'

'A man! A strange man in the window!'

They both spoke at once, words jumbled up with crying and their mouths muffled as they hid their faces against Natalie's legs.

Natalie glanced nervously at the window. There was certainly no-one there. It was unlikely – the bedroom was on the first floor.

She sat down with the twins and stroked their hair.

'Look. There's no man! Nobody is tall enough to walk up to the window! You had a bad dream, that's all!'

'I saw the man!' Caitlin said, her eyes wide with fear.

'And me saw him!' cried Ffion, 'A monster!'

'Just look at the window now,' Natalie coaxed, 'there's no-one there.'

She got up from the bed and walked across to the window while both girls screamed, 'No, Nattee!'

She glanced down on to the patio. There was certainly no-one outside.

'Come and see,' she said and held her hands out to them.

With some whimpering, they ran forward and attached themselves to Natalie once again.

'Look at the window,' she said.

Slowly, they turned their heads and looked.

'Because you're twins, you get the same dream,' she explained (making it up as she went along), 'and sometimes, you get silly dreams, but they're not real. When you wake up properly next day, you know they are dreams because what you thought you saw wasn't possible.'

They started to calm down.

'No-one can get to the window without a ladder,' she said, 'You can't see a ladder, can you?'

They peeped around her.

'Santa Claus doesn't walk up a ladder,' said Ffion with authority.

'No, he doesn't,' agreed Natalie, 'but he's got magic powers and he can see who is being naughty without having to look through windows.'

The twins started to relax and offered other suggestions of fictional characters who looked through windows. Natalie responded with false amazement and agreement.

'Do you remember the story about the naughty penguin when he was looking into the igloo?' she asked.

'Yes!'

'He sitted on the snowman...!'

'He standed on the polar bear's head!'

Their excited voices got higher as they competed with each other for parts of the story they remembered.

'That's why you had that dream. Your brain, inside your head, remembers the story after you have forgotten it. When you went to sleep, your brain gave you a dream that a man was looking through the window. He was probably standing on a snowman!' Natalie said.

This version cheered them up and they suggested other possibilities to the dream.

'Now, back to bed and forget all about the dream,' Natalie said. Her voice was stern. She wanted to get away from the girls. Her heart was still beating very quickly – so fast that she felt breathless. She felt very strange and she could do without the girls' questions.

They went back into their beds without further argument.

Natalie left them and went to the room she used when she slept over. She had put her overnight bag in there earlier and she pulled out her pyjamas. She sat on the bed and put her hand on her chest. Her heart was still beating very quickly. She felt panic taking over. What was wrong with her?

Then, as suddenly as it had started, her heart began to beat normally. Natalie sighed and waited to see if the feeling would come back.

She pulled her book out of the bag and began reading. She did not change into her pyjamas in case the girls did not settle straight away. She intended to stay awake for a while. There was no food up here to tempt her and she had read that staying awake used more calories than sleeping.

Half way through reading she suddenly wondered if the boys were still around and had climbed up to the bedroom window. But why would they, she wondered? They had seemed pleasant enough and if they wanted anything, they would surely have come to the door again...

She began to think more deeply. She saw, in her mind, the hip-thrusting movement the older boy had made when she had suddenly illuminated them by the patio light. And the clinking sound...

She sat bolt upright. The Mars bars! The thieving little shits had taken them from the fridge! And, no wonder the fridge looked empty, she realised, the wine bottles had disappeared from the bottom shelf. Natalie had only half noticed the wine bottles. At seventeen, she was not a practised drinker. She had taken various alcoholic drinks (and had been drunk) when she had been at parties with school friends but alcohol held no fascination for her otherwise. Her anger was replaced by relief. So she hadn't eaten so many Mars bars! She grinned to herself – the relief bloomed even greater – thankful that she had *not* eaten all that food! She had been well and truly caught by the boys' story. She realised that she had not heard any gunshots for a while. They were probably a long way away – relieved to have got away with it, she thought. The travelling fair always brought some petty thieving to the area. Natalie looked forward to telling Llinos. She would have to tell Ben and Rachel, of course, but, in her opinion, they needed to be less laid back about locking doors and closing windows.

She got up and padded out to the landing to look out through the window. The feeble moonlight showed a deserted patio. She could hear sheep bleating in the distance and the sound of an owl nearby. Suddenly, her heart started beating very quickly again. She pressed her hand to her upper chest and tried to breathe slowly. She went back to her bedroom. The palpitations continued.

Natalie started to wonder about the food she had eaten. Had she had enough sugar and salt? Despite her anorexia she knew about nutrition and the workings of the human body, but she did not make a connection between them. Maybe I need a packet of crisps, she thought. She was certain that she had taken enough sugar that day (far too much in her estimation) but salt was something that she had not considered. She did not feel hungry and wondered if she could simply suck the salt off the surface of the crisps... She dismissed the thought of merely sprinkling salt on to her fingers and licking it off – she grimaced at the idea.

Her heart seemed to be slowing down again, but the episode had frightened her and she decided to go downstairs again.

She stepped very quietly down the stairs without putting the light on. At the foot of the stairs, she switched the hallway table lamp on and went into the kitchen. The loud tick of the clock welcomed her and the glow from the microwave and the cooker gave her enough light to see what she wanted. She opened a cupboard and pulled a packet of crisps from a multi-bag. She sat at the kitchen table and took one out. She put the crisp into her mouth and let the salt wash over her tongue. The feeling was blissful. Just as the crisp was becoming soggy, she pulled it out of her mouth, got up and put it into the waste food container. A smell of discarded lasagne wafted at her as the lid flipped open. It flipped shut again with a snapping noise. She stood by the worktop and repeated her actions – sucked the salt off the crisp and flipped the lid to throw it. The routine and sound comforted her – the rustle of the packet, the noise inside her head as the crisp met her tongue and teeth, the sucking sounds as the salt detached and the click of the waste food bin as she flipped the lid open and shut. Rustle, crunch, snap-click. She could almost time each movement.

An extra sound confused her – another tap-click. She looked down at the edge of the worktop to see if her jeans button was hitting the side of the cupboard. The tap-click came again.

She froze with a crisp in her mouth. All she could hear was the beating of her heart – a fast beating that had nothing to do with palpitations. A fearful heartbeat.

Right beside her, a voice said, 'I am sorry to ask, darlin', but I am needing a glass of water?'

Natalie gasped, then coughed violently as the crisp particles broke up and dispersed throughout her mouth and down her throat. She spun around. There was no-one there. The tap-click came again. It was coming from the herbery – she could see the kitchen door handle being tried. Her coughing subsided into lesser gasps.

'What do you think you're doing?' she demanded angrily.

'We didn't mean to scare you, like,' said the other voice, 'we just got a bit thirsty, y'know?'

Natalie recovered her composure.

'There's a tap down by the stables,' she said, 'use that!'

She heard a half giggle from the other side of the door. She heard the tap-click of the door handle being tried again. She felt a wave of gratitude that she had bolted the door.

'That is kind, darlin',' came the voice of the older boy.

Everything went quiet. Natalie didn't know if they had gone. Should she open the door to check? Then she could lock the herbery door at the same time. She cocked her head to one side and listened. Nothing could be heard except the tick of the clock. She continued to lean against the worktop, holding her breath while she listened. Don't be a diva, she reasoned with herself, they're younger than you. You can send them on their way. You could even call the police if they become a pain in the arse. The thought gave her some comfort.

The packet of crisps lay on the worktop – temporarily forgotten. She glanced at it with as little interest as if it had been an ornament. Once again, the thought of the twins' bad dream of the man in the window came to her. Had those two morons climbed up the wall, she wondered? Perhaps she should phone the police now... And say what, she asked herself? That they came to ask permission to go shooting and had been given the go-ahead? And that she had now changed her mind? The sequence of events made her look at it in a new perspective. Phoning the police because someone had called for a glass of water seemed like an over-reaction. What the fuck was she thinking of?

She concentrated again. There was no sound from the herbery. Her mind presented her with an obvious fact – there was a sink and a tap in the herbery! Why hadn't they used that? The mental image of Rachel's pots of herbs came into her mind. Would they have seen the tap? In the dark?

And what about the wine bottles they had thieved? That was enough to warrant calling the police, wasn't it? But was it serious enough to call 999? Wasn't there another number you could call when it wasn't an emergency? But Natalie didn't know what that number was. And, a little voice suggested in her mind (the voice of the girl they called Sensible Natalie when they took the piss at school), that she couldn't be absolutely certain that there had been wine bottles in the bottom of the fridge...

She realised that she was standing in a rigid position, her leg muscles locked in a painful pose. She breathed out, trying to make herself relax. She made a decision – she would sit down at the kitchen table for fifteen minutes. If she heard nothing, she would go into the herbery to lock the outer door. That would prevent any more intrusions from those two idiots, she decided. She pulled out the chair that would place her opposite the clock. The light was still on in the hallway and, together with the various electrical appliances that gave a ghostly green glow, Natalie was able to see the clock clearly. She leaned forward with her arms on the table and thought about the imminent end of the school holidays. Almost automatically, she thought of Jack, too. Avoiding him was an added challenge. She was going to have to find out what universities he had applied to. It would be her worse nightmare to find that they ended up at the same one in a year's time. She wondered how to find out which ones he was likely to apply to. She dropped her head on to her arms and mentally played imaginary scenarios where she had fooled Jack and ended up at the opposite side of the country from him. Llinos was intending to apply to Edinburgh, she knew. Maybe she could also find an equally far flung course?

The next conscious thought in Natalie's mind was when she opened her eyes and saw that the clock had jumped twenty-two minutes into the future. For a few seconds, she could not remember why she was there. Then the sequence of events arranged themselves in her mind. She sat up with partly numb arms and listened for any sound. The side of her face was wet with sweat where she had leaned on her hand. She wiped it with her forearm. She really needed to go to bed.

She got up and crept upstairs. Checking the girls from the doorway of their bedroom, she could see that both were asleep – Ffion turned towards the door and Caitlin curled up facing the wall. Good!

She went into her bedroom and flopped down on the bed. Tiredness kicked in at an all-time high. She began to undress and stopped halfway. Should she lock the herbery door? Just in case those idiots came back...

She stood up and thought about it. She decided that locking the door would be the best plan. That would put an end to any worry.

She got up and stretched. A yawn followed. She listened again. There was nothing to be heard. They had probably gone – not just from the herbery but gone off the property. They were just stupid over-grown kids.

She went downstairs to the kitchen. At the door she very quietly slid open the bolt. It made a low metallic sound and clicked into place. She waited a second; still no sound from outside. She turned the handle, hearing its tap-click as she did so. Very slowly, she opened the door an inch and strained to see through the gap. Nothing obvious was to be seen. She opened it a bit more, her heart hammering loudly with anticipation. After a few seconds of looking, she opened it fully. Everything looked normal in the somewhat darkened room but she put the light on to check. Instantly, she felt relief. The herb pots sat in their usual positions. Everything was fine. She went to the door and clicked the deadlock. She glanced up at the bolt – reachable only to her and Ben or people of similar height. She wrinkled her nose. There was a funny smell in the room, she thought. Had those boys left something in here? She looked over at the sink, though it wasn't a 'blocked drain' kind of smell. It was such a familiar smell. Suddenly, she realised that it was alcohol.

A slurred voice beside her said, 'I have had sleep, darlin.'

She spun around to see the older boy standing in the doorway of the boot room.

19. Anna

Like most people brought up in the countryside, Anna had no fear of the dark. Even after the rape, she did not fear the dark – only those who wandered freely in her view and whose actions or comments had left her wondering if it was the person who had nearly killed her.

But, during the happy time that preceded that trauma she enjoyed the tension of watching films that featured terrifying events happening during the hours of darkness, but it did not carry over to her own life. She appreciated the skill of the film-maker and the need to create suspense by not letting the viewer see all the action. Darkness, in her opinion, was the best way to achieve this.

In her daily life, the despised surroundings in which she lived were minimised when darkness fell and hid the landscape; it dimmed the constant presence of farms and the generic, thickset farmers (with their characteristic almost-lame gait) who could be seen working in harmony with some machine or other.

At the end of a night working at the Beer Tent at Llanefa YFC Show, she relished the thought of walking home and the chance to let her mind wander into Hollywood mode. Though her body felt tired after her long day, her mind was just waking up and offering her ideas about her latest 'project', *Jaws*. After watching this film at home, she had been struck by the need to update the whole production. She had recorded it so that she could look at it again in sections with a notebook at her side. Later she would enter all the data into her computer. In the future, she imagined herself giving a PowerPoint presentation at an interview where she would astound the panel with the improvements she had made to this, and other, films.

Her mind had wandered to such an extent that she was unaware of Owen speaking to her until he repeated her name in a louder voice.

'Anna?'

'Sorry, miles away!'

'Can you put these in the van for me?'

She glanced down at the two small crates of soft drinks by Owen's feet. He continued to pull out heavier crates of empty beer bottles to place on a trolley he had nearby.

Anna picked up the small crates and headed outside to where Owen's van was parked. The side door-panel was open and some of the boxes and crates had already been placed inside. A few people still remained on the showground; men holding car keys talking to men who needed lifts home. Somewhere in the vicinity she could hear the screeching sound of female laughter as small groups of women headed off to vehicles.

One of the men (Anna had named him Vlad – she had forgotten why) called over to her.

'Do you need a ride home, bach?'

'No, it's ok, thanks,' she replied with a happy voice, 'Owen's got the van.'

She caught the not-low-enough remark from one of them.

'If I was twenty years younger, I'd give her a ride home she'd never forget!'

Lecherous laughter followed.

She climbed into the side of the van and began to drag some larger crates to one side to make room for the ones she had brought out of the tent. Small groups of people drifted past and she heard snippets of conversation.

'...by the entrance to Byron's farm...'

She sighed. Always some story about a farm!

'...and then she asked what I had on under my kilt...'

Or some stupid rugby trip, she thought, as she heard the voice of the man she called Angus (so named because of his ridiculous tales of the one time he had been to Scotland).

'...waste of public money! The ambulance should be for ill people not...'

And people complaining about something, she thought as she went back into the tent. Owen was stacking more crates on the trolley.

'You want a lift home with me? If you can hang on until all this stuff's loaded...?'

'No thanks. I need the fresh air and time to wind down,' she replied.

Owen nodded. He was half relieved. Apart from one very rainy show night, when her brother had come to collect her, Anna always chose to walk. Owen had no doubt that taking her back to her parents' house in his van would fuel gossip. Especially, with her parents away...

'Ok, just watch how you go. Lot of idiots about on the road tonight...'

Tell me something new, she thought uncharitably.

'We've had enough excitement for tonight. That girl...'

'What girl?' said Anna.

'One of the fairground girls collapsed. A fit someone said, but I think she must have taken something. Didn't you see the ambulance? Out cold, she was. Gone off to hospital. Gary's bird went with her.'

Anna felt a flash of anger – both for Owen for his use of the term 'bird' and, for some subconscious reason, towards Gary.

'Right, if there's nothing else you need me to do, I'll head off,' she said.

'No. You go, darling. Call by tomorrow so that I can pay you. I'll have sorted the cash by then.'

'Hasta la vista', she said and was gone before Owen had a chance to say anything else.

***

He looked around at the makeshift bar while mentally planning what else needed to go into the van and what could be safely left on the showground until the following day. He felt sticky and weary. He was not normally a man who took a drink when he was working away from the Poacher's, (and even at home he tried to curtail his drinking – it often threatened to run out of control), but he looked longingly at a cold bottle of lager. Just one, he thought. He felt confident that it would keep him under the legal driving limit. Or shall I wait until I'm home, he asked himself. His dry throat cast the final vote and he picked up the bottle and a plastic glass.

***

Anna picked her way across the darkened showground, the field entrance showed up with its white YFC Show banner. Occasionally, a car's headlights would illuminate it even more. Several other people offered her a lift, which she declined. Within minutes she was alone and walking along the road which ran adjacent to the show field. Road lights lit up the main stretch and she could see small clusters of people walking ahead of her – some with an unsteady gait that betrayed their attempt at sobriety. Every so often, a shout or loud laugh would resonate from one of the groups. One person carried someone else in piggy-back style. Anna could not see who they were and had no wish to become involved. Her mind had reached the sanctuary of the film making world.

The trouble with '*Jaws*', she reflected, was the way it had become dated; not old enough to be what she would have called a *classic,* but certainly old fashioned in an ineffective way. She would keep the music that signalled the shark's presence, she conceded, but the rest of the film needed a major overhaul. She mentally made a list of who she thought should be cast in the main roles.

Throughout the evening a late summer mist had rolled over the landscape and now slowly lifted to reveal the silhouettes of the well known Llanefa landmarks – the castle ruins and the standing stones on opposite hills – the faint orange glow of minimal light-pollution gave them a gothic quality. Anna halted in her tracks and stared with an appraising eye. That would be perfect for a Guillermo del Torro production, she thought. A car approached her from behind and slowed down.

'Need a lift?' a male voice called.

She looked at the driver, another local farmer. His car was already full with those who had been drinking. A woman's hysterical laugh came from the direction of the back seat. Anna noted that Gary was sitting in the front passenger seat.

'You can sit on my lap!' someone called from the back seat; a comment that was followed by laughter.

'No thanks, I'm fine,' she said, 'the path is just down here.'

The car drove off and she saw a stocky arm wave from the driver's window as it went.

She turned on to the narrower road where there were no roadside lights. Anna breathed a sigh of relief as the blackness gave her imagination the freedom to wander. In a few minutes, all she could hear was the thap-thap of her feet on the tarmac. It was a comforting sound and she glanced down at her feet – a faded vision in the darkness. It made her think of *Pretty Woman* once more; her own introduction to the film – the feet clad in various high-heeled footwear as the working girls strutted their stuff on the dimly lit streets. She hummed *'Pretty Woman'* as she matched her steps to the tune.

At that brief moment, just before she turned off the tarmac road and on to the earthy public footpath, Anna felt that life was good. Much later, she would remember that feeling as she tried to cling mentally to the time before bad things had happened to her.

20. Anna

Anna listened to the sound her feet made on the grassy path; a *swish-thup* as her shoes brushed the long grasses before hitting the hard, dried-out earth. She paid particular attention to the sound her feet made. She wondered how it could be generated artificially if the sound needed to be used in a theatre production. She stopped and broke the movement down into two parts – the lift of her foot, then the contact with the ground. She stamped her feet on the earth to see how loud it could be made before sounding contrived. Some of the grasses left stripes of dew on her bare legs; it provided a cooling relief after the heat of the day.

The noise she made alerted the horses in the adjoining field and she saw the familiar milky-grey shape of the friendliest pony emerging from the darkness and heading slowly towards her. She took a few further steps forward – noting the different tone to the *swish* as her feet moved through the grasses that had no seed-heads.

A snorting sound broke her reverie. The white pony was nearly at the fence, walking with purpose, certain of a snack. Anna took a few running steps to compare the different effect of the noise at speed. Nothing much, she noted.

Another snort from the pony made her put aside her research.

'I suppose you want some grass?' she asked the pony. She knew it was ridiculous to talk out loud to an animal, but one thing she had learned on her grooming course was that words spoken in a normal tone relaxed animals. It was also a habit she had picked up from watching films. Actors *spoke* to animals, though she acknowledged that this was in order to convey some plot fact to the viewer. She had no audience or need to reassure the white pony, but the habit prevailed.

The pony leaned as far as he could over the fence, while Anna rubbed his face and inhaled the sweet smell of him. He shook her hand off impatiently, clearly wanting the main prize.

'Ok, Mr Greedy!' she said with a laugh, 'Just let me get some for you.'

She turned and plucked some greenery from the hedge that the horses were unable to reach because of the fence. Its acrid smell made her wrinkle her nose as the stems broke. She offered it to the pony; he only sniffed at it and continued to wait. Anna pulled her mobile phone from her pocket and switched on the torch. She saw that she had offered a handful of fern to the pony.

'Fussy, are we?' she said before throwing the fern away and picking some other shoots. She turned the phone-torch off and wondered if fern was poisonous to horses, just like ivy. That was probably why she never saw them eating from the base of the Devil Tree. She automatically glanced that way, but the total darkness plus the distance involved meant she could not see it.

She heard the other horses getting closer – soft thumps giving them away; she saw their white faces moving like ghosts while the rest of their dark brown bodies remained camouflaged. The dry weather had made their field short of grass, while the unreachable hedge held tempting lush plant-life.

'Right, last bit of grass for you,' she told the white pony, 'or *they'll* all want some as well!'

He took the last bunch of grasses offered and Anna began to walk away. Somewhere in the distance she could hear car engines and a dog barking. A pinprick of light from a farm high up on the surrounding hill was the only other sign of human life.

The pony walked alongside the fence with her – an optimistic gesture that he hoped would gain him another snack. Anna tried to ignore him and kept walking. The white faces in the field were also getting closer. She increased her pace. She had once let them all come up for bunches of grass, but her kindness had misfired when one of the horses had turned on the others, biting and kicking while it held its ears flat against its head in an aggressive pose. She had been fearful that one of them would be badly injured and no wish for that to happen again.

She walked a little faster but the white pony kept up with her. The footfalls of the others sounded nearer; Anna glanced over her shoulder quickly. The white faces moved up and down – one of them shaped like an asymmetrical egg-timer. Close by, another white facial marking took on the shape of a map of Africa.

'Now you've started something, sweetie-pie,' she said to the white pony. Her heart rate increased as she desperately tried to out-walk him. A squeal came from one of the others – the sound of an argument beginning. Anna started to jog; anxiety and fear combined. What if they killed each other? What if their stampeding broke the small fence and they trampled her as they escaped?

The horses broke into a run, the thumping sounds becoming louder and a vibration developed through the ground under Anna's feet. Reasoned thinking told her she should slow to a walk, but the fear of being trampled kept her jogging. Suddenly a louder squeal and a thundering of hooves dispersed the horses in all directions and Anna glanced back in some relief to see that most of the shapes had vanished into blackness.

She fell back into a walk, panting slightly. Every few strides, she looked over to see if they were coming back and was relieved to see no more moving white shapes. The path took a slight dog-leg under some trees, putting the horses' field partially behind her. She began to relax as she again took note of the sound her feet made on the stonier ground. She was thinking of how to develop the sound if it was to appear threatening – for a pursuit and attack scene, for instance – this was another memory that stayed with her after the rape. She would later wonder how she had been so stupid as to tempt fate with her vivid imagination.

Before she had slipped into her other, creative world, she was aware of more footfalls. She turned her head and saw a single white shape moving towards her. She marvelled at the shape which was almost like the top part of a shirt. At least there was only one horse this time, she thought gratefully.

'So you're determined to have some!' she spoke to the shape, 'but you'll have to hurry up, mate!'

As the words came out of her mouth, she realised that the white shape *was* a shirt. Fisherman, her brain suggested – it happened, very occasionally, that she passed a fisherman on this path, though never at night. (Fishermen were a weird breed of humans, in her opinion - grunting a greeting at best and often not saying anything to her.)

A slight embarrassment came over her but, before she could say anything else, the shape was right beside her, strong hands grabbed her upper arms and a face attached itself to hers. A beer-flavoured tongue pushed into her mouth – the force of it all shoved Anna backwards.

She tried to lift her arms but they were clamped to her sides. She brought up a leg to kick the person away but his body was too close to hers. They fell back into the hedge; Anna underneath. The face detached itself from Anna's.

'Get off!' she shouted angrily.

'Stop!' a man's voice said; beer fumes and spittle hit her face.

He grabbed at Anna's breast through her shirt and pressed himself against her groin.

'Stop!' he growled again.

'Please don't... I don't want...' she tried to say, her voice no more than a whimper but her words were stopped by the mouth covering hers, the tongue pushing against her lips. Anna clenched her teeth together to stop his tongue going into her mouth, but the tongue simply slathered over her face before sliding past her lips and into the side of her cheek.

She tried to roll away, but with his weight on her, it was impossible.

As soon as his face was away from hers again, she yelled 'Noooooo!' as loudly as possible. The man shook her.

'Don't!' he said in a high voice and she realised that he was excited by the struggle. He put one hand around her throat. She was aware of his thumb moving quickly back and forth over her Adam's Apple.

'Don't,' he repeated.

Anna began shivering; her fury had turned to terror. Deep tremors ran from her head to her feet. A shoe had come off and she felt the dewy, slimy grass on her foot.

The weight on her was oppressive. She tried to wriggle her shoulders but the hand tightened on her throat. Another hand ran down her leg and then up under her skirt. She clamped her legs together.

The man tugged at her skirt, pulling one side upwards while the other side tightened against her leg. His knee came up between her legs and forced Anna's thigh to one side with a powerful shove; she heard the sound of material tearing – the brutal strength of it added to her terror.

'Please don't...' she repeated.

'Up!' he commanded, while trying to lift her left hip. Anna turned the other way in an attempt to confound him.

He roared an animal-like noise and shook her; at some point the hand that had pulled at her skirt had taken hold of her shoulder. Her fear intensified and she suddenly wanted to obey the man; do whatever he said; self-preservation took over any other emotion she had felt.

The man thrust at her lower body with his groin and made a low noise, deep in his throat. Some saliva fell on to Anna's face. She froze into complete stillness.

He removed one hand from her shoulder and delved down between her thighs. Her shivering continued even more intensely and she fought to stop it. She realised that he was undoing his trousers and she began to cry; the only sound that came out of her mouth was a barely perceptible, weak grizzling.

He breathed out loudly – a mixture of a sigh and a laugh. The act brought a further onslaught of beer odour combined with some other half-familiar sweet smell. He hauled Anna's skirt even higher; she lifted her hips obligingly while trying to mouth some pleading word at him. He felt around underneath for her panties, rubbing his fingertips over the area to find the edge of the material. His hand slipped under it and found pubic hair. He groaned softly and leaned more heavily on top of her before slathering her face with his tongue again. Anna's cries became louder sobs. Suddenly she felt the brutal ripping away of her panties, the scrape of the material against her skin.

'No!' she wailed.

The material gave way, tearing at their weakest point and burning welts into the top of her thigh. A further scratch from his torn fingernail (where it had caught on the edge of her panties) stung the side of her hip. Cool, night air made its way on to Anna's skin. She continued to sob, but lay as still as possible despite the shivering and the constant movement of the man on top of her. He let go of her throat and Anna seized her chance to try to get away – a futile rolling upwards while her hands pushed at the man's face. In an instant, he had the palm of his hand on her chin and shoved her back on to the ground, (like a sheep being prepared for shearing, Anna remembered thinking). The back of her head hit the solid mass of the hedge where something sharp poked her ear. She cried out and a stronger shove under her chin made her bite the side of her tongue. An anguished sound came from deep in her throat.

'Quiet!' he commanded. She stopped instantly. The hand moved on to her throat again; its grip got tighter as the man became more engrossed in his actions. Anna was focused so completely on that hand that she was almost unaware of the other hand and what it was doing. The grip on her throat relaxed and she realised that the smooth hardness of the man's penis was rubbing against her thigh. His other hand was holding it there and jabbing it against her. He let it go and gave another pull at the torn panties (making her scream in pain) until they fell completely apart at the side seam.

Anna's mind accepted that there was only one outcome; she prayed that the man would get what he needed from her – and quickly. She dared to hope that it would end then.

A raw pain went through her as a finger and torn fingernail was forced into her dry vagina. He gave an impatient sigh before trying again, this time working his finger up and down rapidly – the movement created a hot poker of pain inside her. Anna tried to wriggle away from the direction of the pain but the action only produced a pleasurable groan from her attacker.

The man pulled his hand away, lifted it near his face (Anna could see the vague shape of the pale hand in the darkness). She tensed herself for a blow or a punch but instead, he spat on the hand. Some of the saliva ran on to her neck in thin strings.

The hand returned to its destination and rubbed roughly against her vagina before a finger was inserted again. The pain was less this time.

Then, he pulled his hand away and very quickly grabbed his penis and thrust it against her, his fingers were still around it as he tried to force it inside her. She had a moment of hope as she felt the softening and bending of his penis (he would surely give up now, she thought), but he made some swift movements with his hand and the jabbing continued. The torn fingernail caught the tender skin on her labia and she half-screamed with pain as the tear stretched as he continued to push against it. Again the face clamped on to hers, the tongue lashing up and down. Mercifully, he pulled the finger away from his penis and Anna felt the immediate relief as the pain level dropped. Fear took over from pain once more and she began to shiver even more violently. Suddenly, he tightened his grip on her throat and delved deep underneath her with his spare hand. Anna gasped and tried to yell but before she could attempt to squeeze a sound from her throat, another pain took over. The man had grasped her from underneath and thrust a finger into her anus. Anna screamed and fought to roll away from him even as the hand closed around her throat. The torn fingernail felt like broken glass inside her anus. In the few seconds that remained, Anna had a mental vision of a metal spike being driven into her body – a subconscious image from some film she had seen – her screams were trapped inside her chest as her throat failed to squeeze them out past the pressure of the hand. She heard the remains of the scream emerge as he suddenly removed his left hand from her throat and grasped his penis instead. Anna realised afterwards that this was the time she should have attacked him and tried to push him off, but the pain and intrusion of the sharp nail in her anus took away any rational thought. While she froze in pain, she hardly noticed the additional ripping feeling as he forced his penis inside her. He gave a few hard pushes with his lower body and Anna felt the telltale signs as he came. The cessation of pain was instant as he pulled his finger out of her. He rolled off and sat up with his back to her – she knew he was turned away from her as the faint paleness of his face was not visible. She lay very still. She could smell the half familiar aroma of his soap and could feel fluid seeping down the inside of her thigh and on to the grass. She did not know if it was his semen or her blood. She still felt pain deep inside her – a raw ache rather than the previous ripping agony. Her head thumped and her throat felt dry in a way that she never thought was possible – she tried to swallow her spit but her stomach threatened to eject anything that passed that way. She coughed and was aware of a glob of thick saliva clinging to the side of her cheek.

The man half turned towards her – a vague grey image in the darkness. Anna tried not to look at him in case it provoked him into violence. He patted her leg – a conciliatory gesture such as Anna had seen dozens of times when the farmers rewarded their sheepdogs; a gesture accompanied by the words 'Good dog' or 'Good bitch'.

'Darlin', he said.

He got to his feet and fumbled with his clothes. Anna whimpered very quietly on the floor. She closed her eyes, forcing the tears to stay inside but they ran down the side of her face and over her ears and throat. The sound of the fumbling stopped and Anna was aware of no other noise at all. She froze again, waiting for another, worse, assault. She kept her eyes closed. She felt a sudden thud that made her jump – he had dropped onto his knees and she could make out the indistinct black shape of his upper body looming over her. Before she could even mouth the word *no*, he slapped his hand against her vagina and roughly rubbed at it. His breath carried the nauseating smell of beer towards her face. She flinched.

'Please don't...' she murmured.

He appeared not to notice but moved nearer – the vague body shape became larger as he got closer. The rubbing got faster and rougher, the pain intensified. Anna was aware of him doing something else too but the darkness was a blessing. He leaned even closer and, while she clamped her legs together, he pushed a finger into her again. This time, Anna screamed out a howl of pain and threw her upper body to one side. The finger came out and the man's body threw itself on her again. She could feel more frantic movements from him; it became clear that he was masturbating. She felt herself fading away from it all – *it's not real, it's not real,* she kept repeating to herself. *It's just a film – it's not real.* These thoughts went around inside her head, keeping her sane. There was hardly any new pain – only the remnants of the previous internal injuries. Her mind kept her a distance away from the reality – *it's not real, it's not real.* His weight was pressing on her again, but she was hardly aware of it. *It's not real,* she repeated the mantra in her mind; she could not think of anything else except that phrase. Suddenly, all the movement stopped and he had lifted himself away as if he had suddenly given up. She was not aware of what had stopped him, but she continued to lie very still on the dewy grass. She kept her eyes closed – *it's not real.*

She could hear her heart beating. A pulsating pain in her groin matched the heartbeat. A wet trickle of some kind had also run down from her anus. She felt as though her insides were slowly leaking until there would be nothing left inside her. The sharp plant that dug into her ear seemed to be a pleasant pain in comparison; she tried to focus on it (pressed her head harder against it) while her body kept up its uncontrollable shivering. She heard a 'hff-hff-hff' sound and realised it was the sound of her own breathing as the trembling affected the pattern of her respiration. She waited on the damp, grassy floor, feeling the trickle of *stuff* from her insides... and waited, for another assault or the final hand around her throat...

She had no idea how long she had lain there – awake but not awake; she had moments of wondering if she had died and this was the result – a perpetual vision of her last minutes. She was aware of noises nearby and felt the ground thump with footfalls; she braced herself but kept her eyes closed. So, I'm not dead, she thought. The sound came nearer; she whimpered again. This was what it was like to know you were going to die – another sob broke out of her mouth before she could stop it.

'Please don't...'

A snort close beside her forced her eyes open.

All she saw was the familiar shape of the white pony looming over the fence, his sweet scent a relief to her senses. There was no-one else there.

Anna gave way to noisy crying; hysteria took over and she cried until she could not breathe properly.

She forced herself to sit up, but the effort was too much and she lay back down once more. The white pony snorted again. The sound drove her to roll over on to all fours and very slowly got up. Her legs could barely hold her. She crouched down to cast around for her missing shoe. Her shaking hand came to rest on her bag before making contact with a familiar rectangular object – her mobile phone. She pressed a key and saw the screen light up – the Hollywood sign that she kept as her screen saver glowed back at her. She pressed her Contacts button, scrolling down to Home. Her need to speak to her mother was the only thing in her mind.

The house phone rang and rang before Anna remembered that her parents had gone away. She considered her brothers – though that thought was dispelled almost instantly. She had never had a close relationship with any of them and the thought of telling them what had happened made her insides recoil in horror. She realised that she had no idea who the man was. And yet, she felt that she *did* know him... She began to cry again. She wiped her forearm over her face and in doing so, smelled the beer, saliva and some other scent from the man. The reminder was too much and she suddenly leaned down and retched into the hedgerow. The smell stayed in her nostrils and she retched a few more times, though nothing came up from her stomach. A few strings of saliva hung from her mouth and the feeling made her retch again – the memory of the man's saliva turned her stomach – she convinced herself that it was his spit she was getting rid of. This thought brought about another bout of retching until she collapsed forward into the grass. She lay there with the side of her face against the cold, damp grass, her knees drawn up defensively towards her stomach. The grass was uncomfortably cold – she relished the feeling of discomfort that did not involve the pain of her attack. It was so tempting to just stay there and let her mind reach blankness.

The pony suddenly snorted again - a loud noise in the comparative silence and Anna jumped nervously. What was wrong with her? What if the man was still waiting for her on the path? She looked in both directions. There was no sign of movement. She needed to go from here, but she felt incapable of moving from her safe location (she thought, later, how stupid she had been – sitting in a hedge was not safe). Her mind gave her options - should she continue homeward through the path and its overhanging trees (and more intense darkness) or return to the road where she had just come from (a shorter distance), but, uppermost in her thoughts was the need to stay where she was. Where had *he* gone? Was he waiting for her? Waiting to finish what he had started? The memory of the hand on her throat made her shivering more intense. What she really wanted to do was curl up on the floor and let sleep take away this horror; she wanted to wake up and find it had just been a nightmare. Or even, she thought, she could lie there until she died.

We're going to have to get a bigger boat, she thought, before wondering where such a stupid phrase had come from. You're in shock, that's why, she told herself. Been watching *Jaws* too many times. And yet there was something nudging at the edge of her memory...

The pony snorted again and swished his tail impatiently before starting to walk away.

'Don't go!' Anna called to him, 'Have some more grass!'

She bent and pulled frantically at the grass. Her body protested at the movement. The pony re-considered and halted. Anna gave him grass with her hands shaking. She switched on her phone-torch and glanced nervously about her while the pony ate. No sign of anyone. She started to walk in the direction in which she had just come from – her pain became more intense as she moved. The pony followed at the side of the fence. Every time he began to lose interest, Anna pulled more grass for him. When he became bored with that, Anna remembered the packet of mints in her bag and dug around to give him those – spacing them out to keep the pony close for longer. She did not understand why she thought she should keep him beside her, but his presence was company and comfort of a sort.

A desperate need to urinate made her squat suddenly in the clumps of fern. The flow of urine brought another breath-catching pain and she sobbed while her bladder emptied its meagre amount. While she squatted, her body added another insult to her predicament and she felt her bowel move. She tried to stop herself but the sobbing had weakened her internal muscles and she was helpless to stop the passing of a small pile of faeces – its air-filled bubbling sound adding to her disgust. Her bowels cramped several times and she strained to rid her insides of anything that bore traces of him, though each movement increased the pain inside where she had been torn.

When she felt that there was nothing else inside her, she got up and continued, like a sleep-walker, in the direction she had chosen.

Shortly, she came to the end of the path and the minor road came into view.

What am I doing here? Anna thought, as she looked through the darkness. The cottage on the junction looked like a badly developed photograph in the darkness. There was a faint light at one of the windows but no obvious sign of life. She was even further away from home. Her lower body ached as if she had been sitting in acid. The thought of a clean bathroom inside the cottage made her long to get rid of her filthy clothes and his filthy... stuff – her stomach clenched a warning as she thought this. She stared at the comforting shape of the lit up window. She pictured herself being welcomed inside – a hot bath being run. Reality chipped in with the questions she would be asked by the old lady who lived there. There was a crushing feeling in her stomach as she imagined telling someone the details. Panic, shame and fear all lurked in the forefront of her thoughts. A swift suggestion of a name half showed itself in her mind – the man's name – and then it was gone again. Try harder, she thought; *you know who it was*. But, the more she thought about it, the further away from her mind it went. She thought back to when she first realised the white shape was not a horse – was there anything familiar about it? She went over it in her mind – what she had said when she thought she was speaking to a horse. Had he said anything then? His familiar scent kept returning to her nostrils (and turning her stomach) – of course, it was... and there her brain would let her down again.

'So, you're determined to have some. You'd better hurry up, mate!'

The words returned to her; then went around in her mind repeatedly. She tried to stop the process by thinking, *it's not real, it's just a film,* but as soon as she reached the last word, *you'd better hurry up mate,* replaced them instantly.

Crushing self-doubt took over. Did he think she was...? *Hurry up, Mate! Determined to have some...*

No way! The memory of the sharp fingernail, the hand around her throat.

Hurry up, mate!

So, you're determined to have some.

The comforting little cottage suddenly lost its appeal. She broke down again – crying until she was weak and had to sit down at the side of the road; and all the time the words, *'We're going have to get a bigger boat',* swirled round inside her head, driving her mad with every repetition.

***

Dilys Bowen was regarded locally as a 'funny old spinster', an ex-school teacher who had *gone a bit odd* since retirement. She had lived in the cottage that sat in Anna's view since she had moved from the school house after she had retired. Although Llanefa folk thought she was 'a bit strange', Dilys was far from it. What affected Dilys the most was her deafness. The fact that she had never sought help for this condition meant that she lived in a quiet world, not quite keeping up with what people said and often assuming an inaccurate conclusion when someone spoke to her. Some people thought she was being unapproachable but unfortunately, Dilys was simply unaware of conversation directed at her.

Like many people who found human relationships difficult, Dilys had directed her focus on her pet dog, Toby. His ancestry was a mixture of breeds and Dilys had adopted him from a local sanctuary when he needed a home. Toby's presence in her life was a great benefit to Dilys; he ensured that she walked several times a day and his other needs meant that she had a living being to care for. Occasionally, she would take him in the car and give him a walk at different locations where she met other dog walkers (though her conversation with them was limited due to her deafness).

On the night of the Llanefa YFC Show, Dilys had been aware of vehicles driving past her house until quite late. She saw the beams of lights that temporarily lit up the living room window as the cars turned into the junction. Her normal practise was to take Toby out for his last walk of the night – a chance for him to empty his bladder – by walking along the minor road for a hundred yards before turning around and going back to her house. Because of the added hazard of Show traffic, Dilys had waited until it was later than usual so that she was not blinded by car lights and the even more worrying thought that some drivers had been drinking. There were no pavements on the country lane outside Dilys's house and she was conscious of the need to be careful.

Once the movement of vehicles past her house seemed to have come to an end, Dilys got up from her armchair and took her teacup and biscuit plate to the kitchen and washed them. Toby knew the routine and walked round in circles as he waited for her to finish and fetch his lead. As the final item was put away in the cupboard, Toby jumped on to the kitchen chair, from where Dilys would attach his lead without having to bend down. She pulled a small torch from her coat which was hanging behind the door and set off down the small back garden with Toby jumping up and down beside her.

Out on the tarmac, Toby sniffed at various wild plants and duly watered them. Dilys told him to hurry up. They progressed at a normal pace down the lane – several strides then a stop and a cocking of Toby's leg before it was all repeated again. Dilys directed the torch towards the ground so that she could see where Toby was walking – she always tried to prevent him from stepping in anything that would necessitate a wipe down when they returned home. He had a particular fondness for fox droppings – a source of great angst between them.

Suddenly, Toby halted - one front leg still in mid-step. The brown hairs on the back of his neck stood up and he growled softly. Dilys did not hear the growl but she saw his stance and felt a vibration coming from the lead. She pointed the torch in the direction he was looking – expecting to see a fox. A heap of clothes lay at the roadside by the turn off to the public footpath. Dilys looked again – her cataract-clouded eyes gave her only limited information. It wasn't just a heap of clothes – there was someone still in them. She hesitated – considered turning back towards her house – when a face, *a girl's face*, looked up at the beam of light. Dilys went towards her. The girl was sitting at the side of the road; her clothes looked as though she had fallen. Her face was shiny with tears and mucus.

'Are you all right?' Dilys said, from a safe distance.

The girl laid her face on her arms and began to cry.

'I've been attacked,' she sobbed.

But to Dilys's ears, it sounded like 'I've been sacked'.

'Are you hurt?' she asked and tried to go nearer.

The girl covered her face and cried some more. Jumbled words came out from behind her fingers and Dilys went closer.

'You'll have to speak up, bach,' she said.

The girl's wailing became louder and the words even more indecipherable.

Dilys thought she would hear her better if she bent down right beside her. But as she started to go closer, a mighty tug on the lead stopped her. Toby was pulling backwards and rearing like a horse. With only one hand to control him, while the other held the torch, she almost lost her grip on the lead. Dilys called to him and tried to pull him towards her but he panicked even more and tried to bite his lead. She remembered that when she had first seen him at the dog sanctuary, the owner told her that he had come from a home where there had been domestic violence and would need to be homed where there were no men or young children as loud noises appeared to frighten him.

Toby continued to throw himself around on the end of his lead, Dilys could see saliva frothing at the corners of his mouth. She began to worry that he would strangle himself.

'Wait. Stop it. It's all right,' she said to the dog. It was no use; she would have to take him back to the house.

'He's very frightened. I'll have to take him back,' she told the girl.

She turned and Toby launched into a galloping gait, though his feet scrabbled repeatedly against the same part of the ground as Dilys held him back as much as possible.

Dilys reached the safety of her house and put Toby inside. He ran into the living room and hid in his bed as soon as the lead was unclipped. Dilys turned around to leave the house once more. Her heart was beating forcefully in her chest. At seventy-eight, she was giving her body an extreme test. Once more she made her way down to the edge of the path, but by the time she had arrived there, the girl had gone.

Dilys looked around but saw no sign of anyone. She remembered the nearby show and concluded that the girl must have been drunk. She headed back to the house to take care of her dog.

21. Arwel.

The activity in Llanefa Police Station usually remained at a relatively sedate pace throughout the year. The only exceptions were the Agricultural Show days, when the coming together of farmers, feed mill workers and agricultural contractors caused a tidal wave of drinking, celebrating and, inevitably, quarrelling.

Those who spent most weeks of the year taking a social drink in one of the Llanefa pubs were ill-prepared for the beer-fest that Show days provided, while the seasoned drinkers used the opportunity to increase their intake Added to the alcohol was the level of competitiveness that spurred them on to out-do each other in various activities.

The night of Llanefa YFC Show was no exception. During the day, there had been the usual calls for the Emergency Services as people were kicked by horses, were drunk and become unconscious, or simply sunburned and dehydrated. An added incident had been an accident at the junction on to the bypass when a caravan had been annihilated by a careless driver losing control after turning in the wrong direction on the one-way system. But, as far as Llanefa Police were concerned, the real activity started in the evening once the consumption of alcohol had reached a peak.

Although the police station was staffed twenty-four hours a day, it was often locked up during parts of the night while officers patrolled the small town and outlying districts. The only exception to this was if there were prisoners in the cells, when it became necessary to have an officer on-site to check on them at regular intervals. This dubious honour was bestowed upon Arwel Moses on the night of Llanefa YFC Show. The reason for his confinement to the Station was the presence of two men who had been arrested for fighting outside the showground. Both had been drunk and disorderly (or D&D as they were commonly known). Once they had both been searched and placed in adjoining cells, the arresting officer had returned to patrolling by car and left Arwel to be entertained by the two miscreants as they yelled insults at each other and at Llanefa Police in general from the confines of their quarters. Arwel had a log sheet in the Charge Room and ticked off his observations of the men at fifteen minute intervals. Once they were deemed sober enough, they would be charged, given a court hearing date and sent home. But for the moment, their serenading and catcalls were evidence that this particular time had not yet come.

One of them was trying to sing *'Tie A Yellow Ribbon'* in between responding to the suggestions from the next door cell that he was a fucking wanker. Arwel used the time to complete some of his overdue reports and tried not to let *'Tie A Yellow Ribbon'* lodge itself into his brain – otherwise he knew it would still be there when he went home at 6am and would, no doubt, stop him sleeping.

As they had been fighting as well as being drunk, it was important that they were monitored for any sign of injury that needed medical attention. So, at each fifteen-minute interval, Arwel would go to the small observation hatch in the door of each cell and speak to both men in order to record their response. If there was no response, it meant that he needed to enter the cell to make a physical check of the prisoner. More modern police stations had Closed-Circuit Television in each cell but Llanefa still relied on the old fashioned method.

While still under the influence of beer and adrenalin, the answers given to Arwel were varied and almost amusing. When they heard his steps approaching the cell door, each man would yell random commands such as 'Let me out of this shit-hole' or 'Get me a curry!' Arwel was used to it. He had the benefit of nearly twenty-years police service and very little made him outwardly angry or flustered.

As he made his way down the narrow corridor that housed the cells, Arwel was pleased to note that the shouts were getting less vociferous; a sure sign that the beer was wearing off.

He looked in at Steve Robins, in the first cell; he was standing in the middle of the floor, executing some slow-motion, if uncoordinated, Kung-Fu moves.

'All right, Steve?' said Arwel, out of habit.

'Bastard!' he replied.

Arwel wasn't sure who he was referring to and cared even less. The salient fact was that Steve was on his feet and obviously healthy.

He moved on to the next cell. Carl Thomas was sitting on the edge of the bunk. He looked up as the metallic clunk of the viewing hatch opened slightly as Arwel looked in.

'Ok?' Arwel asked.

'Want to go home now,' he said.

Arwel recognised that the fight was going out of him.

'Have a sleep. Sober up. Then you can go home. You and your mate!'

'No mate of mine!' he said, 'Owes me two hundred quid. Lying bastard said he's paid me back...'

Arwel slid the hatch back to its smaller dimension. He turned and made his way back to the Charge Room to fill in the log.

Inside the cells were buzzers that would ring in the main office if a prisoner needed to call an officer in an emergency. Those well used to bed and breakfast in Llanefa Police Station also used them to wear down the officer on duty in the hope that they would be released sooner. Once the dulcet tones of *Tie A Yellow Ribbon* died down, it was replaced by constant operation of the buzzer. Arwel ignored it as much as he could. At random intervals, a yell of 'Open the door! Let me out of this fucking shit-hole!' would carry through in between buzzes, but Arwel ignored that too.

As he trawled through his reports he heard Steve shouting through to Carl that 'it may have been a misunderstanding about the money he owed', and wondered if sober progress was being made. Though, that progress halted when Carl responded by calling him a 'fucking liar who would rob his own mother'. Each time Arwel went to check on them, they appeared a little quieter; Steve sat on the bunk and Carl lay down on his, but both answered him in an almost civil manner. It wouldn't be long, Arwel thought, before he could call in the Sergeant to charge them and boot them out.

Back at his table, Arwel continued with his paperwork. He was attempting to complete a report about Bara, who had acted out of character earlier that evening by assaulting a local farmer and dog breeder, Meirion Jones. Unusually, Meirion had refused to make a complaint even though he had an impressive black eye as a result. Bara had been shouting the word 'wolf' repeatedly as he was hitting Meirion and Arwel was trying to word this in such a way that would not result in Bara being detained under the Mental Health Act. Everyone knew that Bara had worked for Meirion and most were convinced that he had either not been paid or had perhaps been bitten by one of Meirion's German Shepherds. Either way, Arwel felt sorry for Bara's parents when they had come to collect him; although they were elderly they were extremely protective of their son and would not cope well with him being detained.

He heard banging and wondered if the two drunks were having one last attempt at hitting the cell doors before they sobered completely. They would soon give up, he thought as he struggled to find the words to put on paper.

The banging went on until he realised that it was coming from the door to the station. The security lock was on and any officer coming in had to tap in the current code number to unlock it. He puffed out his cheeks; he obviously was not going to get any peace to finish his reports. That twat, PC Dominic Beynon, had forgotten the code, no doubt! He got to his feet and went into the reception area by the front desk. The banging was getting louder and faster.

'Hang on! Fuck's sake!' he said.

As the door opened, a young woman fell past him into the reception area. She was crying noisily and grabbed Arwel by the upper arms, then, with a complete change of heart, threw herself away from him.

'I've been... attacked. Rape,' she said this last word in a strangulated and elongated tone as she gave in to racking sobs.

Shit, he thought, while trying to calm the woman – girl even, he realised – and guided her towards the room where he had been completing his reports.

She threw herself down on to the seat and covered her face with her hands. Arwel glanced at the clock automatically – everything would need to be logged.

'Can you tell me what happened, bach?' he said gently, but keeping a non-threatening distance from her.

'He came back... from the Devil Tree. I thought it was over but he *came back!*' The last few words came out as a scream. 'He followed me home... and I... had to hide and then I ran... there's no-one home... He called me...' some uncontrollable crying followed this rapid speech pattern.

'Take your time, bach. Try and start at the beginning,' said Arwel, knowing how important it was for victims to unleash their feelings but at the same time wanting her to hurry up and tell him the whole story.

'By the Devil Tree. The white faces. I thought it was a horse. The white pony came with me and he went. I saw the white face coming back and... and... he jumped on me and put his tongue in my mouth and I thought I didn't know who it was. And then... The white face. And then he...spat on his hand. I couldn't see...'

'Wait a second... let me catch up here... Who was it? Did you know him?'

'No, I didn't know who he was then... then I tried to run back down the path... and the white pony stayed with me... my legs hurt and it hurt where... he put his hand around my neck and he was pushing me and I was saying, please don't, but he was lying on top of me and he stopped and I thought he was still there. I could feel the footsteps and I thought he was going to kill me but it was the white pony... And after he'd gone, I thought it was over, but he came back when I thought it was safe. *HE CAME BACK*! And followed me home... calling me all the time... standing outside my house... and the door wasn't locked and I was just scared he would...'

Arwel leant forward slightly – the body language of someone who wanted more information, but this caused an alarming reaction from the hysterical girl; she pulled back and put her hands over her face again.

He leaned back immediately. He could hear the buzzer sounding from the cells – it was like an alarm reminding him to keep his distance from the distressed girl. He needed to get things started – call a senior officer, CID, a female officer, a doctor – it all went around in his mind as the crying girl sobbed uncontrollably. The buzzer from cells became more insistent. He got up and shut the door.

The girl shot to her feet and put the table between them.

'Open the door! Open the door!' she shouted. Spit flew out of her mouth as she did so.

'Ok,' he said calmly and reached out for the handle so that he was not blocking the doorway. In the background the sound of the buzzer increased as soon as the door was opened. Steve was yelling that he had to 'get down here now!'

'It's all right,' he said reassuringly, 'Ignore them. They're just a bit drunk. Now, can you just take some deep breaths and tell me what happened. You were on the path by the Devil Tree?'

The memory of it sent her into further disabling sobs that shook her upper body. Arwel noted that she was wearing a dark skirt and white shirt top. Both appeared to be wet and dishevelled. Her legs looked bare and were streaked with earth. She carried a bag across her shoulder – it looked grubby.

'I want to... I can't... he hurt me with... I thought he had gone... I ran home but I heard him calling me outside the house...he could have opened the...' again the crying took over. Arwel wondered if he could leave her there to go and radio the Sergeant.

'Look, I'll just need to get someone else...' he started.

'No, don't... please don't... they'll say it was my fault...they'll never believe he could do that...' she looked up in panic and Arwel wondered if the noise from the buzzer was upsetting her even further. The shouting from the cells was getting louder and more agitated and one of them was yelling that he was dying.

'It's ok,' he said in a reassuring tone, 'They can't come in here...'

'Fuck sake! He's dead and it's your fault!' the shout came through clearly.

The girl looked towards the doorway – her eyelids stretched to almost cartoon proportions; she seemed to have forgotten Arwel completely and he was certain that she was close to running out of the room.

'Let me just go and shut those idiots up,' he said with a little smile, 'They just say anything to see if I'll let them out. Then I'll come straight back get some help for you.'

Her eyes were still wide and focussed entirely on the direction the shouting was still coming from.

Arwel considered whether to go to the radio or the cells first, but the shouting had reached a screaming pitch and he decided to go and completely shut the observation hatch and tell them – *even ask them* - to be quiet.

He strode quickly in the direction of the shouting which, he now realised, was coming from Steve's cell only.

He pulled the hatch back fully – Steve's face was right beside it, eyes wild and his face covered in sweat.

'He's dying! He's dying! I heard him! Do something! *Please*'

Arwel went to the second cell and pulled back the hatch. He could see Carl lying on his back on the floor with a pool of vomit around his head.

'Fuck!' Arwel shouted. His hands became useless appendages as he tried to open the cell door quickly. The seconds felt like minutes as he made simple errors caused by panic. Steve's shouting continued and Arwel's world became filled with sound – his own heartbeat being the loudest inside his head.

'Carl! Carl!' he shouted and tried to get a response. Nothing happened so Arwel dug his fingers around Carl's nail beds and squeezed – the First Aid Trainer's instructions to 'give them some pain to wake the brain' floated into his mind.

He put his hand on Carl's stomach – he could detect no movement. Quickly, he turned Carl's head to one side and tried to clear his mouth. The slippery feel of vomit made his stomach clench. Deep in his mind, a voice was saying – *no, no, no – not mouth to mouth!*

Turning his head back, Arwel positioned him so that his airway was clear and began to carry out chest compressions. Breathe, *please breathe*, he thought. There was a sterile mouth to mouth kit in the First Aid box in the corridor and Arwel had decided that he would have to get it when Carl gurgled. A small spurt of fluid came out of his mouth followed by a gasp and small cough. Arwel continued chest compressions until some arm movements made it clear that Carl was partly conscious again.

Thank God for that, Arwel thought. He turned Carl into a recovery position and again checked that he was breathing. Arwel breathed out in relief. He glanced in disgust at his slime-covered hands – the need to rinse them quickly under the tap (before phoning directly to Ambulance Control) was uppermost in his mind. He half backed out of the cell, expecting Carl to stop breathing again. Go now, he told himself. Tap, Ambulance, Sarge – in that order.

Shit! The girl! He had left her alone in that state! He strode up the corridor, holding his hands away from him. He would have to say something quickly to reassure her before he did anything else. The door to the report room was closed so he used his elbow to open the handle.

Inside the room was empty. Apart from a faint smell of urine, there was nothing to suggest that the girl had ever been there.

22. Tegwyn.

The sound of the phone began as part of a vague dream. In seconds, Tegwyn was awake and had the receiver in his hand.

'Yes?' he said.

Tony Jenkins spoke to him.

'Sorry to bother you, boss. Had a very distressed young woman in here claiming she was raped down by the Devil Tree. But she's gone. Out the door without a trace. I wasn't in the nick at the time, but Arwel Moses was here - dealing with D&D prisoners – bit of a busy night. One of them had to be taken to hospital and while he was trying to revive him, the girl just vanished. I've got the cars out looking for her, but I thought you should know...'

'Do we know who she is?' Tegwyn was fully alert in an instant.

'Not really. Arwel said he's seen her around but can't remember where from. I didn't see her at all.'

'Ok. You've called Alun James I suppose?'

'Yes. He's on his way here. He said I should tell you as well.'

'Ok. I'm on my way.'

Gwenda was awake and looked across at him as he put the receiver down.

'Call out?' she said.

'Yes. Thought it was too quiet to be true. Go back to sleep. I'll ring in the morning if it's going to be a long one.'

Gwenda turned over as he swung out of bed. His mind had switched to the routine he needed to establish as soon as he arrived at the station. He padded downstairs barefoot in an effort to keep Gwenda's disturbed sleep to a minimum.

He grabbed a light jacket, though he could tell that it was not likely to be needed. The kitchen clock glowed in the darkness - 01.52am. Great!

He let himself out of the back door and unlocked the car. His actions were completely automatic – his mind was already ticking off a to-do list.

He started the car, drove out through the gateway and left the engine running while he went to shut the driveway gates.

A movement at the periphery of his vision stopped him from completing his task. A man's figure lumbered along on the opposite pavement in his direction. Before Tegwyn could form any thought, the man pirouetted in a half circle like a dancer before plummeting off the pavement. His body appeared to have suddenly lost any bone and muscle and he lay in a crumpled heap on the roadway. Tegwyn rushed towards him as the man regained his ability to move and attempted unsuccessfully to get to his feet. Close to him the beams from his car headlights showed him that the slumped figure was Edgar. The tell-tale fumes of alcohol pointed to the reason why he was there.

He looked up as Tegwyn knelt beside him.

'Mr Prydderch! Missed my footing! Bit slip-slip slippitty tonight...'

'Are you ok?' he asked.

'Me?' said Edgar, as if there were a dozen candidates for Tegwyn's concern, 'I'm fine. Tha's the problem. I'm fine...'

Tegwyn recognised the pattern of how things were going. He sighed quietly.

'Can you get up?'

'I'm ok. I'm ok,' he repeated, 'but I'll tell you something else, Tegwyn. You don't mind me calling you Tegwyn, do you? I'll tell you something else, Tel... Ten...

Mr Prydderch. I'm fine. But the caravan...' a half sob stopped him from saying more.

Tegwyn held his upper arm and elbow to assist him but Edgar seemed to want to stop where he was. He turned his face towards Tegwyn; there was more he needed to say.

'Never even got out of Llanefa,' he said sadly, 'Idiot driver. Straight into the side of the caravan. Bang!'

'Yes, I heard,' Tegwyn said, as if conversations held with people sitting in the road in the middle of the night were entirely normal. 'But, you need to get up from here in case another car comes...'

This was not strictly true as no-one would turn into the cul-de-sac at that time of night unless they lived there.

'But I'm fine,' Edgar repeated in a slurred voice.

'Come on, up you get!'

He struggled to his feet, blasting Tegwyn with more alcohol fumes. He swayed somewhat and turned fully to face Tegwyn again.

'Thing is, I'm fine,' he repeated, 'But the caravan... Let me tell you, Mr Prydderch, the caravan's fucked. Kaput. Knackered. In bits!'

Tegwyn was so surprised at Edgar's use of a profanity that for a moment he wondered if he had heard right.

'Don't worry. Insurance will sort all that.' he said, 'You and Marg are ok. That's the important part. Once you've sorted the insurance, you can look for another caravan.'

Tegwyn had heard about the accident earlier that afternoon. It had sounded clear cut; another driver's fault and no-one injured, but the road had been partially closed for a while as the debris was cleared up.

Tegwyn held on tighter to Edgar's arm as he felt him stager sideways.

'It's the only holiday we get,' he said morosely, 'No point going abroad. Marg won't fly any more. Lot of things she won't do any more...'

Tegwyn tensed. This was a familiar scenario from years before when he had been a uniformed constable attending to drunks and domestic disputes.

'Oh, well, let's get you into the house,' he said, cutting off whatever unwelcome statement Edgar had been about to make.

'You com... commitate your life to one person. Things go tits up. I've tried to be a good husband, but what for...?'

He looked at Tegwyn as if the right answer was about to be given to him.

'I don't mean to be rude, Mr Pry... Telwyn, but what happened to my... my... conjungal rights? I'm still healthy and able to...'

'Up the step,' Tegwyn interrupted in his haste to stop the words from reaching his ears.

'I know I can oblige in the bedroom compartment because...'

Marg's voice came sharply out of the darkness at the side of the house.

'Oh Edgar! You promised me! No alcohol – that's what you said!'

Edgar turned his head jerkily, his eyeballs followed a fraction of a second behind.

'Ah, my lovely lady wife!' he exclaimed.

'Edgar! Stop making a fool of yourself,' she said, as she walked up to them. Tegwyn saw that she had enormous Ugg-boot type slippers and a Scottie-dog patterned dressing gown on.

'It's all right, Mr Prydderch,' she said, 'I'll take him from here. I'm sorry if he was a nuisance.'

'Are you sure you can manage?' Tegwyn asked her.

'Oh, she can manage. Very capa-capabilical woman,' said Edgar with a lecherous leer, still slurring his words

'Stop it, Edgar,' Marg said, 'Come indoors with me now...'

Edgar began to say something else – Tegwyn had an idea that it was something he would rather not hear – but Marg stopped him before the damage could be done.

With a final, 'We'll be all right now,' from Marg, she and Edgar disappeared into the darkness. Tegwyn could hear Edgar murmuring terms of endearment as they went. He quickened his pace back to the car. He didn't want to hear any more and he was conscious of the need of his presence at Llanefa police station. On his way there, he reflected that it hadn't been as much fun as he had imagined to hear Edgar swearing.

23. Natalie.

It felt to Natalie as if the herbery was full of people. The older looking boy stood in the doorway and rubbed his eyes while Striker hovered behind him.

'What are doing in here?' she asked angrily.

'Oh, you must not be angry. We just had small sleep,' he replied.

As he spoke, Natalie was aware of a stronger smell of alcohol wafting from him.

'Ok, well you'll have to go now,' she said, 'I'm going to bed.'

Then, with an added flash of inspiration, she continued, 'My boyfriend is asleep upstairs. He'll be annoyed if you wake him.'

The boy's face broke into a leery grin.

'That is very nice. He is tucked up in the bed. You will ask him to come down and we can explain and say sorry, yes?'

Natalie knew he didn't believe her.

'He must be sick in his head if you are down here and he is asleep in the bed. On his own...'

'Yeah, well, he's tired,' Natalie said, floundering a little.

His grin became bigger.

'You have made him tired!'

'Right, well, I have to go to bed...' she said, opening the door to the patio.

'Oh, we will not disturb more,' he said, 'we will collect our stuff and leave all here as we found it.'

Natalie's anxiety increased. Striker, still partly hidden behind him, gazed sheepishly at her.

'You really will have to go now,' she added, 'the children will be frightened if they hear you.'

'Don't you worry yourself. We'll head off now, right enough,' Striker said.

Natalie stood in silence. The two boys mirrored her.

Striker belched. The other one appeared to find this funny. He started laughing, though Natalie didn't know whether to describe it as a laugh or a giggle. Cold tendrils of concern took hold of her imagination. What if she couldn't get rid of them?

'I'm going to go back in there, now,' she said, 'You really have to go.'

They continued to stare at her.

'Or I'll have to call the police,' she said while trying to inject some authority into her voice.

'Ooo – are you a bitch now,' the older boy said, while behind him Striker made an attempt to pass by him in the doorway.

'Where you go?' he demanded of Striker.

'We should go now. Listen, Pablo, we should just...'

Pablo looked at him in disbelief.

'You are fuckin pussy!'

'Ok, ok but let's go...'

Pablo looked at Natalie.

'I'll make deal,' he said, 'you show us tits and then we go.'

He collapsed into giggles as this statement struck him as the wittiest thing he had ever heard.

Natalie's heart thumped harder in fear. She tried to work out if she could step back into the kitchen and bolt the door before Pablo could make a move.

Striker began to look nervous and started to say something but Pablo shut him up with a glare. Natalie could see a bottle of wine lying on its side on the floor of the boot room. She swallowed hard but her throat had become dry.

'Well?' Pablo said, 'shake!'

He held out his hand as if he had just suggested a bet on a horse race.

'I'm giving you one chance to go or I *will* phone the police,' she said.

'Ok, phone cops and *then* show us tits,' he said and giggled again. Striker half laughed with him but stepped towards the door. Pablo's hand shot out and grabbed him by the upper arm. Striker gave a yelp of pain.

'Get in here, you fucking baby!' he said and pulled Striker nearer to Natalie. She froze.

'You ever shagged a tall girl?' he asked Striker conversationally.

Striker started to look uncomfortable.

'Loads,' he said, with a perceptible recovery of confidence.

'Lucky bastard!' said Pablo, his European accent becoming stronger so that it sounded like 'Lakee bass-tart'.

'Not even one tall bird I have shagged!' he shook his head sorrowfully.

'What is like, Striker? With tall girls? Did you do stand-up shag?' he continued, looking sideways at Striker.

His speech was getting broken up and Natalie had to try hard to understand him.

Striker just shrugged. He could not have been older than fifteen, Natalie thought, with Pablo a year older maybe... If it had not been for the severity of the situation, she would have found it amusing, the way they talked – like men from another generation. Somewhere in the background, she thought, the boys obviously had a dubious male role model.

Pablo reached out and put his hand on Striker's shoulder.

Striker flinched.

'Your arm. You hurt it, you big pussy!'

Striker looked down at the back of his hand; Natalie looked too. There was a bruise developing.

'Should have do what I say,' Pablo said, 'the gun, it kick you. You hold the gun wrong.'

To demonstrate, he swung around and picked up his gun. Natalie stared in disbelief – fear now making her immobile.

'You are holding gun like this!' he said and gave a pathetic impersonation of Striker.

'You must hold *like this!*' he added and swung the gun around to point at Striker.

'Jesus! What are you doing?' Natalie felt her hands reach out to grasp the gun, her fingers making a weak contact with it before she realised that her actions could cause an accident. She snatched her arms back to her sides.

'You are good with gun?' he asked Natalie curiously.

She shook her head first, not trusting her voice, 'No, no... just leave it...'

Pablo shrugged and looked at Striker.

'You must learn to use gun right way – then you do not hurt arm,' he said, his voice becoming mellower.

Natalie breathed a little easier. Pablo seemed to have changed his focus.

'I will make arm better for you,' he said and, before anyone had a chance to move, he had picked up Striker's arm and thrust the hand against Natalie's breast. She flinched backwards against the doorframe and the hand fell downwards over her abdomen. Striker looked horrified and snatched his hand back. Pablo laughed again then put his own hand, palm outwards towards Natalie's breast, (stopping a millimetre away from making contact) while placing his other hand on his groin and making a slow thrusting gesture. Natalie pulled back as far as she could go. Despite her shock, deep in her mind she hoped that he would not touch her tummy and ridicule her fat.

Pablo unexpectedly came closer and seemed to reach out for her waist. Natalie lashed out at him and a sudden clatter stopped them all as Pablo's canvas bag slid off his shoulder and crashed to the floor, dispensing various contents onto the tiles.

'Get out!' she growled at him.

Pablo looked sadly at Striker.

'Tall girls, too much hard work,' he said.

Pablo turned around to the entrance to the boot room and picked up some of the spilled items. Natalie seized her chance and slipped sideways through the doorway into the kitchen and slammed the door, bolting it almost immediately. She braced herself, waiting for an attempt to barge the door, but none came. She stayed behind the door and listened. No noise came from the other side. She double checked the bolt with shaking hands.

She leaned with her ear against the door but apart from some muffled swearing and the sound of a bottle rolling over the tiles, there was nothing.

'I'm going to phone the police now,' she shouted through the door.

No reply came back to her. Natalie stood where she was. She wanted to phone the police but she was afraid to leave the door. While she stood beside it, she felt protected. She ran through the events in her mind. Did she have a reason to call the police? She checked her pocket, though she knew that her mobile phone had no signal in this house surrounded by hills. Unless she phoned 999, she thought, you didn't need a network signal for that. Was it serious enough an incident to do that? She stopped half way through searching her pockets. Did she want to go through all that fuss? Apart from stealing the wine bottles, they had *sort of* touched her breast. Well, Pablo had *almost* done so. How many times had she been felt up by boys who tried to cop a feel at parties? She felt anger at their nerve. Bastards, she thought, I *will* phone. They deserve to sweat for this.

She recommenced her hunt through her pockets. Had she left her mobile phone upstairs? Still she kept her vigil by the door. There were no more noises coming from the herbery. Go to the study and phone the police, she told herself, but her courage failed her and she felt incapable of leaving the door. Her imagination leaped forward to her contact with the police. They would want to know what they had done to her – *almost* done to her, she reminded herself. There would be some kind of examination. She cringed inwardly at the thought of police doctors examining her body and noting the rolls of fat. She imagined the conclusion they would come to when they had finished – no wonder the boys had done no more, they would say to each other; that girl was so *fat and lumpy*... it must have put them off!

Natalie leaned her head against the door. She no longer cared that the herbery door was unlocked. She was not intending to go out there again. Ever! Maybe she should ring Rachel. They would come home immediately from their dinner. They could be back in a few hours. She thought of the times she had looked after the girls in the past. Ben and Rachel liked a drink and sometimes had even had a taxi to bring them home to this far flung location. Would they both drink at the dinner? Ok, then – they could come back in the morning, she consoled herself. She could stay up all night until they came back.

But, she could still phone her mother now, she thought. Oh God, no! Her mother would want to know what the boys had done! Natalie's mind went around in circles. Why couldn't she think straight? She was usually able to make decisions, remain calm. She breathed in deeply. Think it through, she told herself. Break it down! Yes, break it down - that was what her Physics teacher advised them when they had a seemingly unsolvable problem.

So, they took some wine bottles, she accepted. What about the other *touchy* stuff? Could she just pretend that had never happened? She felt a lightening of her spirits – yes - that was the answer! In a minute she would go and phone her mother and see if she would phone the police for her if she thought that the theft of some wine bottles was serious enough to warrant it. She took half a dozen steps away from the kitchen door and halted. She was convinced that as soon as she was far enough away from the door, the boys would barge at it and force the bolt off its screws. Even though all was quiet on the other side of the door, Natalie believed they were still there. She went back and leaned against it. A weakness came over her as she did so. Her vision narrowed into thin tunnels and she slid down into a squatting position until her sight returned to normal. She glanced at the worktop where her abandoned packet of crisps lay. The sight of it did nothing to tempt her, she realised gratefully. She straightened up against the door, her hip bone pressing uncomfortably on the wood.

The beginnings of a solution had presented itself to her. She needed to know if the boys were definitely there. If not, she *would* leave the door and phone her mother.

'You still there?' she called through the door, 'Sorry I was so pissed off. Do you want a coffee before you go?'

She had no intention of making them coffee but it seemed to be the only way of finding out if they were still there.

No replies came back to her. They had gone. Or were they just keeping quiet so that she let her guard down? They had caught her out once before.

'Or tea, maybe?' she added.

Still no answer.

'I think there's a can of coke in the fridge, if you prefer...'

Answer me, you fucking scumbags, she thought.

She waited another few minutes then started to walk slowly backwards away from the door. Halfway across the kitchen, she stopped. Every nerve in her body tensed, waiting for the crashing, breaking open of the door. She held her breath, then walked a few more steps, keeping her eyes fixed on the door. This time, she reached the doorway to the hall. She swung round to check that they were not hiding in wait for her there. She knew that this was not really possible but her reasoning powers had ceased to work. She turned around once more to watch the kitchen door and backed out into the hallway. She stopped. In another three steps, she would not be able to see the bolted door. She had talked herself into believing that *this* was when the door would be broken down – when she no longer watched it. She hesitated. She could hear nothing. *Were* they still there?

She could not have said how long she waited in the hallway, watching the kitchen door but a sudden muffled bang made her jump.

With relief, she realised that it was a gunshot in the distance. They *had* gone from the herbery. She turned and went towards the study. The possibility of only one of them remaining in the herbery came to her as she opened the study door. She wheeled around, still worried that it was some kind of trick. She thought she had also heard a shout in the distance. That was good – it meant that the two of them were together, she hoped.

In the study, she picked up the phone and pressed the 'Call' button. With the receiver still in her hand and her thumb poised over the number pad, she had second thoughts. Should she phone her mother? Was there any need now that the boys had gone from the house? Could she just phone for a chat and mention it in passing? Don't be such a numty, she thought, she will have been in bed for ages! Once again, the possibilities ran through her mind. Perhaps she should just leave it for tonight and tell her mother in the morning – providing that the boys didn't come back...

She pressed the 'Off' button and put the phone back in its charger unit. She went back to the kitchen and pressed her ear against the door. A slight embarrassment came over her as she remembered her offer of coffee to an empty room!

She went to the worktop and picked up the abandoned packet of crisps before tipping its contents into the food waste bin. The reassuring click-click as it opened and shut had a calming effect on her. She walked over to the other waste bin and put the packet in there. The flip top made a *whurffing* noise. She tried to pretend it was late evening and that she was just doing normal things, running the tap, wiping down the worktop – all the little noises that comforted her now but would have irritated her at other times.

She suddenly froze in her actions. Why, in this silence, when every noise registered at twice its normal volume, had the phone not given its irritating beep-beep-beep while she had hesitated about phoning her mother? The noise it made to tell you that it was *'off the hook'* as her mother called it?

She ran back into the study and picked the phone up. She pressed the 'Call' button while it rested against her ear. There was no dial tone.

Bastards! They had made certain that she could not phone the police. She jabbed at the button a few times to check but all she heard was the sound of her rapid breathing.

24. Natalie.

Natalie leaned back into a rigid position on the bed. She was still in her clothes. In this tense position, she let her mind investigate *comfortable* reasons why the phone didn't work. She felt desperately tired but her eyes refused to stay shut. At intervals, she heard phantom noises that made her creep out on to the landing and peer through the window. The episode with the boys had unsettled her and she could not relax.

An equal worry was that she could not find her mobile phone. She considered that it may have fallen out of her pocket during the scuffle in the herbery, but she had made a definite decision not to go beyond the bolted kitchen door. Its solid oak panels gave her a feeling of security though she still imagined the boys breaking it down at the hinges if they decided to do so.

Thankfully, the twins had stayed asleep throughout, but she had still crept into the doorway of their bedroom to check – glancing nervously at the bedroom window at the same time -neither had moved from their previous positions and there was a soft snoring coming from one of them.

She felt the softness of the pillow under her head and her eyes closed once again; this time sleep prevailed and she fell into a dream where her mother was forcing her to eat home-made bread by pressing it into her mouth with a toy gun. She jerked awake almost immediately, expecting to hear the sound of the boys running up the stairs. She sat up, feeling jittery as if she'd had too much coffee. There was no other sound and she lay back down again with her heart beating too quickly to be conducive to sleep. She turned on her side to face the door of the bedroom. She closed her eyes but they automatically opened and stared at the shadowed shape of the doorway. She forced them shut again but a loud *TICK* from the old floorboards set her body on high alert for the umpteenth time. It was a sound she was used to when she stayed at Ben and Rachel's house but all noises now had the power to alarm her.

Her leg felt numb from lying on one side but she was reluctant to turn the other way with her back to the door. She rolled on to her back instead and sighed. You never knew how easy it was to become scared of something, she realised. It made her think of her lie about being scared of horse-riding – she half smiled in the darkness. The thought that she had not weighed herself for hours also bothered her. She had been too nervous to do it while the possibility of the boys still being around and maybe breaking in had a grip on her mind. (The even more shocking thought of them catching her on the weigh scales and registering her bulging belly and *vast* weight, made her catch her breath in panic). Now, the scales began to feature more strongly in her thoughts. Surely, all this activity and adrenalin would have a telling affect on her weight? Maybe she should do some exercises and then sneak into the bathroom?

She slid off the bed and lay on the floor with her hands behind her head; she pulled herself into a sit-up and lay back down again. Her muscles trembled as she did it. She began the repetitions, relishing the effort as she imagined the calories as a digital reading that was running backwards.

A loud banging noise and shout from downstairs made her shoot upwards with her hands out; she scrambled to her feet, feeling the pressure enveloping her eyes – even in the dark room she knew that her vision was blackening as the familiar feeling pressed behind her eyes and inside her head.

A loud exhaling 'Huh!' had come from her mouth and she felt the beat of her heart pulsing deep in her throat.

Another shout came. Natalie slapped on the light switch with her hand at the same time that she opened the door. On the landing, she stopped; there was no noise. She listened again – the twins were quiet. Had it been an animal outdoors? The bedroom windows were open so the sound would have carried easily enough...

The next sound was a despairing, muffled moan, 'Pleeeeeease!'

She made her way downstairs with every hair standing on end while her thoughts repeated the phrase, *little shits, little shits!*

This time, I really *am* going to phone the police, she thought briefly before remembering the dead phone line. *What* have I done with my mobile phone?

She switched on every light as she went; her eyes were stretched wide open, she expected to see the boys somewhere in the house. Beyond that, she feared what would happen if they were...

Another cry came, 'Pliss!'

It was Pablo's voice, she was certain. He was back in the herbery.

As the kitchen light went on, he must have seen the line of light around the door as he changed his words to, 'Thank Got! You must help!'

Natalie went close to the door, 'What. Do. You. Want?' she said as menacingly as she could.

'Pliss call for help. Striker has accident with gun!'

Natalie's hands flew up to the bolt before she froze in her tracks.

'Oh yeah?' she said, 'What a load of bollocks! I'm phoning the police.'

'Pliss, pliss, you must help...' his voice broke slightly. Crying or trying not to laugh, Natalie thought.

'Piss off,' she said, 'Go away. You understand that, do you?'

'There is much blut,' he said in a calmer voice.

'There is much bullshit,' she fired back at him, her temper was up and she'd had enough of their stupid nonsense.

But, what if..? She considered this for half a second. No way! They had fooled her too many times. The memory of his hand reaching out for her breast reinforced her decision.

'Use your phone, if you need help,' she said, 'or use mine. You've probably taken that with you!'

There was a silence for a few seconds as he took in her words.

'I have no phone. There is no signal in this... *shit place*,' he spat out, 'So I don't bring my phone.'

Natalie could hear him breathing heavily.

'Pliss, I am sorry. Pliss help.'

'Let me think about it,' said Natalie, 'Right, I've thought about it. NO!'

She could hear the crying noises again. She listened intently. Yes, it was a laugh. The wanker won't fool me again, she thought. She wondered where Striker was and whether he was also part of this latest con.

He hammered on the door making it shake.

'Stop that!' Natalie called, 'It won't make any difference. I'm not opening the door!'

'Please call for ambulance,' he said with another cry.

'I can't call for anyone, you moron! You cut the phone line!'

'No, I have not cut phone. Pliss try,' he said.

Natalie wondered if he was telling the truth about the phone. If so, maybe the phone was now working...

'Wait there. I'll check the phone,' she said, 'and then I will phone the police.'

He did not reply and Natalie again went to the study. This time she went directly without fear of the kitchen door being kicked open. She picked up the phone and pressed the 'Call' button as she put it to her face. There was no sound coming from the handset. In desperation, she called 'Hello, hello.' a few times in the hope that some unknown voice would reply. Nothing happened. She jabbed the button repeatedly before putting the handset back in its holder.

She rushed back to the kitchen, holding her breath until she saw that the door was still intact.

'There is no phone line,' she said, 'what have you done to it?'

Pablo's voice broke into sobs, 'He will die. He must have help!'

'Yeah well, life's a bitch,' she said, though a grain of doubt had worked into her mind. The sobbing sounded very convincing. But what if it was the truth, she thought, without a phone he's fucked.

He yelled and hammered the door repeatedly before breaking into crying sounds again.

'Go away! I can't help you,' she repeated.

The hammering and whimpering stopped.

'You are a beetch!' he said.

Natalie waited for more to come but he was silent. She could hear some moving around, but nothing else. That was probably Striker sneaking out.

She wondered what they would do next. She realised that all the downstairs windows were either closed or the opened parts were too small for them to get in – courtesy of Ben and Rachel's insistence on restoring the house's original features. She glanced at the floor, wondering where her phone was. She began a systematic search of the house, up-turning cushions and rugs downstairs. She crept upstairs and looked more quietly. Although reluctant to disturb the twins, she tip-toed into their bedroom and knelt down to check under the beds, but throughout her search Ffion lay on her tummy with arms and legs out in starfish style while Caitlin remained on her side facing the wall and neither showed any signs of being woken. Natalie sighed. The possibility of it having dropped out of her pocket in the herbery seemed to be the most likely answer. She went to the kitchen door and leaned her face and ear against it. There was no sound from the other side. Maybe, she could very quickly... No! Sensible Natalie intervened and quashed the idea before it could form properly.

She listened again. Surely, they had gone away? She weighed up the circumstances; while they were not in the house and not bothering her, she had no need of her phone. *Ergo – dim problemo*, she told herself, before the pain of remembering whose phrase that was flashed through her mind. An image of Jack filled her thoughts. She remembered lying to the boys that her boyfriend was upstairs. Two lies, she reminded herself – he wasn't there and he certainly wasn't her boyfriend anymore! Bastard! But, wishful thinking was showing her how much easier it would have been to deal with the boys if those two facts *had* been true.

What to do next? Natalie felt tired but was afraid to go back upstairs. For some illogical reason she felt safer being downstairs near the kitchen door. She sat down on the hard chair at the table but her body craved more comfort that it could provide. Instead, she got up and made her way into the sitting room, leaving the hallway light on. There, she pushed her hands down under the cushions again to check if her phone was there before she lay down on the sofa and stared at the beamed ceiling.

No more unusual sounds disturbed her and her exhausted, malnourished body eventually switched off.

25. Jack.

When the source of Natalie's unhappiness had been a little boy with long dark eyelashes and dimples, during his first few years at school, he had suffered with a bad stutter. The harder he tried not to stutter, the worse it became. As a very young child, it would make him lose his temper and cry, but as he got older he retreated into silence and was labelled as 'shy' by his class teacher.

Eventually, Jack's parents followed advice and took him to see a Speech Therapist. He was taught to breathe in before speaking on the outward breath. As he became older he controlled it more effectively, so that by the time he started secondary school, the stammer appeared to have disappeared altogether and almost everyone had forgotten that it had ever existed.

Most of the time, even Jack himself forgot that he had ever had a stammer. Though, if he was in a particularly stressful situation, he would feel the tightening of his throat and the rapid working of his tongue before he spoke. On those occasions, he either said nothing or tried to remember to breathe in. When being reprimanded by teachers, the former option was not only effective but convenient as he tried to avoid saying anything that would get him into further trouble.

Towards the end of his GCSE years at school, he was smitten by Natalie and spent some time trying to 'accidentally' bump into her. He had known that she had a boyfriend but he bided his time until that particular relationship ran its course before he made his move.

In his eyes, Natalie was perfect! That fact that most girls in Llanefa School thought that, with his dark good looks and tall muscular body, *he* was perfect was no longer relevant to him – he had eyes for no-one but Natalie. He had admitted to himself that he loved her. He had even said as much to her. They were planning to go to the same university even though their chosen careers were different – he had decided on Sports Science while she had chosen Medicine. Jack had never put it into words but he envisaged them being married in many years to come. He loved her looks – dark hair and eyes, she was tall and not too skinny as some girls were. Just thinking about her gave him a small flutter of happiness in the pit of his stomach. Sometimes, thinking about her gave him another flutter of feeling further down than his stomach – she was just *so* sexy!

His school friends teased him about her, but all in good fun. He took it all and teased them back. Even the men in the saw-mill, where Jack worked at weekends and school holidays, would wind him up by asking whether the wedding date had been decided. Jack was a popular boy and reacted well to their comments thus endearing him to them.

Since being dumped by Natalie, Jack was a lost soul. He put on a cheerful front for customers at the saw-mill and was his usual self with friends, but deep inside he was distraught. He had no idea why he had been dumped and Natalie refused to speak to him. His heart leapt in shock if he saw her talking to another boy – he feared that she would soon be snapped up by another boyfriend (how could they resist her?) and he could not bear to think of that happening.

Like all tragic love stories, Jack and Natalie's relationship had come to an end due to a cruel misunderstanding – though neither of them were aware of it.

One night many months before, while driving Natalie home from a night at the bowling alley, Jack had taken a turn off the main road and parked the car in the lay-by at the end of the Devil Tree path - a few hundred yards from Anna's parents' house. If nowhere else was available, they would have sex in Jack's car and the deserted lay-by was a safe option.

The car was a rather old and shabby model with a defective locking system but its back seat was perfectly adequate for the lustful couple to have sex on it. Unknown to them, some of Jack's friends were also travelling on the same road that night and, when they saw the familiar car parked (with its steamed-up windows), it was an ideal opportunity to have some fun. They stopped behind Jack's car and tumbled out in a hurry – four boys all wanting to be the first to embarrass the pair.

Having heard a car stop behind them, Jack and Natalie had panicked – Natalie convinced that it was her father – and tried to scramble apart and rearrange their clothes. In the confusion, they tried to move in opposite directions and Natalie had to partly climb over Jack to get to the hedge-side door – feeling less exposed by heading that way. At that exact moment, Lloyd Carter, one of Jack's friends, opened the door and shone his mobile phone torch on them, while the others broke into hysterical laughter and tried to get a better look.

Jack pulled the door shut quickly and the boys, having had their fun, got back in the car and drove away with much hooting of the car horn.

'Scumbags!' said Natalie, before they both burst out laughing. For the next fifteen minutes, they voiced embarrassing potential scenarios of when they next saw the boys in school, but in between every suggestion, they were helpless with laughter – partly with relief because it had *not* been Natalie's father!

As expected, the next time they were in school, there was some teasing and hip-thrusting gestures directed at them and that seemed to be the end of it.

Later that week, as Jack was getting off the school bus, some of his classmates began talking about a new film that they had seen. The plot had been exciting but the major talking point had been the way the actress was shot while having sex with the hero in the film. More to the point, she had been 'on top' at the time. It had been a fairly graphic scene and before long, despite being adults in body, their minds were that of schoolboys and there were many joking remarks about the practicalities of having sex with the woman on top.

'If she tucks her knees up, I could just spin her!' Lloyd Carter suggested, to hoots of laughter.

'Or drop her from the jib of a JCB!' Steve Jones said, his voice changing its tone from boy to man and back again as he struggled to speak through his bout of hysterical laughter.

Jack gave Steve a light smack around the side of his head, 'I hear you prefer JCBs to women anyway!'

When they had finished laughing, Steve, not to be outdone, turned to Jack and said, 'You know all about it anyway! Natalie was on top when we caught you at it! Excellent girlfriend choice!'

It was not something that he had expected (after all, Natalie had not been on top – they had only ever had sex in the conventional way) and his body went into meltdown. His emotions went through a dozen changes as he tried to think of what to say. He was angry that they were making fun of Natalie and surprised at the way the conversation had led to the supposition. He let anger lead the way.

In his brain, the words he wanted to say was, 'What the fuck would you know?' but at that moment, his stammer returned with a vengeance and all that came out of his mouth was 'Wooo, woo, wha... woo...'

As they disembarked the bus near to Mrs Jenkins's garden and saw the dog patrolling its usual beat, it was too

186

much for the other boys. They burst out laughing when one of them said 'Woo, woo, doggy fashion as well! Way to go, Jack. Woof, woof wooooooo!'

And so the joke was carried on and added to like Chinese Whispers as each new person heard it. Jack never made the association with Natalie's decision and they both went their separate unhappy ways. The joke had never included Natalie's weight or body shape (both of which were completely unremarkable), but, at the fateful moment that Natalie had overheard the conversation that was to change her personality, it was the pudgy, flabby shape of the dog that had seared an image in her mind.

On the day of Llanefa YFC Show, Jack had been working at the saw-mill during the first half of the day. After finishing work at lunchtime, he went home to take a shower before heading over to the show field. As he arrived there, he realised that he was having yet another crappy day. Every day was a crappy day while Natalie was not part of it.

He expected to see Natalie at the show – she had been a regular sight in the horse ring at previous shows. He was determined to have another attempt at speaking to her and finding out what was wrong. He had sent her several text messages during the day but none had been answered. It was to be his last attempt that day. If he could actually get to talk to her for some length of time, he was certain that they could resume their relationship. He drove his car to the showground in the hope that he could persuade Natalie to speak to him in the privacy of the car. In the back of his mind, he had a vision of them both driving away from the showground to some remote spot where she would come to her senses. If she refused, he was going to have to accept that having crappy days was the way it was going to be from now on...

When he arrived at the showground, he was disappointed not to see Natalie anywhere. The showground was well spread out and he was certain that she would be near the horse ring, but he was unwilling to ask anyone if they had seen her – he was beginning to feel like a stalker and did not want to be humiliated further. He saw Llinos in the distance and was even more surprised to see her clad in horse-riding gear and taking part in competitions. But, Jack's popularity meant that he was soon included in a gang of similar aged friends who roamed the showground in search of entertainment. They spent a while trying to outdo each other on the Reverse Steering quad bike as they drove it round a course of cones and make-do gates, before trying their hands at the Logging Competition and the Tug-o-War. Then they headed off to the fairground where they dared each other as to how many times they could go on the Spinning Seats without throwing up. As the afternoon turned into evening, they ate hot-dog and chips from the Burger Van and washed it all down with lager which was bought by one of the over-eighteen boys in their company. The evening Disco began and things took on a new level of entertainment. In readiness for their eighteenth birthdays (which, in some cases, were not due for a further ten months), they had decided to practise for the Famous Five Challenge. Some of the friends had already turned eighteen and many embellished tales were told by those who had already taken the Famous Five Challenge (which involved drinking a pint each of four different lagers, ciders and beers before finishing with a pint of 'top shelf' spirits). Jack was glad that he had the excuse of having brought the car; he had an inkling that drinking large amounts of alcohol would make him maudlin and reveal just how crappy his days had become.

'You could always leave the car here,' one of his friends suggested.

'Nah, too much hassle,' he'd replied, though he drank two pints of lager throughout the evening and was close to agreeing to leave the car at the showground.

As a group, they drifted apart throughout the evening, while other people joined them. One couple who came to sit with them was Llinos and her new boyfriend, Kyle. Llinos tried to keep her distance from Jack (she had seen the wistful, questioning look on his face) but Kyle was a friend of one of Jack's other companions so the situation was unavoidable.

Eventually, Jack managed to get into the seat next to Llinos and chatted neutrally to her. Kyle gave him a quizzical look and Jack heard her tell him in a relatively low voice (despite the noise from the disco) that it was 'my best mate's ex-boyfriend'.

'Saw you in the horse ring today,' he said to Llinos, 'bit of a change!'

Llinos answered cautiously, she could see where the conversation was heading.

'Yeah, thought I'd have a go! My legs are like soggy pasta now!'

'Natalie not riding then?'

'No, decided against it...' she said eventually.

'Away, is she?'

'No, she was here, helping me. She's gone now. Babysitting.'

'Oh, bad timing for her! Where's she babysitting?'

Llinos looked at him pityingly.

'Jack, you know I'm not going to tell you that. Just move on...'

He gave a feigned astonished look and held up his hands.

'Just making conversation. It's no odds to me where she is! She would have told me herself if she wanted to... It was just a... Well, whatever...'

And so the evening passed. At one point, Llinos got up to go the porta-loos and when she came back, she swapped seats with Kyle so that Jack would not be able to converse as easily with her. When they left the table to dance, she made certain that Kyle was positioned between her and Jack on their return. Jack consoled himself by accepting another pint of lager – the Famous Five Challenge was looking like a definite diversion to him. He felt a small spike of hate for Llinos. Fuck her, he thought as he gulped a third of his lager in one go, who did she think she was? Natalie's grandmother?

Another girl in their group lost her neck chain and Llinos was soon helping to search for it on the ground (I see you're not too up-yourself to help another *girl*, he thought uncharitably!) Meanwhile Kyle started chatting to him about the upcoming soccer season. Jack suddenly saw his chance.

'Where's Llinos's friend, Natalie, babysitting tonight, then? She's normally here.'

'Dunno,' he said, 'she swapped with Llinos. Otherwise, she would have had two days looking after triplets or something...'

He gestured his thumb over his shoulder at Llinos as he said it.

Jack shrugged in a couldn't-care-less way and tried not to lift his arm in a triumphant gesture. He didn't know of any triplets that Natalie babysat, but he certainly knew of twins! The vet's children! He mentally counted out how many hours he needed to wait until he was safe to drive, but he knew that once that time had passed, he would drive over there and sort out his crappy days once and for all.

26. Natalie.

The sound, the awakening and the thought all happened together.

They're back, she told herself.

She realised that she was sitting bolt upright on the sofa, heartbeat increasing and muscles tensed. For a few more seconds, while she held her breath, she wondered if it had been a dream. She breathed out. Then the noise came once more - a laboured sound.

She swung her legs on to the floor and froze again. It was a noise she recognised. While her father and her uncle had been putting down patio slabs in their garden the previous autumn, she had been in the kitchen, making car-shaped cupcakes for Llinos's seventeenth birthday. She had heard them as they advised each other as to the best position to place each slab, then the shuffle of work-boots as they scuffed over the grit and sand, the dull clunk of the slab as it landed; the tap of the slab being gently hit into position. But the sound she heard now was the other one that had accompanied the patio work; the sound of men breathing with effort – a mixture of grunting and exhaling as they lifted and bent with the extra weight of the slab.

She listened again. The breathing came in short gasps and sounded as though the person had his mouth open. What were the boys bringing into the house, she wondered? A deep seated fear took hold and she kept quiet.

The gasping was accompanied by the sound of something being dragged across the tiles. Natalie crept out of the sitting room and huddled on the floor by the entrance to the kitchen in an attempt to... she had no idea what she was trying to attempt. The instinctive obsession to see the kitchen door had returned, though she did not think beyond that action if the boys managed to get in.

She heard another noise – a voice – a single word. Not so much spoken as a vocal reaction to whatever physical effort the speaker was engaged in.

'Ark' was what it sounded like to Natalie.

She crept a little closer, going on to hands and knees across the kitchen floor.

'Ark, guff!'

Then the sound of a cough followed by a cry of 'Wugh!'

Natalie had come to a halt by the table legs. Her instinct was now to turn and go – up to the safety of her bedroom – the sound was scaring her. She tried to turn around on all fours, being careful not to hit the table legs. The absurdity of her situation struck her and she realised that she could stand up and walk out quietly. She came up into a crouch and then up on to her feet. The faintness hit her immediately and she went to her knees in a crumpled heap and landed sideways on the floor. She waited for the feeling to go, all the while listening for the sounds from the herbery. She turned her head to look in the direction of the door and slowly got to her feet. In her eagerness to get to safety, she forgot how close she was to the cooker – a large, double fronted Aga lookalike – and as she came half way up, she hit her shoulder against the rail that ran around the front. The pain and her yelp were instant. She clamped her mouth shut and put her other hand to her painful shoulder, but it was too late. From the herbery came a distinctive voice.

'Help me...'

Natalie stayed silent.

More shuffling noises outside the herbery door followed by another plea for help, stopped her in her half upright position. It wasn't Pablo's voice.

Her mind swung back and forth with indecision. She *knew* they were trying to fool her into opening the door. And they *knew* that she did not have a phone.

'Help me,' came the voice again.

Was it Striker? It didn't sound like his voice...

'Who's there?' Natalie said eventually.

'Help me, please. I've been shot.'

'Striker?' she said.

'Had accident. Pablo gone...'

She recognised his voice more easily now. She went to the door and hesitated.

'What's happened?' she asked through the door.

'Gun went off. Wouldn't work then... Pablo messing with it... ooough...'

He continued to groan for a moment. It sounded theatrical to Natalie. They must think I'm stupid, she thought. How many times were they going to try to get her to open the door?

'Sorry! Don't believe you!' she said briskly.

More groaning came from the other side of the door – a different tone – maybe Pablo was adding his fake groans to the charade?

'Need ambulance and...' he said in a very convincing tone.

Natalie stared up at the bolt. Should she?

'You cut off my phone,' she said, 'I can't help you...'

'Please, try...'

'Stop it! You're not going to fool me again! Just get out!'

No reply came back to her, but she could hear the laboured breathing though its volume had reduced.

She slid down on to the floor; despair came over her. *What* was she going to do?

Within a few minutes, she had almost weakened. What if Striker really was injured? She had no phone, but would she be able to help him if he was bleeding? The possibilities weighed themselves up and down in her mind. If he had *really* had an accident, would he have been able to walk to the farmhouse? And if so, surely his injuries could not be that bad. Unless he can't stop the bleeding, some wise voice – a strain of the old, pre-anorexia, Sensible Natalie – told her. Then you could help. Maybe...

It had gone quiet outside the door. Natalie began to wonder if they had gone again. She leaned over and put her ear to the door. There was a suggestion of *some* kind of sound...

She braced her feet beneath her body and got up slowly, mindful of the faintness that had hit her earlier. Perhaps she should unbolt the door after all.

She had reached up towards the metal catch when a different noise came through – the distinctive sound of a moaning retch, followed by a thump.

Natalie pulled her arm down immediately. A vision of the missing wine bottles took the place of her doubted concern.

'For fuck's sake!' she said sharply, 'You come here, steal wine and get pissed. If you puke in there, you'd better clean it all up... I swear I'll...'

Whatever threat she had in mind, had evaporated. She pictured the explaining she would have to do when Ben and Rachel got home. And I *will* tell the police... or someone official, she told herself. Thieving bastards! She hoped they would have never-to-be-forgotten hangovers after this.

Once on her feet she went again to the study to check the phone – it was still silent.

She circled a few times while she wondered what to do. The obvious answer – there's nothing you *can* do – calmed her somewhat.

She went back into the living room and sat on the sofa. She still felt uncertain about going upstairs while the boys were still in the house. She wondered if they would fall into a drunken sleep and leave once they had sobered up. She folded her legs under her and leaned sideways on the sofa – she was *so* tired. Her breathing slowed down and she felt reassured by the silence. She felt her eyes closing and gave in to the feeling. She stayed in this half-asleep state for several minutes before her exhausted body gave in and her head lolled to one side.

She woke suddenly, instantly alert. She listened for any sound. A feeling of déjà vu hit her. This had happened before.

'Did you?' Striker's voice called from a distance,' Did you hear me?'

She got up slowly and made her way through the hallway and into the kitchen.

'What do you want?' she asked ungraciously, 'I've already told you that the phone doesn't work.'

'I said, I'm sorry we scared you,' he said.

'Bit late for that now!' she snapped back.

'Really. Just some fun that went a bit wrong, y'know?'

'Oh yeah! Fun! I'm pissing myself laughing here!' Natalie was ready to deal with whatever he said, 'And it sounds like you've made a good recovery from your *accident*!' She placed a sarcastic emphasis on the last word.

'It doesn't hurt so much now,' he said, 'I'm sorry about the mess, like.'

'I bet!' she said, 'Anyway, where's your lovely friend?'

'Gone. I told you, did I?'

'Took my phone with him, did he?'

There was a silence for a few seconds.

'I don't know nothin' about your phone, like.'

'Like you don't know *nothing* about the phone cable here, I suppose?' Natalie was relishing the sarcasm she felt – it was one way of dealing with the tosser without being in the same room as him.

'We were trying to climb up the wall, y'know. To give you a bit of a scare – just in fun. But Pablo caught his foot in a wire on the wall – just under the window. That might have been the phone cable...'

'Very brave of you,' she snarled at him, 'you frightened the children, you pair of shits!'

Natalie could feel her temper rising. Get a grip, she told herself, you know what happens when you lose it. She was likely to explode and open the door in an attempt to confront them face to face and maybe threaten them with... Her mind ran through a list of items in the kitchen that she could use. Just calm down, she told herself, going out to them is a very bad idea. She felt her rage seeping away. Good!

'The little girl, is she ok?' Striker asked.

Instantly Natalie's temper flared again.

'What did you do? What did you fucking do to them?' she shouted and hammered on the door until her head began to develop the familiar floating feeling inside.

'No, no, no! Nothing!' he said, 'I was just asking, like, about the one who's sick in the heart?'

'Neither of them are sick,' she yelled back at him, 'What do you mean? You must have done something to them! Tell me what you did, you fucking wanker!'

'I swear; we didn't even touch them! We only went up the wall and they screamed...'

Natalie made another effort to calm herself. They're winding you up, she told herself, ignore them.

She sat down again, worn out with the effort of shouting and her lack of nutrition.

She listened out for any cries from upstairs and was relieved that the noise had not disturbed the twins. Silence fell once more.

A strange burping sound came from the other side of the door.

'You'd better not puke in there,' Natalie said.

He did not answer and Natalie half dared to hope that he had gone outside. She lowered her chin on to her chest and began to cry quietly. How long could she keep this up for? Everything seemed to be going against her – Jack's insult about her to his friends, her weight that refused to go lower, her greediness (the vision of the Mars bars came back with a vengeance) and now these morons who refused to leave.

Her heart began its racing again, the force and speed of it shocked her into raising her head and letting out a gasp. She pressed her hand to her chest – she could feel the rapid beats hitting her palm – it felt as though her heart would burst out through her skin.

'Got the flutters. Need to drink some Coke,' Striker's voice came through the door.

The shock of his voice made her heart return to its normal rhythm.

'There *is* no Coke,' she said in an almost normal tone – the timing of his statement had been spookily correct. She suddenly had a yearning for Coke – not just a yearning but a certainty that its ingredients would stop this weird heartbeat. That's why you're so *fat*, the internal voice told her.

'And the little girl is ok?' he said.

'Oh, don't start all that again!' Natalie said, losing patience.

But, her thoughts had already turned in the direction of the twins. They had been quiet, so she hoped they were sleeping rather than cuddled together in terror. She pictured the scene – they were four years old, for God sake, if they were frightened, they would scream and yell! But...

'If you've done something to them...' she started.

Suddenly, a terrible realisation came to her. Where was Pablo? She had not heard his voice for a long time! What if he was up there in the twins' bedroom right now?

She flew to her feet, clinging to the worktop while her faintness tried to get the better of her. She used the few seconds to grab a bread knife from its holder on the worktop. Bastard!

Fighting the faintness, she went upstairs – her only thought was concerned with making Pablo cry in fear. She would teach him to run around in the middle of the night, scaring little girls! An instant shot of reality broke through this vision as she remembered the build and obvious strength of the boy. She gripped the knife a little tighter.

She crossed the landing and pushed the door fully open from its ajar position. She was relieved to see that the children were unharmed; Ffion was lying on her tummy with her head facing towards the door. One leg was thrown over the edge of the bed. Caitlin was still lying on her side facing the wall. There was no-one else in the room. To double-check, Natalie opened the small wardrobes and peered under the beds. Nothing. She glanced at the bread knife in embarrassment and held it flat against her leg in case the girls woke up and saw it. The window was still in the same position that Natalie had left it. She tip-toed out of the room and stood on the landing. Could he be in one of the other rooms? She went quietly to the bedroom that she used and put on the light. Everything looked normal.

Then she checked the bathroom – her eyes flew to the weigh scales as if drawn by magnetic force. Later, her mind promised. The two spare bedrooms had open doors but Natalie went in and put the lights on to reassure herself. The fifth bedroom was Ben and Rachel's. She felt uneasy about checking in there – it felt like an intrusion of their privacy. She had never so much as opened the door to their room before. She knew that there was also an en-suite bathroom beyond it. She hesitated at the door, the knife back in its ready-to-attack position. Was this *really* necessary? She put her palm on the door handle and angled it downwards; the door held its closed position. It was then that she noticed a keyhole below the handle. Her curiosity engaged – what did they have in there that made it necessary to lock the door? All sorts of bizarre suggestions whizzed through her mind – the result of her relief that Pablo was not in the house. Unless... it was Pablo who was in there and *he* had locked it? She dismissed the thought immediately; the 'Sensible Natalie' reasoned that if Ben and Rachel had gone to the trouble of putting a lock on the door, the chances were that they would keep it locked when they went away.

She let her arm hang down, letting the knife rest against her leg once more. Obviously, Pablo was *not* in the house – or certainly was not in the upstairs rooms, though Natalie was suspicious that he remained in an alcohol induced sleep in the boot-room. She clenched her fingers around the knife handle as a result of thinking about him.

She quietly made her way downstairs where she stopped in the kitchen entrance and sat on the floor with her back to the door frame. She kept the knife by her side.

'I said, so I did', came Striker's lowered voice from the herbery.

Natalie held her breath. Was he talking to Pablo?

'Did you hear me? I said we didn't do anything. Just climbed up the wall, y'know?'

'Whatever,' Natalie said.

'We wouldn't do stuff like that, y'know. Especially with a sick little girl. We just wanted to play a trick on you...'

Natalie felt a coldness creeping down from the base of her skull and as far as her shoulder blades. Why did he keep saying that? And yet, something was sounding an alarm in her mind. She shook her head. The bastards were trying to freak her out.

She was letting them get to her. She was tired and upset. Their childish, stupid games had found an easy target in her. If only she had the courage to go upstairs and sleep – safe in the knowledge that they wouldn't get into the house. But she knew that even if she talked herself into going up to bed, she would not be able to switch off the fear and ignore the fact that they were still a possible threat. Maybe in the living room, then, she bargained with herself. A little sleep on the sofa – that might make her feel more in control of the situation; near enough to hear if they tried forcing the door. She got up slowly and began to walk towards the sitting room. The knife lay on the floor.

'Need some zeds,' Striker said.

Could he see her, Natalie wondered? This was the second time he had timed a statement to her actions.

'That'll be the wine you stole,' she said, 'Go ahead and sleep! But I want you gone when you wake up!'

'I can't go from here,' he said.

Natalie thought about responding and telling him that she knew he was faking his injuries but decided to leave him without an answer. Engaging in an argument with him was not going to solve anything, she realised. She felt a calmness come over her – Sensible Natalie was back. She continued into the living room and lay down on the sofa.

At first, she lay back in a rigid position, staring at the ceiling. This is hopeless, she thought, I don't want to sleep. But as the minutes ticked by, her muscles relaxed and she could feel the tiredness creeping back. She turned on to her side and pulled her knees up. The action reminded of her of the twins – Ffion sprawled half out of the duvet and Caitlin turned on her side. How wonderful it would be if she could just block out all that had happened and sleep as easily as the twins did!

'Shit!'

The cry was out of her mouth and she was on her feet before the word had completed. She half ran towards the hallway, her vision blackening, but only slowing her slightly as she felt her way along the wall towards the stairs. Her foot missed the first step and she stumbled. It gave her body a chance to recover from her faintness and she grasped the banister as her vision cleared. She took the steps two at a time, her breath carrying small cries of 'No, please, no'.

She crossed the landing in three giant steps and, catching hold of the doorframe, swung into the twins' bedroom in one fluid movement. Caitlin was still in the same position.

'Caitlin! Ffion!' she yelled.

She threw herself on to her knees between both beds, simultaneously shaking at both girls to wake them.

She let out a louder cry before she could speak their names again.

Ffion began to move, throwing her arm backwards. Still, Natalie continued to shake them.

Ffion turned a confused face towards her, 'Penguin fallen,' she mumbled.

Ignoring her for the moment, Natalie concentrated on Caitlin and shook her harder. Natalie began to cry and tried to pick Caitlin up. She folded limply as Natalie moved her.

'Wake up!' Natalie screamed.

Somewhere in the background, Ffion had started to wail in fright but Natalie took no heed of her.

'Caitlin! Caitlin!' Natalie continued to call, 'please wake up, please, please...'

She rolled Caitlin on to her back. When she saw the little girl's unresponsive face, she knew that something was terribly wrong.

27. Natalie.

Shut up!' Natalie screamed at Ffion, 'Shut up!'

Ffion wailed even louder and tried to climb on to Caitlin's bed.

'Get off!' Natalie snapped and gave her a push.

Ffion rolled on to the floor while her crying reached a glass-shattering pitch.

Natalie had her face against Caitlin's tummy. She could feel a faint beating of the child's heart and with relief she realised that the small tummy was moving up and down. But *why* wouldn't she wake up?

The colour of her skin was sickly pale and she felt cold.

'Please, Caitlin, please wake up! Don't do this, for fuck's sake!'

Ffion's crying stopped suddenly with a hiccup.

'*Naughty* word, Nattee,' she said before another sob took hold.

Natalie rubbed Caitlin's hands roughly in an attempt to warm her up. She still hoped that the action would be uncomfortable enough to wake her, but Caitlin remained unresponsive.

In desperation, Natalie yanked the duvet from the bed and rolled Caitlin on to it; then she wrapped her up tightly to keep her warm. Somewhere in her brain Sensible Natalie was reminding her of a conversation her mother had had with a neighbour about Cot Death following a tragedy suffered by a celebrity mother. *Don't keep them wrapped up too warm,* was the phrase that stuck in her mind. But Caitlin was too old for Cot Death, wasn't she? Don't, her mind warned; don't tempt fate.

She began to loosen the duvet.

'Wake up, Cay-tin!' Ffion said in a tearful voice. She had her knuckles jammed against her mouth.

'Ok, just sit there quietly,' Natalie told her, while her mind whirled around the possibilities of what she could do. She automatically patted her clothes again, where the *fuck* was her phone?

'Wait here. Don't touch her,' she told Ffion and ran downstairs to the study. Again she tried the phone, hitting it and jabbing violently at the number keys. When it was clear that nothing was happening, she raced back out to the hallway. Halfway up the stairs she thought she heard Striker's voice calling, 'Is she ok?'

She ignored him and kept up her pace. At the door to the twins' bedroom, the faintness hit her violently and she felt herself folding bodily towards the floor.

In a faraway place, she could hear Ffion screaming, 'Don't die, Nattee, don't die,' but she was powerless to answer. A darkness and muteness fell before she was once more aware of Ffion's screaming and the sight of the twins' bedroom came back into focus. She scrambled on to all fours; her knee throbbed as she did so. Ffion threw herself at her, clasping her around the throat to the extent that her breathing felt restricted. She caught hold of Ffion's hands and pulled them away.

'It's ok, it's ok,' she said, though her eyes were on Caitlin's still body on the bed.

'Make Cay-tin wake up!' Ffion screeched.

'Ok, I will,' Natalie said automatically, 'just let me...'

She got up and felt Caitlin's tummy and chest once more. For a terrible moment, she thought that there was no breathing, but then came the reassuring, if weak, beat of her heart.

The boys! Natalie suddenly thought of them asleep in the herbery. They had taken her phone – now they would have to give it back so that she could phone for an ambulance! Even with no signal, she was certain that emergency calls would get through. And if not, she could make them walk to the top of the hill until they found a signal.

She got up and waited a few seconds. She expected the faintness now – she had to be careful – she would be no good to Caitlin if she fell down the stairs and broke her neck! As if to surprise her, her head remained clear and she went towards the stairway. Suddenly, Ffion launched at her legs and clung on.

'No, Nattee, don't go!'

'Just wait here – I'm going downstairs again...'

'Noooooooo!'

'Just for a minute...'

'Nooo. I wanna come with you...' more was added to this wail but Natalie could not make out what she was saying.

'Ok, ok, just stop crying and don't touch anything when I speak to the man...'

Ffion stopped and sniffed.

Natalie held her hand and they went downstairs. In the kitchen, Natalie stood in front of the door to the herbery. As she reached up for the bolt, she called through the door.

'I've got one of the little girls with me, so just behave yourselves, ok? And I'm going to need my mobile phone to call...' she glanced at Ffion, not wanting to say the word 'ambulance', '...nine, nine, nine.'

'Why you talking to the door, Nattee?' Ffion said, her face streaked with tears. It was eerie, how she could change instantaneously from distressed crying to curious child.

Natalie slid open the bolt. She had gone past the fear of what might happen when she opened the door.

She pulled the handle towards her and, before her eyes had assimilated the information, her nostrils took in the unpleasant smell of vomit and an added sweet aroma.

'Stay behind me,' she commanded Ffion and opened the door fully.

The sight that met her would haunt her nightmares for years. She turned her head away and realised that Ffion was trying to see past her.

'Stinky poo!' Ffion commented.

'Don't look, cariad. Don't look. Turn around and don't...' Natalie failed to complete the sentence as she felt herself gag.

'Why?' Ffion said, her eyes wide with interest.

Natalie swallowed to rid her throat of its need to gag again.

'There's a mess on the floor, cariad, and I don't want you to fall in it. Just stay here.'

Ffion continued to try to see around Natalie.

'Go and sit at the table,' she said, 'Go on. Now!'

Something in her voice triggered obedience in Ffion and she turned away from the doorway.

Natalie braced herself to step into the herbery. Although she was certain that there was vomit *somewhere*, there was no obvious sign of it. However, the two obvious things that *were* on the floor, were copious amounts of blood and the still body of Striker.

28. Natalie.

Natalie had never seen a dead body before, but she had no doubt that Striker was her first. The amount of blood she could see on the floor, even before she put the utility room light on, (she was already thinking of it as a utility room – an emergency such as this threw silly phrases like 'herbery' out of the equation) told her that no-one could lose that much blood and still be alive. The floor was covered in large black pools. When she put the light on and saw the full extent of the situation, it confirmed her fears. He was definitely dead, she thought. His blood covered a large area of the utility room floor; Striker himself was slumped against a wall; only one shoulder making contact. His head hung down against the corner of the room. If it had not been for this half-effective support, he would, most likely, have slid fully to the ground.

But, even if his body had contained far more blood than the average person, Natalie knew that he would not have survived the injury that glared at her from under the light. Somewhere in the region of his ribs, there was a large hole where his clothes had torn. Natalie could see beyond that and quickly looked away - there had been something *meaty* nestling inside the hole.

'Nattee, why...'

'Get back in there!' she yelled at Ffion, 'Don't come out here!'

Ffion's face crumpled into an offended pose and a forced cry began to ascend the noise scale.

'Shut up! Get back in there! Now!'

Ffion continued to cry but went back towards the kitchen table.

Oh shit! Oh shit! Oh shit! Natalie's mind could form no other thought. She stood in the doorway, trying not to look at Striker. But, she reminded herself, maybe her phone was in there. Oh God, what if it was *underneath* him? She would have to... Another gagging feeling hit her. The smell was nauseating. She folded her arm across her mouth and nose to keep the odour at bay.

Pablo! Where was he?

'Pablo?' she called.

There was no reply.

'Stay there!' she shouted at Ffion again and stepped into the black patch on the floor. She expected it to be slippery, but instead, she felt its stickiness against the soles of her trainers. It made a sound like Sellotape being peeled off the roll.

'Pablo!' she called again and, looking deliberately straight ahead, she stepped over Striker and went into the boot room. The blood had seeped into the doorway there too.

She switched on the light expecting to see him asleep on the floor, but all she saw were some shoes that had been knocked off their rack and an empty wine bottle on its side. Natalie's heart was thumping heavily and she held on to the door frame. Don't faint! Just don't! She tried to breathe deeply but the smell created another gagging feeling. She pressed her arm harder against her face and drew in air through her mouth. Surely her phone had to be in here? Stop being a wimp and look for it, she chastised herself.

'NATTEEEEEE!'

She spun around to see Ffion in the doorway of the utility room. Natalie rushed back to her, ignoring the 'prrrrt, prrrrt' of the blood as it stuck to her soles and stepped unceremoniously over Striker.

'Get in the kitchen!'

Ffion wrapped her arms around Natalie's legs and began crying hysterically.

'Sssh, it's ok, it's ok...' Natalie led her back to the kitchen table and lifted her on to a chair. Her head thumped a warning so she crouched on the floor beside Ffion's chair. Don't faint, she pleaded, not now.

'The man...' Ffion's sobs were broken up by occasional words.

'Yes, I know. He's sleeping,' Natalie said, 'he's only sleeping. You have to be quiet. We don't want to wake him.'

Ffion clung to Natalie, her sobs slowing down a little.

'He's been... working... painting the room, but he fell asleep and now he's... he's... tipped the paint all over the floor. What a silly man! But you mustn't go out there and get paint on yourself.'

Natalie glanced at the kitchen floor where her bloody footsteps had left irregular marks on the floor.

Ffion looked Natalie straight in the face. She suddenly looked much older than four years old. Natalie half expected her to say, 'What a load of bollocks!' but she only gulped a few times.

'Now I've got to find my phone because Caitlin needs to go to see the nurse.'

'Why?'

'Because she's got the flu and she needs medicine.'

'Mam got medicine for her...' Ffion said helpfully.

'Yes, I know but she needs a special medicine now so I have to get my phone from...'

For fuck's sake, you're wasting time, Sensible Natalie, reminded her.

'Now stay here!' she finished firmly.

She left Ffion sniffing and wailing at the table and forced herself into the utility room once more. Just to ensure she was left alone, she pushed the door shut behind her. A louder cry from Ffion followed.

'I'll be right back' she called.

The sight and smell of the blood had less effect on her the second time while she had the immediate urgency of Caitlin's condition in her mind. A quick look around the utility room convinced her that the phone was not there. She glanced at Striker's body – no, she couldn't do it. You've got to, she thought, you've got no choice.

She knelt beside him, trying to ignore the patch of vomit that clung to the clothes on his upper chest. The smell hit her nostrils and she folded her arm over her face once more. She ran her other hand over his pockets to try to detect the tell-tale shape of a phone. When that revealed nothing, she pushed her arm under his body, closing her eyes and holding her breath as her face became closer to his. His eyes were partly open and she did not think she could go ahead with her search if she had to see those dull fish-like eyes at close quarters.

Ffion's crying had reached a crescendo and Natalie hurried, shoving her arm more roughly under Striker's legs, but her hand came back empty. There was no phone.

She pulled back in a hurry, a sob working its way up her throat. What if Caitlin dies, what if Caitlin dies, what if Caitlin dies? The words refused to leave her mind.

Ffion's crying sounded nearer and Natalie could see the door handle moving.

'Stay there. I'm coming!' she called.

She leapt to the doorway and, with a swift opening of the door, she was back in the kitchen with Ffion before her vision blackened. She went to her knees and Ffion clung to her as she tried to stay focused.

In a few seconds, the faintness had cleared and Natalie saw that her arms and clothes were stained with Striker's blood. The glint of the bread knife on the floor also caught her attention and she grabbed it and lobbed it into the sink in case Ffion noticed it.

'We're going to have to take Caitlin to the nurse,' she told Ffion.

'Why?'

Natalie took a breath and counted to five; screaming at the little girl, *because I bloody say so,* would not help.

'She has to have some special medicine and the phone doesn't work.'

'Why?'

Patience, the Sensible Natalie reminded her.

'I don't know why the phone doesn't work. Maybe...'

You're wasting time, Sensible Natalie said.

'Put your shoes on. We have to go. I can't leave you here.'

Ffion started wailing again and clung to Natalie.

'Don't leave me, Nattee! Don't leave me!'

'Come on. We have to get your shoes, but we must be very quick, ok?'

She grabbed Ffion roughly by the hand and led her out of the kitchen and up the stairs.

Once in the twins' bedroom, Natalie rushed to check Caitlin's breathing; there was no change.

'Why Caitlin sleeping?'

Natalie closed her eyes. Questions, questions.

'Just put your feet in here quickly. Hurry!'

Natalie held socks out for Ffion to put her feet into, but her eyes never left the still form of Caitlin.

'Put that on!' Natalie grabbed a thin hoodie from the chair beside the bed and threw it at Ffion.

Natalie felt as though each movement was performed through a vat of syrup. Her mind was willing Ffion to hurry up but she knew that shouting at her would only delay matters. Meanwhile, she rolled the duvet around Caitlin once more and tied a dressing gown belt around the middle. The top gaped open, but Natalie was helpless as to what else to do.

She tried to pick the child up but the bulk of the duvet was too thick.

'Put your shoes on!' she shouted at Ffion.

Caitlin rolled helplessly on to her side. Natalie pulled the belt loose and released her from the duvet. There was a blanket box at the bottom of the bed and Natalie threw it open. Some clean sheets lay folded in there. She grabbed one and yanked it out.

'Mam does that when we do a sick on the bed!' Ffion commented, with a shoe half on and off.

Natalie ignored her; she continued to wrap the sheet around Caitlin and once again tied the dressing gown belt around it to keep it in place. She had another attempt to lift her and found it easier with less bulk. She prodded at Caitlin again to try to make her wake up but nothing happened.

She turned her attention to Ffion, who was struggling with her shoes.

'Sit still,' she said and, with shaking hands, fastened her shoes, 'Ok, let's go.'

Natalie picked up Caitlin and positioned her over her shoulder. The weight was unbelievable, she thought.

'We have to go downstairs. Stay behind me and don't get in the way,' she told Ffion.

Step by step, she carried her unconscious burden down the stairs while Ffion kept up a stream of questions that gained her only grunts as answers. At the last step, Natalie felt her vision narrow briefly but she leaned over and clung to the banister until it passed.

Ffion stepped past her and headed towards the kitchen.

'Not that way,' Natalie said, 'Let's go through the front door.'

'Why?' said Ffion.

Natalie's exhaustion stopped her from replying – a well-timed impediment that kept the harsh words from being voiced and making the situation worse.

There was an old oak settle in the hallway – an antique that was so hard and uncomfortable that no-one wanted to sit on it – and Natalie gratefully lowered Caitlin on to it as she approached the front door. Then, a second later, lowered her own frame on to it, relishing its presence as if it had been a feather filled mattress. Her arms trembled deep in their muscles as she let them hang down. She quickly checked Caitlin's breathing again; the only way she knew for certain that she had not stopped was when she put her ear near the child's mouth – a slight dampness of breath moistened her ear lobe.

Don't waste time, she thought. She got up immediately and opened the front door; the pale view of the stable-yard made her insides feel as though they had folded over on themselves.

I can't do this, she thought.

Rachel's car, Sensible Natalie suggested. She felt her heart leap. Of course! It was parked in a bay under a hay barn. In typical testimony to the old fashioned, trusting way of life they enjoyed in Llanefa, Ben and Rachel used to leave the keys hanging on a hook near to some implements on the wall of the hay barn. Ok, so I haven't passed my driving test yet, but I *can* drive, she thought.

'Wait here. I'll get the car,' she told Ffion.

'No...' Ffion started to say, 'Car...'

Natalie cut her off with a stern 'Shh' and exited the door before any further questions delayed her.

She made her way down through the stable yard, jogging and half waiting for a bout of faintness to stop her. Her heart beat forcefully but she ignored it. She reached the hay barn and swung around the corner of a supporting beam that formed a right angle between the tack room and the barn. Visibility was even less due to the roof and side of the building blocking out the feeble moonlight. She stopped and stared – certain that the car would materialise in her vision at any second. She felt around on the wall until her hand made contact with the plastic covered switch and pressed it. The empty space in the barn seemed twice as large as it should have been – the void mocking her. Where...? She turned around and ran across the yard to check other, less visible areas; no car. She began to think of possibilities – was it in a garage for repairs or a service? Had Rachel parked it somewhere else? Where?

A flashback of Caitlin's unresponsive face cancelled out all other considerations. *You're wasting time, Sensible Natalie warned.* Natalie felt a sob forming again. She wanted to curl up on the ground and wait for someone else to materialise and solve the problem.

'NATTEEEEE!' a wail came from the direction of the house. Natalie jumped. Had Caitlin... Please, no, she thought. She ran back towards the house. The front door was still open. Caitlin was on the settle where she had left her. Ffion was standing in the doorway with her fists rubbing her teary eyes. She threw herself at Natalie.

'Don't go, Nattee,' she said in between sobs.

'Ok, ok, come on, we've got to go,' she replied.

'Car gone,' Ffion said.

Great! Why didn't you tell me before, Natalie thought, while automatically tucking the bed sheet around Caitlin.

She pictured the long rutted driveway up the hill; the constant questions from Ffion and the increasingly heavy weight of Caitlin. Could she risk leaving Caitlin here while she went for help? *What if she stops breathing Sensible Natalie asked, how would you know?* What will I do if she stops breathing on the way, Natalie asked herself. She did not need her mind to provide the answer.

Ffion was looking up at her expectantly.

Don't ask me another question, she thought.

Ffion's face worked itself into a question-forming shape.

'Let's go,' she said before the child could say whatever she had intended to.

She turned back to the settle and picked up Caitlin; the weight felt as if it had increased since she had put her down there. Despite her efforts, the sheet had twisted and was dragging down near Natalie's shins.

Natalie and Ffion stepped into the weak moonlight and set off towards the driveway.

29. Natalie.

She was struggling. The weight of the child slung over her shoulder seemed so much greater than it should have been. Her bodily weakness and lack of nutrition added to the daunting task of walking uphill for three-quarters of a mile in the dark. She tried not to think about how far and how taxing the journey would be; the reality would have halted her completely.

Ffion, meanwhile, was treating it like a school trip; she skipped along beside Natalie, keeping up a stream of childish anecdotes interspersed with questions about where they were going and why they were doing it.

Natalie stopped at regular intervals and put Caitlin on the ground while she tried to regain some strength. Each stop was also a chance to check the child's breathing – Natalie's fingers shook and her heart raced as she attempted to detect a pulse in Caitlin's neck. Her nerves, already fully stretched, took her to a new level of anxiety when Caitlin suddenly gasped during one such rest. Natalie shook her and called her but the moment had passed and she returned to her previously limp state.

Ffion was also alarmed by this behaviour and started crying – a result of over-tiredness at being forced out of bed in the middle of the night rather than due to any genuine concern for her sister. Natalie found that her patience was running low and constantly shouted at the child – which made Ffion cry even more. The constant grizzling seemed to lodge itself in Natalie's brain; her degree of worry escalated to match the sound of crying.

She tried to picture how far away the nearest house was. Once she had completed the gruelling climb up out of the valley, she had to find someone who could phone for an ambulance. The occasional cottages they had passed on her way here in Ben's car felt as though they were on the other side of the world. Maybe someone would be driving at this time of night, she thought. She would have to flag them down. Sensible Natalie reminded her how seldom cars passed along the road at the top of the drive – a reason that Ben and Rachel had bought the place.

It was no good, she would have to stop again; the stops were getting more frequent and Natalie's arms were reaching their limit. She was cautious about fainting and dropping Caitlin, but to her surprise she felt no more than the vague beginnings of wooziness and that only happened when she got up to walk each time after a rest.

The sheet she had tied around Caitlin kept becoming unravelled; she tucked it around her and re-tied the belt each time she stopped. Caitlin did not feel noticeably colder and there was even a sweaty patch on the side of her face that Natalie suspected had rubbed off from her own skin.

'When we going back to bed, Nattee?' Ffion asked. It was obvious that the adventure had lost its appeal to her.

'We've got to get Caitlin to see the nurse,' Natalie kept repeating. If she asks me why again, I swear I'll fucking leave them both here, she thought.

'Bedtime now,' Ffion reminded her.

'Mmm,'

Ffion stopped and gasped.

Oh no, Natalie thought. Not her too! But before she had a chance to say anything, Ffion's gasp turned into a huge, gaping yawn. Natalie's heartbeat returned to normal.

How much further? Her arms trembled so much with the effort of carrying Caitlin that she could not stop them shaking after she had put the child down to give herself a break. She began to feel helpless. Would it be better if she left them here and went on to get help? She pictured the scene; two little girls left in the countryside in the middle of the night (or probably just one – Ffion would cling to her if she tried to leave). What was wrong with her? She couldn't leave them here! She imagined coming back to them, both seriously injured after being attacked by badgers and foxes. She recognised that her imagination was giving her fantasy scenarios, but stress and weakness were fuelling the idea that there *were* creatures waiting for her to abandon the twins on the darkened track.

She stopped suddenly and almost dropped Caitlin. I'm done, she thought. I can't go any further. A pitiful sob escaped from her as she let Caitlin slump to the floor. She's going to die, she thought. I can't do it. She's going to die. Her breath came in whooping gasps and there was a line of sweat running down the middle of her back.

'Why you laughing, Nattee?' asked Ffion.

Natalie cracked.

'I'm not bloody laughing,' she cried, her words coming in between sobs, 'Caitlin is very ill and... and... you're too bloody slow!'

Ffion's face registered a variety of emotions despite the limited light. The choice between berating Natalie for swearing, being upset about her sister and taking offence at being shouted at, all battled for supremacy within the space of a second. Her face folded in on itself and she opened her mouth to let out a loud wail.

Natalie immediately felt terrible and grabbed Ffion.

'I'm sorry, I'm sorry. I didn't mean it. I'm just tired. Please stop crying,' she said, while inside her head she understood how close she was to walking away from it all.

Ffion was reluctant to forgive and she wriggled away from Natalie's touch.

'You nasty, Nattee,' she said in a tearful voice.

'Come on. Let's go. We have to try to make Caitlin better,' she cajoled.

Ffion half turned away, expecting Natalie to come after her, but Natalie had dismissed her. She had to get Caitlin on to her shoulder again. She bent down to lift her, but she just felt drained of strength.

She tried again but she could not get her off the ground. Caitlin's head rolled to one side and the sight of it brought on a fresh bout of crying.

I just can't do it. I can't do anything. I can't lose weight. I can't stop eating. I'm too fat to lift her...

As the self-destructive thoughts ran through her mind, Ffion wailed even louder in an attempt to gain attention and a further apology. Natalie continued to ignore her.

'Going to bed now,' Ffion stated eventually, when the crying had failed to get the desired attention. She turned back in the direction they had come from. Natalie still ignored her; she had her hand under Caitlin's chin, trying to find her pulse.

Ffion stomped off in the direction of home, getting about ten steps before she realised that Natalie had not stopped her. In the distance, a vixen called – an eerie sound to those not accustomed to it. Ffion halted. She could not see where she was going; and Natalie and Caitlin were not coming with her. She spun on her heels and ran back to Natalie, throwing her arms around Natalie's legs and screamed.

'Shh!' Natalie said automatically, though she paid little attention to her – the presence of a pulse on Caitlin's neck was still evading her fingers. Fuck, her brain said. *Try again, Sensible Natalie said, try further forward. Her head is in a different position now.* She put her fingers around Caitlin's jaw until her fingertips prodded deep into her neck. Suddenly, she felt it – the thrup, thrup – faint but definitely there. Thank you, thank you, she thought, though she had no idea who or what she was thanking.

Now, you've really got to get her up and get going, she thought. The reality made her aware of her weakened arms and legs. She bent over and grasped the little body and heaved it towards her. It was no good. She could not lift her.

Drag her, then! Whether it was the real Natalie or the Sensible version, it was a good idea. She pulled Caitlin's arms up and grasped them. Natalie stood behind her and wrapped the sheet around each of Caitlin's wrists, then caught hold of both together before dragging her backwards over the bumpy ground. Her head lolled to one side but Natalie kept going while watching that her head did not slip off the sheet. Within ten steps, she had run out of steam. That's the secret, she thought, ten steps at a time.

Ffion was beside her once more – her affront and tiredness gone – chattering away about the stars and the moving light shining down from them. Natalie made some noises of agreement but had no real grasp of what she was saying. Every ten steps, she stopped dragging Caitlin along the ground and checked her pulse or re-adjusted the sheet. The ten steps reduced to five steps and Natalie felt the hopelessness overcome her.

'Look at the magic light, Nattee!' Ffion said, pointing upwards.

Natalie grunted in reply.

She took a few deep breaths before bending forwards once more. Ffion was almost dancing with excitement and pointing upwards. Natalie had passed into a different plane and could safely ignore her comments without losing patience.

'Look, look, Nattee,' she said, 'Look!'

Natalie turned her head in Ffion's direction – an automatic reaction.

Suddenly, the 'magic light' caught Natalie's attention. It wasn't coming from the stars, she realised. It was coming from uphill! There was a car coming down the drive! She pulled Caitlin and her sheet to one side.

'Stay close to me!' she shouted to Ffion.

Pablo, she thought. He's come back in a car. He's got to help.

The beams of light concentrated into two bright tunnels that appeared through the trees at both sides of the lane. Natalie leapt out onto the track, waving her arms and hoping the driver would see her before it was too late. She jumped up and down and yelled 'Stop!'

The car lights bumped unevenly over the track, temporarily blinding Natalie. She turned her head away but continued to wave her arms.

As if the driver had suddenly caught sight of her, the car's lights dipped as it braked. The loose gravel on the track prevented it from slowing gradually and the headlights came alarmingly closer to Natalie with a telltale skidding noise.

'Stop! Stop!' she screamed.

With a foot to spare, the car slewed sideways to a halt.

Natalie ran forward to the driver's side.

'You've got to help me...' she said, though the engine was still running and it was unlikely that the driver could hear.

She reached the driver's side and continued her plea of, 'You've got to help me,' when the driver's door opened and someone stepped out.

30. Jack

Jack made his way to the car park of the showground. Being nothing more than a large field designated as a temporary measure for the event he was forced to wander blindly through rows of other vehicles as he searched for his car in the weak moonlight. He had not drunk the remains of his third glass of lager and had simply left his crowd of friends without comment. No-one had noticed his absence while they all came and went freely from the dance area or bar.

He got into his car and sat in darkness. He checked his watch and tried to work out when it would be safe to drive. He knew that the police were always keen to check motorists on show nights and he did not want to add a driving ban to his troubles. He pushed his driver's seat back and put the car radio on. When he felt sleepy, he switched the radio off and drifted into a doze while occasional raucous shouts disturbed him. With the radio off, he could hear the faint sound of the disco music from the tent. At intervals he fell asleep again with the ease of the young.

He awoke suddenly to the sound of shouting. He sat up in some alarm and realised that he was listening to some argument between several men.

'You don't expect me to believe that, good boy?' a voice boomed close to his car.

A sudden laugh reassured him that the argument was not a serious one. He kept his head ducked down; what he did not want was for some of his friends to realise that he and his car were still on the showground or they were likely to want him to act as their taxi. He wasn't certain if he was safe to drive, but more significantly, he did not want to waste time with them while he had a plan to follow. He checked the clock in the car – could he risk it? He mentally planned his journey to Ben and Rachel's farmhouse; if he took a slightly longer route, he would avoid the main road (and the police patrol). He reasoned that if all was in darkness when he got to the house, he would simply sleep in the car on the drive and speak to Natalie in the morning. Again he worked out the timing – nearly three glasses of lager – how many hours did he need from the time he had started drinking? Jack and his friends all had a basic knowledge of how to calculate drink-drive times – the need of a driving licence was paramount in such a community – and few of them flouted this guideline.

The aforementioned lager reminded him that it was accumulating in his bladder and he got out of the car to urinate on to the grass. In the darkness, he was aware that some activity was still going on in the Beer Tent; it was probably a good idea to wait a little longer rather than attract attention by driving past his friends if he saw them walking on the road. There were some street lights along the main road and it would be difficult to drive past them if he saw them – plus, they would know it was his car. He got back in the car and leaned back in the seat again.

Some unknown time later, he jerked awake. He sat up and looked about him for a few seconds before remembering where he was. He glanced to one side expecting to see Natalie (they had fallen asleep in his car on previous occasions) before the rest of his memory caught up.

He checked the clock and saw that he had slept for longer than he had planned. He opened the car door and listened. There were no sounds of voices and he could not make out many vehicles left beside him – the ones still there had probably been temporarily abandoned by their 'over-the-limit' owners.

In his more sober condition, he began to wonder if it was such a good idea to carry out his plan. What if Kyle had made a mistake and Natalie was now back home, having been babysitting for the evening only? Though why would he make such a mistake? He thought back over the past few months – he had been to Natalie's house and she had refused to speak to him. He had attempted to speak to her in school and that had also failed. This was his only chance. If this failed, then he was going to have to accept it, but he refused to give in until she had at least told him *why* she had dumped him.

His pulse increased with anticipation – what if she still...?

He swallowed. Fuck it, if you're going to do it, then do it, he told himself.

Before he could change his mind, he started the ignition and drove carefully out of the bumpy field.

He glanced cautiously at the road – no traffic in sight and, more importantly, no police cars. He turned left, away from the direction of home and towards the Pwll y Coed road. After half a mile, he turned on to a very minor road so that he could avoid any police who were stopping vehicles – he was still not certain that he was entirely safe to drive.

He put the car into a low gear as he climbed the hill and wound round the bends between the trees. The road was very narrow and he was mindful of the wild deer that sometimes leapt out on to the road. Hitting a deer would be disastrous as there would, no doubt, be damage to his car that he would not be able to explain to his parents. Also, hitting a deer was a reportable offence, he believed; he thought he remembered such a question in his Written Driving Test. It was not just the idea of being caught by police that worried him, but the reason *why* it had happened. If Natalie still rejected him, he would look like a fool – chasing after her and getting himself into trouble

with the police as a result. He wanted to keep it private –
if Natalie rejected him again, he did not want anyone else
to know that it had happened.

He continued to scan the high hedge-bank for deer
and kept his speed low. He began to increase the speed as
the trees became fewer and he had a better view of the
bank. He realised that he had been holding his breath, so
he gave a sigh and pressed harder on the accelerator.

At the bottom of his peripheral vision an unexpected
movement alerted him - the shape of something lying in
the road.

'Fuck!' he shouted and slammed on his brakes. The
fact that he was travelling uphill was an advantage as he
stopped instantly. The animal, or whatever it was (he
hoped it was simply a broken branch), had disappeared
from view in front of the car bonnet. He heard an ominous
thud against some part of his car.

Leaving his headlights on, he leapt out of the car.
Instinct warned him that it might be a badger or fox and
that he needed to be careful in case he was bitten, but he
did not slow his pace as he rounded the front of the car.

The shape moved and Jack halted, expecting the
animal to dart past him to safety. The headlights were
partly blinding him and he could see midges hovering in
the beams. A cry came from the animal and he looked
more closely. The shape moved again and became the
sitting figure of a woman.

'Oh fuck, no!' he either said or thought – he could not
have determined which if anyone had asked him later.

The woman was making a wailing noise. Jack knelt
down beside her.

'Are you all right?' he said, 'Are you hurt? Are you ok?'

He seemed unable to stop the questions that would
provide him with the answer he wanted to hear. The
wailing continued.

Jack was still unable to see her properly but she looked to be a strange shape. He felt sick.

The woman pulled her hand away from her face.

'I can't even do that!' she cried.

Jack panicked further; if she wasn't even able to move her other arm (as that seemed to explain her words to him), then she really was seriously hurt. He turned around towards his car.

'Try not to move. I'll phone for an ambulance,' he said.

The wail that followed froze him to the spot.

'Nooo-ooo-ooooo...' broken up by sobs.

She scrambled on to her knees, moaning as she rekindled various injuries.

'Stay there!' Jack yelled. 'Don't move in case you've broken something!'

'Don't phone anyone,' she said with a further sob, 'please don't!'

Jack went back to her and slowly helped her to her feet. To his relief, he saw that she was able to walk and use her arms. He could see traces of blood but nothing that caused him alarm. The 'funny shape' he had seen had been caused by a canvas bag that she wore around her shoulder and under the opposite arm.

'Can you get in the car?' Jack asked.

She nodded.

He helped her into the passenger side, realising that it was Anna who had worked in the Beer Tent that day; he had seen her in the Poacher's Rest on several occasions.

Jack got into the driver's seat and looked across at her.

'Do you want me to take you to hospital?' he asked (while praying that she would refuse – it would cause him some awkward questions), 'Or shall I drive you home?'

She began to cry again.

'No, I can't go home. There's no-one there. Only...'

She looked at him in desperation, 'Please don't take me to hospital.'

Jack was at a loss what else to suggest. He had a vague idea that she had older brothers, but had no knowledge of where they lived.

'Where were you going?' Jack asked, 'Shall I take you there instead?'

She was silent for a minute. Jack started driving slowly up the hill, casting his eyes side to side, looking for somewhere to turn the car around.

'I don't know,' she said eventually.

Jack gave up with his questions.

'Ok, well I can't help you if you won't tell me where you want to go!' he said.

'I've... done something... stupid,' she said, 'I just wanted it all to... end. The hillside looked high enough and then I saw the car lights. I thought... one quick leap and...'

'You're taking the piss!' Jack said incredulously, before looking at her face and seeing that she was being honest with him.

'For fuck's sake! I could have *killed* you!'

The words were out of his mouth before he realised that was exactly what the intention was. He could not believe that he had said it.

'I didn't mean... you know. It's just... you can't go round doing that sort of crap...' he finished weakly.

She put her hands over her face again.

'I'm sorry,' she said before dissolving into helpless, shoulder racking sobs.

He said nothing and they continued to the top of the hill where Jack turned in the direction of Pwll y Coed once more. It dawned on him that his crappy day was getting even crappier and he now had an additional problem. He had to drop Anna off somewhere if he was going to go on to Ben and Rachel's farmhouse.

'I'll have to take you somewhere...' he said, 'if you're sure you're ok...'

She was silent for another minute.

'Can you drop me off by the old railway bridge at Pwll y Coed?' she asked him.

She sounded much more positive, he noted.

'Ok.'

They travelled in silence. Jack's thoughts circled inside his head before coming to the obvious conclusion.

'You're going to do it again, aren't you? At the old railway bridge?'

'No,' she said but kept her eyes facing forward.

Jack did not believe her. His mind was in turmoil. What could he do with her? He couldn't just kick her out on the road – it was obvious that she was intent on harming herself. He certainly did not want to take her to hospital and have to answer questions about why and what he was doing when he almost ran her over. His thoughts came to rest on one word – Natalie. She would know what to do! Sensible Natalie – the one who solved all their problems when something went wrong! And even morc importantly, he would have a valid excuse to speak to her. (At this time of night, his mind questioned? It doesn't matter, it's an emergency, he told himself).

'I have to turn off here first. I want you do me a favour. Speak to my girlfriend before I drop you off? Deal?'

Anna stared at him – her eyes small and piggy from crying.

'You're not going to make me see anyone else...? They'll think I'm mad...'

'No. Not if you don't want to.'

She nodded and sniffed. She lifted a hand to wipe at her eyes and nose.

Jack slowed down along the lane. He was trying to remember where the entrance to the farmhouse was. He knew that there was a long driveway, but he had only been there a couple of times. As he slowed the car, he kept a watchful eye on Anna – he was convinced that she was going to leap out of the car before he got to his destination.

'I'm sorry I scared you,' she said.

He smiled at her, 'You fucking did an' all!'

He expected her to return his smile – most girls did – but she just gazed ahead as if in a trance.

'Do you believe in bad things happening like... as a punishment?' she said.

What the fuck was she on about, Jack thought. His experience of girls had been limited to girlfriends (whose questions had been generally simple and shallow), his family members and Natalie.

'Punishment is usually bad,' he agreed, after dredging the extent of his knowledge of psychology.

'I mean, really bad things. Stuff you wouldn't believe would happen?'

'Sometimes,' he said, though he was playing for time – he had no idea what she was talking about. He was beginning to think that she was a nutter. All the times he had seen her in town and even that evening at the YFC Showground, she had seemed like just a regular person. But here, she just seemed deranged; and there was a definite smell of piss about her.

She returned to her trance, Jack was relieved to see. He wasn't certain how long he could keep up the kind of conversation that she seemed to be heading towards. With relief, he saw he had just passed the sign on the gatepost that read 'Coed y Bryn Farmhouse'. He braked and quickly reversed before turning into the rutted track that served as a driveway. He drove carefully to avoid damaging the underside of his car. He remembered that Ben and Rachel had a 4x4 car each – he could see why!

'It's not my fault,' Anna said suddenly, 'but everyone will think it was...'

She hid her face in her hands again.

Natalie, save me, Jack thought.

'I just tried to stop it happening...' she began, 'I didn't do anything wrong... Will you tell them?'

'Tell who?' Jack asked while half his mind was telling him to simply agree with whatever she said.

'Everyone who will be asking questions,' she replied.

Jack had the uncomfortable feeling that she was talking about the time after she had thrown herself off the railway bridge – or whatever else she intended to do.

'Look,' he said, 'don't you think you should... get some help... or something... You know, if you're feeling bad... you know, bad in a...'

He failed to find the right words to describe depression.

'I deserve to feel bad...'

A severe bout of crying followed this. She seemed to be unable to breathe in properly – her outward breaths were extended because of the crying and she whooped air inwards a couple of times. Jack wondered if she was too young to have a heart attack. He glanced at her; he was really worried. This was so far out of his experience that he had no idea how to deal with it.

She took her hands away from her face and began screaming, 'Stop! Stop!'

Jack continued to look at her in great alarm but she carried on screaming. Instantly, he realised that she was looking ahead through the windscreen. He turned to look and saw the unmistakeable forms of people in his headlights. He braked suddenly but the loose gravelly surface slid under the car tyres and the car continued onwards and slightly sideways while Anna screamed on and on.

The car stopped in time and Jack saw, with amazement, Natalie and a small child standing on the track.

31. Tegwyn.

The path by the Devil Tree was a hive of activity. Flashlights were directed in random directions as more police arrived from Carmarthen to help search the alleged scene of the crime. Other police cars had been dispatched to search for the victim.

Tegwyn and Alun James stood at each new section of the path before letting each officer through. Dominic Beynon thumped his way past them, the light beam of his torch jigging up and down as he walked.

'Try not to fuck up all the forensic evidence!' Alun James growled at him, while Dominic simply looked at him in amazement. 'Keep to one side. Clear each area around you before you go on!'

Alun James was not one to deal well with loss of sleep and his patience was greatly lacking.

Jamie Bowen came up to them from the direction of the road.

'Just spoken to Traffic,' he said, 'They've seen a young woman walking along the by-pass on the opposite carriageway to them. Obviously worse for wear. Got denim shorts and black top on. Looks pretty happy, they said. The victim's description isn't anywhere close to that, is it?'

'Not according to Arwel,' said Alun, 'But get them to speak to her – just to double check…'

Jamie turned around to go back down.

'And come straight back here afterwards. We could do with another pair of eyes on the path.'

Everyone present knew that searching the alleged scene of the crime in darkness was probably a futile exercise, but it had seemed necessary. Several other officers had been summoned to search the roadways in case the young woman was still around.

'We'll give it another hour, then pack it in for the night. Tape off the ends of the path – not that I expect anyone to be walking through at this time of night,' Tegwyn said.

At intervals, a shout would alert them to some object that had been found on the path – an empty Coke bottle, part of a shoe, the lid of a peanut butter jar - Tegwyn was unconvinced that any of them were relevant to the enquiry but nevertheless, each item was bagged and identified with a log number.

Jamie returned and included himself in the searching of the scene. He did it meticulously, Tegwyn noted.

After some time of fruitless searching, torchlight could be seen in the horses' field. Alun glanced across in an attempt to identify the person, but the beams of light swept back towards his eyes, temporarily blinding him. Eventually, the light came closer and the torch carrier climbed unceremoniously over the small fence. It was Jamie. Behind him, Tegwyn could see the glowing eyes of the horses as they watched suspiciously.

'Anyone know who owns these horses?' Jamie asked.

Alun shook his head, 'Shouldn't be difficult to find out. Why?'

'Well, Arwel said that she was on about the white pony walking with her or something... I've looked and there is no white pony in there. Brown ones with white faces, but no white ones. Maybe someone stole the white one...? Or, suppose the owner came to get the white one for some reason and then saw the girl. I think we should trace him. He could be the one who carried out the attack.'

Both older men immediately shone their own lights into the field. It was true. A cluster of white-faced brown horses stared back at them.

It was an excellent observation, Tegwyn thought. He started to make arrangements to go back to the station so that the land-owner and, hopefully, the horses' owner could be traced. He walked along the path towards the car. Alun James came behind, stumbling over the ruts and swearing. His words were illegible until he answered a call on his radio. He stood still while Tegwyn walked on.

A thudding of steps behind him made him turn around.

'Boss,' he said, 'got a call from Headquarters. The hospital has reported an incident. Seems that there's a man been shot over at Pwll y Coed way. Who do you want over there?

Tegwyn's pulse shot into overdrive.

It never rains but pours, he thought, before adding another thought. If it had been raining, he was sure none of this would have happened.

32. Jack, Anna and Nat.

The night was filled with voices. Everyone seemed to be either shouting or crying. Natalie was babbling incoherently and pulling at Jack's arm; Ffion was wailing; Jack himself was barking questions at Natalie.

'Help me get her in the car,' Anna's voice, loud but calm, brought them all to their senses.

They looked around and saw her gathering Caitlin into her arms.

Jack opened the back door of the car and quickly helped to carry her in. Everyone else piled in too.

Too many things began happening. Anna phoned 999 and during her brief conversation, turned to Jack and said, 'Just keep going, they said. They'll stay on the line and we have to tell them where we are and how she is... Yes, yes... unconscious.' She switched from talking to the Emergency Operator to talking to Jack every few words.

'Two children. But one is ok. Turn left here – towards the main road... The ambulance will meet us... I don't know. She was like that when we found them...'

'Oh God! Striker! He's dead!' Natalie shouted hysterically from the back seat.

'What!'

Anna held up her hand, 'Ok, ok. I'll put her on.'

Anna gave the phone to Natalie, 'You need to tell them...'

When Jack thought back about the incident, he wondered how he had ever coped with it. He drove the car and listened to Ffion screaming, Anna on the phone, Natalie shouting and believed that he had either gone completely insane or was having the worst nightmare of his life. Who was dead? What had happened to the child?

And how the fuck did he end up with Anna in his car? And just to add to his discomfort, the smell of piss was making him feel nauseous.

Bit by bit, the night's events were becoming clearer to him and he continued driving until the sight of flashing blue lights slowed him down and he flashed his headlights repeatedly while Anna, still on the phone, said, 'I can see them – just coming towards us.'

There followed a blur of activity while the paramedics took over and put Caitlin into the ambulance. Natalie wanted to go with her but the paramedic suggested that she followed in the car.

When they arrived there, Natalie was questioned first by the doctors and then by waiting police who were following up on the death of Striker. She was taken into a relatives' room – the officer insisted that she left Ffion with Anna and Jack.

She went through the shortened version of the evening – the officer making notes and asking more questions.

A nurse came to fetch her and asked if she had contacted Caitlin's parents. Natalie was horrified to realise that she had not given them any thought.

'Is she ok? What's wrong with her?' she asked. All she really wanted to know was that Caitlin was still alive but was too scared to voice that thought.

Another nurse came and, through the open doorway, Natalie saw her try to take Ffion with her. After a short protest, Ffion went with her but clung to Anna's hand and insisted that she came too.

'I've got to ring Rachel!' Natalie said to the officer, 'I've lost my phone with Rachel's mobile number... Oh no!' She burst into tears again, '... I can't remember her number.'

The officer tried to calm her as she sobbed.

Suddenly, she remembered.

'It's the Coach House Hotel! In Newbury! That's where they're staying! It's on the note she left for me!'

The officer used his phone and arranged for someone to contact Ben and Rachel, then continued questioning Natalie.

'How far away was the gunshot do you think?'

'I don't know, I don't know...'

'Do you know anything about a bloodstained knife that was found in the kitchen?' he asked.

Natalie was about to shake her head in denial, when an ice-cold memory materialised in her mind. She tried to put her explanation into words but all she was able to do was cry. Somewhere inside her was a feeling that she should just curl up and close her eyes, shut out all the unpleasant things. She felt herself tilt forward; the officer's voice sounded further away.

'Natalie? Natalie?'

Someone was calling her name. She looked up and wondered why she was on the floor. The nurse held her arm gently.

'I don't think you should ask her much more now,' she said to the officer as she helped Natalie on to a chair. He turned away and they spoke in hushed tones. Natalie heard the words 'possible murder enquiry' – it was enough to set her heart beating at the extra fast rate that she had experienced earlier that night. She gasped.

The nurse turned towards her, 'Can I get you a cup of tea, bach?'

Natalie nodded.

The officer got up and left the room with the nurse. Natalie sat alone, feeling weary and shocked. What was wrong with Caitlin? And Ffion? Why wouldn't they tell her anything?

The door opened. She looked up expectantly, her heart racing again, but it was Jack.

'They said I could come in,' he said. He gave her a smile – the half nervous one when he thought he had overstepped the mark – it was enough to send her into more tears.

He sat beside her and put his arms around her. Natalie's sharp bones dug into him.

'Don't worry,' he said, 'They'll sort everything out. It'll be ok.'

He was still at the age where he considered that those in authority would solve all the awkward problems. Natalie was not so sure.

'What if she dies?' she said in a half whisper, 'What if there was something wrong and I didn't notice?'

'If there had been anything noticeable, you wouldn't have missed it!'

'And Striker. He said she was ill all along!'

'Who's Striker? The one who was shot?'

'I think he was with the fair,' Natalie broke down again, 'there was blood everywhere... I didn't believe him... I lost my phone and now... the knife...'

Jack felt a queasy lurch of his stomach.

'I've brought Anna's bag,' he said, trying to change the subject, 'she's gone in with the other little girl.'

Natalie glanced down – the bag lay in a heap – the zip top gaped partway open in the same way that hers often did. It was a flower patterned canvas tote bag and Natalie saw that it was full of notebooks. She pulled it nearer to her with her foot.

'That policeman asked so many questions,' Natalie said.

'They asked me too,' Jack replied, 'but I wasn't able to tell them much.'

'How were you there, anyway? Thank God you were. I couldn't carry her. Too heavy.'

'I was... just...t-t-t-t... try-t-t ....'

236

Natalie glanced at him in surprise. He breathed in deeply.

'I wanted to talk to you,' he blurted out in one breath.

Natalie's memory gave her a swift rerun of her unpleasant thoughts – though they suddenly seemed far less unpleasant compared to the events of the evening.

The nurse came back in with a cup of tea.

'I hope you take sugar and milk,' she said as she handed her the plastic base with the disposable cup inside. Natalie's instinctive reaction was to say that she did not take sugar and very little milk, but the words that had formed in her head stayed there.

'You want one too?' she asked Jack, 'And where's your friend? The police need to speak to her too.'

'She's gone in with the other little girl,' Jack said and the nurse turned away again.

Natalie sipped at her tea. It tasted wonderful, its sweetness and richness giving her body what she craved. The nurse came back in with some biscuits on a plate. Natalie stared at them longingly until she eventually gave in and took one – nibbling at it and automatically counting one hundred bites.

By the time the nurse had returned with Jack's tea, Natalie was still eating her biscuit and was trying hard not to notice the ones left on the plate.

'Is there any news on Caitlin?' she asked the nurse.

'She seems about the same, I think. Her mother has just been on the phone. They're coming straight back.'

Natalie's heart gave a lurch. She dreaded seeing Rachel and Ben. What would they think of her? The feeling intensified and she felt a little sick at the thought of how they would react.

She stood up warily, waiting to feel the customary faintness, but it did not come.

'Where you going?' asked Jack in panic.

'Loo. That biscuit... Feel a bit yuck...'

Jack pulled his feet out of her way and watched her make her way to the door. She never used to be that thin, he thought. Her eyes were sunken and her skin far too pale. He had a sudden unpleasant vision of his grandmother who had had cancer – a previously stocky woman who had faded before their eyes. He dismissed the thought, but the memory of the way Natalie's bony body had pressed against him while he had hugged her lurked at the back of his mind.

Natalie opened the door to the toilet. She definitely felt sick. The trauma of the night had taken its toll and now she could feel the digestive biscuit she had eaten expanding inside her stomach. She tried not to think of the smell and sight of the blood in the utility room or of the lifeless body of Striker whom she had forgotten about for much of the past hour or two.

She breathed deeply then rinsed her face with cold water. The action made her feel slightly better. She sat on the floor and waited for her nausea to pass completely. In the silence, she realised that there was someone in one of the toilet cubicles. A soft shuffling noise gave it away and Natalie saw the slight movement of shadow under the toilet door.

Within a few minutes, the cubicle door opened slowly. Natalie looked up and saw Anna peering out. She seemed about to close the door again before realising that Natalie had seen her.

'Feeling rough?' she said to Natalie.

'A bit. I just ate a biscuit.'

'Oh.'

'Are you going back in now? Is Ffion ok?' Natalie asked.

'They've got them in the same room,' Anna said, 'She was happy to stay in there when she saw her sister.'

'Is Caitlin awake?'

'I don't think so. Not when I came out... they didn't say anything...'

Natalie burst into tears again.

'They'll never trust me again. They'll think I neglected her.'

Anna squatted down beside her. Despite her anguish, Natalie was aware of a smell of urine coming from Anna.

'Don't be silly! You couldn't have known! I heard you tell them on the phone.'

'I tried to stop her seeing Striker's body and all that blood... And before that I couldn't get them to settle down. They wanted water and then they were too hot...'

Anna put her arm around Natalie. The smell became stronger.

'I'm sure you did all you could. It's been a... scary experience... for all of us.'

Natalie stared intensely at her, 'But I should have noticed something was wrong. I should have! And all I was worried about was them two coming into the house. I was scared. I thought they would have...' She sobbed again, '*Show us your tits*, he said. I thought he was going to... if he got in... he would have... I was just so scared...'

Natalie cried into her palms, noisy slurping sounds. She stopped suddenly and heard another similar sound. She looked up and saw that Anna was crying too.

'I'm sorry,' Natalie said, 'I'm being silly. I'm so worried about Caitlin.'

'It's not that,' Anna said, 'It's what you said... about what they might do...'

A knock on the toilet door halted her. Jack's voice came through.

'Nat? Are you ok?'

'I'm fine,' she called back, 'We'll be out in a minute.'

'Tell Anna that the policeman wants to speak to her.'

'Ok'.

Anna grabbed Natalie's arms.

'Please don't tell the police where I am! I don't want to speak to them!'

'But, you... it's only...'

'Please don't!' Anna began to cry, 'I did something really stupid tonight. Please don't tell them...'

'Ok...' Natalie said doubtfully.

'Look, will you go out and say I'm still in the loo. Tell them I'll be out in a few minutes...'

'Why...?'

'Please don't ask. I just can't tell anyone...'

Natalie got up from the floor and wiped over her face again. She felt better.

She opened the door to find Jack waiting outside with a concerned expression.

'Are you ok?'

She managed a small smile.

'Have they said anything about Caitlin?'

'No. The doctor wants to speak to you. Where's Anna?'

'She's still in the loo,' Natalie said, 'She'll be out in a minute.'

They walked up to the waiting room to meet the doctor who wanted to know if Caitlin had been given any medicine.

'No, nothing. I haven't given her anything!' Natalie's voice rose in some panic before her memory kicked in, 'Apparently she had some medicine for a cough, but I think that was last week... I'm not sure.'

The doctor questioned her some more while the police officer came in and stood tactfully nearby. As soon as he had left the room, the officer began more questions of his own. What time had the two boys been in the house? How long before she had found Caitlin had she been speaking to Striker? When did she hear the sound of a car engine? Natalie struggled to remember the order of the happenings as she relived the events of the night.

'Ok, I need to speak to your friend now. Where is she?'

'She was in the toilet,' Natalie said, 'She'll be out in a minute.'

The officer left the room and moments later she heard him walk by while talking to a nurse.

In less than a minute, he was back again.

'She's gone!' he said, 'do you know where she is?'

He looked sternly at Natalie.

'I don't know,' she said, starting to panic, 'I don't really know her...' She turned to Jack.

He shrugged his shoulders.

'I just... gave her a lift... then all this happened.'

The officer hurried out of the room again.

Natalie and Jack sat down.

'I thought she was with you...' Natalie said.

Jack glanced about him to check that no-one was listening.

'I was coming to talk to you. I took the shortcut because I'd had a pint... trying to stay off the main road and she was just... lying in the road in front of my car.' He lowered his voice even more, 'I don't think she's right in the head. You know, trying to kill herself. She wanted me to drop her off by the old railway bridge but I asked her to speak to you first...'

He shrugged again.

Natalie stared at him with wide eyes.

'Oh no! What if she tries it again?' She got unsteadily to her feet, 'You've got to tell them. They've got to stop her... She said she'd done something stupid and she didn't want to talk to the police...'

Natalie spun around in confusion.

Jack put out his hands to steady her.

'It's ok, it's ok. I'll go and tell them. Just wait here.'

While Jack went to speak to the nurses, Natalie wrapped her arms around her upper body. She felt cold, tired and confused. Surely nothing else was going to happen tonight? She glanced down at Anna's bag which was still on the floor. The longer she stared, the more curious she became. She reached down and pulled out a notebook. Inside its hard cover, the edges of a sheet of paper poked out. Natalie opened the cover and saw that the folded-over side bore the words 'For Mam and Dad'. An unpleasant jolt went through Natalie's body. She opened up the sheet and began to read.

33. Anna's Letter.

The scrawl was barely legible and contained lots of scribbled out parts. Some sections of the paper had been wet and dirty when it had been written on and parts of words blurred into indecipherable shapes. All around the paper were scrawled words – the same word – a man's name repeated over and over. In some parts, the name had been over-written as if the writer had been afraid of it fading or disappearing. It reminded Natalie of how the twins sometimes wrote their names on a drawing.

'Mam and Dad,

I'm sorry you have to read this and I'm sorry that you will be hurt.

I can't see any other way out and I can't ------ like this.

I was raped on the path by the Devil Tree – it's so hard to say this, so I just can't tell you ---- it happened. I thought it was over afte------------------- and I was safe but he followed me home and I was --- scared. He was calling my name outside the house and I knew -------- would try to get in and do it again.

When I couldn't hear him anymore, I ran into the road and ------ to the police station.

I spoke to the poli---- there but----- I was really stupid - I just lost my nerve and ran out. I was so frightened and I started to think --------------- ould all blame me. My mind was just going around a---- ---------nd and I didn't know where to go to be safe. I just feel that he will always be watching out for me and he'll never go away. Even if I go to Newport, ----------fraid he will follow me or he will be waiting for me when I come home to visit you.

When I left the police station, I walked for a long time and I made up my mind to end everything. I couldn't see any other way out. I never wanted to stay in Llanefa and I couldn't bear to stay here any longer.

I went up to the quarry road ---------- writing this while I sit on the high bank. I am using the light from my mo----- phone. When I have the cour----- I----- jump down. I'm scared --------- will hurt, but I'm more scared of what will happen if he comes after me again.

I love you. And the boys. But I can't go on ----- this.

I want you to cremate me and send my ashes to Hollywo---------.

Please don't blame me. The only one who should be blamed is the man who raped me. I know you'll find it hard to believe that he would do such a thing.'

At the end of the note, the same man's name was scrawled in even larger untidy letters.

Natalie took a moment to register what the name meant, then gasped as she realised the implications. No way, she thought!

She stared at the diaries and notebooks. Should she read them? It seemed wrong, but in this situation...

Rape! No wonder Anna had been so upset when she had heard about Pablo! Natalie felt her stomach clench at the thought.

But, still, it couldn't be true! Could it? She could not believe what she had read. What other fantasy scenarios had Anna written in her notebooks? Natalie wasn't certain that she wanted to know. The only thing that seemed real was the fact that Anna had lost the plot and was in imminent danger of harming herself.

She heard new voices outside in the corridor – men with urgency in their tones – but she dismissed them as she continued to stare at the re-folded note.

Suddenly, the door opened with some force. Jack stood there with two men behind him.

'Here she is,' he said, 'Someone wants to talk to you, Nat.'

One of the men was tall, thin and wore glasses.

'I'm DCI Prydderch and this is DC Bowen,' he said, 'I know you've had a terrible night, but there are a couple of things I'd like to ask you if that's ok.'

'Is Caitlin ok? The little girl?' she asked, her panic resurfacing.

'I'm afraid I don't know,' Tegwyn replied, 'But I wanted to ask you about the shooting...'

'Anna!' Natalie almost screamed, 'You've got to find her! She going to do something to herself. She was raped!'

Tegwyn blinked twice. The night's events clicked into sections in his mind.

'Ok, just take it easy and tell me. Where has she gone?'

'I don't know... I can't... But you've got to find her before she does something,'

She waved the note.

'She's written this.'

Jack was gaping at her in astonishment.

Tegwyn took the note and opened it.

He quickly read it and only one word formed in his mind. No.

He read it again but before he could say anything else, his radio-phone beeped. He answered it abruptly and turned away into the corridor in an attempt at privacy. The other officer, Jamie Bowen, spoke to Natalie.

'I remember you, now,' he said, 'you do a lot of horse-riding; competitions and stuff...'

'Not anymore,' Natalie replied automatically, while Jack stared in bemusement.

'Well, maybe you can help me. There are horses in the field by the Devil Tree. One of them is a white pony. Do you know who owns it?'

'There are bay – brown – ponies there,' Natalie said, 'I think they are owned by the people in Castle Farm. Owens, I think...'

'Is the white pony owned by the same people?' Jamie asked.

Natalie looked at him as if he had gone mad; Caitlin was dying – she was sure of it, Striker was dead, Anna was missing, intent on killing herself and he was asking her about *ponies in a field!*

Jamie realised how bizarre it sounded. 'It might help our enquiries,' he added.

'There is no white pony,' Natalie said, 'There used to be, but it's dead now. It was ancient...'

Jamie blinked. His face did the question forming expression again but the words did not come out for a few seconds.

'Could they have had a new one recently?'

Natalie just closed her eyes before more tears came; the only thing she could think of was Caitlin's unresponsive face. The faint feeling was creeping up on her again.

Tegwyn suddenly reappeared in the waiting room.

'We need to go,' he said to Jamie.

'We'll speak to you tomorrow. When you've had some rest,' he added to Natalie as he left the room.

As he walked away, Natalie could hear him telling Jamie, 'Traffic have picked up Pablo and are bringing him in. The girl's been spotted too – hiding in a garden. We'll get down to...' the rest of his words were not loud enough for Natalie to hear.

She turned to Jack, burst into tears and allowed herself to be hugged by him.

'Don't worry,' he said, over and over.

She put her arms around him and clung to him gratefully. She didn't know how long she had stayed there but a female voice interrupted.

'Do you want to come and see the girls now?'

Natalie jumped away from Jack.

'Are they ok?' she gasped, 'Is Caitlin awake? What's wrong with her?'

The nurse smiled at her.

'Just come and see them. Caitlin is still very sleepy but Ffion is asking where Nattee is.'

They followed the nurse along the corridor and up some stairs.

'We've taken them up to the Children's Ward,' she explained.

Natalie walked increasingly faster, wanting the nurse to hurry, but she refused to rush and they made their way towards the double doors of the Ward.

'Just wait a sec,' the nurse said and tapped a security code into the electronic lock at the doorway. Natalie was almost dancing with impatience – especially when the nurse tapped a wrong number and had to start again.

She felt herself straining at the doorway – hurry, hurry, she thought.

She glanced up and saw a security camera above the double doors. The screen showed three people standing at a doorway – a slim, smart nurse (Natalie noticed all slim-bodied people), a tall good-looking boy and a painfully thin young woman. Natalie realised that the boy was Jack and a fraction of a second later, understood that the thin girl who stood beside him was her. She looked again. There must be some flaw in the screen, she thought. She moved to one side so that she stood beside the nurse. That move only served to show her how thin she looked while standing next to a regular sized person. She turned slightly sideways. The image scared her. Was that really what she looked like? She continued to look upwards until she became aware that Jack and the nurse had gone through the, now open, doorway. She walked towards them, giving one last horrified glance at the screen before she passed underneath it. Her heart beat forcefully against her ribs. Even the joy of seeing the twins in their safe setting did not dispel the image she had just seen on the security camera.

34. Manon.

Manon lies in bed. Her eyes feel gritty and sore. Beside her, creating a small bump on the mattress, Gwenllian sleeps contentedly, fingers twitching and mouth pursed into a rosy coloured knot. Manon feels a yawn building up. She would love to go back to sleep but she has duties to fulfil. Just because she has had a disturbed night doesn't mean she can have a lie-in this morning. Last night was very noisy – sirens from police cars or maybe (she thinks hopefully) ambulances or fire engines. They all sound the same to her. She has tried to convince herself that it had been the latter, but the distant noise was enough to keep her awake and on edge. There would be no reason for the police to come here, surely, she thinks? Or had someone said...?

She thinks about the day ahead and starts to feel nervous. Is it really necessary, she asks herself? Why can't she just be allowed to enjoy her baby in the safety of her house?

She swings her legs out of bed and feels her head thump with tiredness. She remembers Sadie who used to work in the same office as her. Manon recalls her coming into the office with her eyes ringed with black shadows.

'Jasmin had me up all night!' she used to say, 'She just can't sleep for more than two hours at a go! I'm knackered!'

Manon had made sympathetic noises and suggested that things would improve when Jasmin became older; offered to make coffee for Sadie and attempted to make her working day easier. But, secretly, she had resented Sadie's attitude. How could she be such a wimp? She had the best reason in the world for having her sleep disturbed! Manon thinks about this as she sits on the side on the bed. She feels a smile working its way to her face; yes, being kept awake because of your baby was the only way to appreciate life! She wishes she could moan half-heartedly to someone: 'Gwenllian was disturbed by the traffic last night. I've hardly slept a wink!'. (Though, she accepts that this not strictly true – it was her, not Gwenllian, who has been kept awake by traffic noises.)

She realises that being able to share baby stories is part of the deal – still, she has Gwenllian and that is a bonus in itself.

She dresses quietly, checking on Gwenllian before leaving the bedroom. Should she put her back in the other bedroom or leave her in the large bed where she has spent the night? Horror stories of babies falling out of beds fill her mind and she gets extra pillows and blankets from the cupboard. She lays them either side of Gwenllian to give her a barrier to stop her rolling off the bed. Despite this, she halts at the door and lets worry work its power on her mind.

Just go quickly and put the kettle on, she thinks, then straight back to check.

Everything takes twice as long as she dashes back and forth from her chores but Gwenllian continues to sleep peacefully.

Eventually, a wail breaks through the peace of the little bungalow – a sound that chills Manon's scalp before she rushes to the bedroom.

Gwenllian is building up to a major protest at discovering she is alone. Manon wonders how far the noise carries; the elderly people next door are quite deaf. She swoops in to pick her up.

'Did you think I'd run off and left you?' she recognises that cooing tone again, 'I wouldn't leave you for anything, cariad! Not for a million pounds!'

She lifts her to her shoulder and rocks her while making comforting noises. Gwenllian's yells begin to subside and she looks about her with wide eyes.

'Ssh, ssh,' she says while still swaying side to side.

'Do you want some breakfast now? Do you? Shall we get you some brekkies? Can we get some brekkies together?' She mentally admonishes herself for her repetitive baby-talk.

The baby looks at her in astonishment, then burps.

'Windy-bops!' Manon remarks, 'More room out than in,'

The baby continues to look about her as if wondering where she is.

'Right! Let's get you sorted, my little dumpling! We've got an important day today!'

She shuffles the baby onto her hip and goes through to the kitchen. She does not attempt to put Gwenllian in her playpen, but prepares the breakfast one-handed – marvelling at how good it feels to be multi-tasking with her baby held safely to her side.

Gwenllian eats her breakfast and allows herself to be washed and dressed with little protest. Manon inhales the smell of newly washed baby like a drug addict taking a fix. They ought to bottle that smell, she thinks.

Once all the necessary chores are completed, she begins to think of the task ahead. It makes her feel anxious.

She puts Gwenllian in the playpen while she gets herself ready. She talks loudly to the baby from each room and leaves the TV on for added company.

'Don't be afraid, little cariad,' she says, 'I won't let anyone hurt or frighten you. It might be a bit strange but there's nothing to be scared of. I promise. I wouldn't let anyone hurt you for anything. I'd rather be hurt myself than let you be harmed...'

A sob breaks from her mouth. A huge feeling of sadness is coming over her. She thinks of all those other babies she has lost and the sob turns into a torrent of crying. She pulls herself together when she hears Gwenllian crying too.

'Don't be sad because Mam's being silly,' she says between sniffs, 'I know you love Mam very much and it makes you sad when she's sad, but I'm ok now. As long as you're here...'

Gwenllian continues to cry. To anyone else it would have sounded like the discontented cry of a child who is in need of entertainment or activity, but Manon goes to her and strokes her face. The child cries louder.

Manon picks her up and swings round in large circles while singing '*Jac y Do*'. It is a song that her grandmother used to sing to her but she hasn't thought of it for many years. She reasons that such knowledge and ploys come as inspiration to women in this very special club called Motherhood.

By the time they are ready to leave, Gwenllian is calm and attentive. Manon takes the baby and the carrier out to her car and secures her into the seat. She is breathing rapidly and her fingers refuse to click the straps together. She constantly looks over her shoulder in case one of the elderly neighbours should appear. She sees no sign of movement. Gwenllian begins to frown and Manon realises that her own face is probably contorted with stress and is scaring the baby. Instantly, she switches into '*Jac y Do*' again and, to her relief, the baby relaxes into a wide-mouthed smile.

She quickly gets into the car and starts the engine. Her pulse is on a high-speed setting and she wishes this did not have to be done. It will be unpleasant – she will not be able to say that Gwenllian is hers and this is what bothers her most. And what if she is seen by someone else who will ask themselves why she has a baby with her...? The beginning of a sobbing episode makes its presence felt – her throat is tight and her sight is blurring. Gwenllian gives a squeal of delight and the sobbing fades away.

Instead, Manon breaks into *'Jac y Do'* before she drives away to her unpleasant task.

35. Manon.

On the way home, Manon battles between the urge to drive faster and the need to be more careful with a young passenger.

Gwenllian is crying from her baby carrier; loud cries that describe her feelings of protest. The ever increasing volume of 'Waah, WAAH', is getting to Manon. Her nerves are on edge and she is conscious of the time of day – the time when the police are changing their shifts. If she does not hurry up, she will have missed this ideal window of not being stopped for a random check. Not only that but... she halts the progression of thoughts before they get out of control.

'Waaaaaah!' Gwenllian yells, 'Waaah-uugh-waaagh!'

'Ssh, don't cry. Ssh!' she tries to stop the noise. It is breaking her concentration as she drives. She needs all her wits about her on this homeward journey.

She pictures her arrival at her bungalow – the crying baby being taken out of her car – attracting the attention of her neighbours.

'Please be quiet,' she pleads before breaking into song, *'Mi welais Jac y Do, yn eistedd ar y to...'*

But Gwenllian does not want to hear about jackdaws on a roof. The crying increases to compete with the singing and soon rises above it.

Manon's hold on her frustration snaps.

'SHUT UP! SHUT UP!' she shouts and half swings around in her driver's seat.

There is a shocked half second of silence before Gwenllian takes the game to a new level – screeching at the top of her voice.

Oh God, what have I done, she thinks? How *could* I have done that? She does not attempt to appease the child – there is no point at this stage; Gwenllian is beyond hearing anything except her own wails.

As the distressed sounds start to recede and be replaced by soft hiccups, Manon sees her chance.

'Sorry, bach. Mam's a bit stressed out and we've been through a lot today, haven't we?'

It occurs to her how confusing and upsetting it must have been for the baby when they met their collaborator - far more for the baby than for her. She feels ashamed. The child has been through a previously unknown experience and she should not be shouting at her! That makes her no better than those smoking, mobile-phone using women she's so despised in the past.

'We'll be home soon, cariad. Then we'll watch CBeebies.'

Gwenllian's head jerks at the familiar word.

'Yes! CBeebies!' Manon repeats, 'then we can watch the world go by, safe in our little home...'

The child stares in fascination – Manon can just about see her while continuing to drive safely. She turns into the road that will eventually lead off to her quiet street and gives a small gasp as she sees a police car coming towards her. It slows down as she approaches. There are cars parked at the side of the road – belonging to residents who do not have garages. The police car headlights flash on twice. Manon holds her breath. Does the driver mean for her to keep going towards him or is he signalling her to stop? She half glances round at Gwenllian – how visible is she? Manon forces her face into a grateful smile and drives towards and past the police car. She lifts her hand in a thank-you gesture as she goes by. The police officer nods in acknowledgement. She speeds up and then remembers the speed limit; she brakes slightly – rushing away will attract attention.

She breathes out as she puts some distance between them.

She continues down the road and is about to turn into her own street when she sees the police car appear behind her in the rear view mirror, closing the distance. Manon's heart does a flip. Blown it now, she thinks. End of!

The headlights of the police car are flashing behind her again.

Maybe he's had a call to go somewhere else in a hurry - she tries to comfort herself with this thought. She pulls into the side of the road and waits for him to pass. He pulls up behind her. Manon's heart is pounding now. She wonders how much more she can take. Her eyes stung as her tears threaten. She should have stayed home; she should have left sooner – a list of regrets line up in her mind.

She half glances around at Gwenllian who, miraculously, is now asleep. She winds down her driver's window as the officer approaches her car. He is speaking on his radio or phone – Manon cannot see which. His tone is urgent although she cannot hear his exact words.

He ends his call and walks to the driver's door. Manon peers out anxiously through the open window.

'Hallo. No need to look so worried,' he says with a smile.

She swallows and attempts a smile in return.

'Did you know you had a brake-light out?' he asks.

Manon wants to hug him with relief but a cautious inner voice suggests that he will notice the baby at any moment.

'Have I? Oh what a pain! I wonder when that went...?'

The officer goes to the back of the car and seems to be tapping the plastic cover.

'Try it now,' he says.

Manon complies.

'Nah, still the same,' he says, 'Sorry.'

'Oh well, I suppose you'll have to book me now,' she says with an attempt at false cheer (though in reality she is hoping that being booked will be worst thing that will happen today).

The officer grins.

'We're not all that bad!' he says,' Usually, I would give you a form to get it fixed within fourteen days, but, well... we're a bit busy today. So if you don't tell – I won't! Just get it fixed. Could be dangerous if someone behind you doesn't see you braking... And you've got a little one in the back. Got to keep them safe!'

Manon's anxiety levels begin rising again.

'How old is she?' he asks, 'I'm assuming *she* with those pink clothes!'

'Eight months,' she says, 'A Christmas baby ... more or less... arrived a bit early...gave us all a surprise... she wasn't due until three weeks later...' She knows she is babbling, but she feels that if she stops talking the officer will ask more questions and then...

'It won't seem long until she'll be staying out late and asking for driving lessons! Take care now. Don't forget to get that brake-light sorted!'

'I will. Thank you, thanks. You're very... Thank you...'

She feels the tears coming now and she inclines her head to stop him seeing them, but he has already gone.

36. Manon.

Manon has never felt so tired.

Gwenllian has also given in to her busy day and is ready to go to sleep. But, it is too early, Manon thinks. If she lets her sleep now, she will be awake too early.

The child's face is pink with heat. She is irritable and does not want her supper, pushing the spoon away as Manon tries to persuade her to eat.

'Here comes the magic spoon – wheee!' she sings, swooping it like a toy plane, but Gwenllian smacks it sideways sending the food to the floor.

'You naughty girl!' she says fondly, 'My Nanna used to say, there are thousands of children starving in Africa! You have to eat *some* of it!'

But Gwenllian just gets more upset and redder in the face.

'I know, bach. It's been a busy day for you. One more spoonful and then we'll put you to bed...'

But Gwenllian does not accept this deal. She wants the spoon *away* and *now!*

'Ok, if you don't really want it...' Manon starts to accept that she is losing this battle. She feels relieved – it has been a trying day. The incident with the police officer has rattled her nerves and she still expects a knock on the door. Maybe she should put the baby to bed and try to unwind.

'Ok, bath-time,' she says.

She switches the television channel to something more entertaining. Sunday evenings are not great for her idea of viewing – too many programmes like *Songs of Praise* and *Countryfile* reminding her of her upbringing.

She switches instead to Sky. The perpetual news channel is broadcasting with an update on the latest unrest in an overseas country. Then a printed red band runs along the bottom of the screen 'Mother of missing baby to give news conference at 18.20...' Manon holds her breath. She has heard it on the BBC News too. She wants to hug Gwenllian close to her. How *dare* careless mothers make such a public fuss when they only have themselves to blame. She quickly changes channels to something that looks like a feel-good family film – something with children in the main cast...

Gwenllian is watching her. Her eyes are staring but there is a glazed quality to her expression.

'Are you ready for bed?' Manon asks.

Gwenllian stares back at her with no response. There are two spots of red on each of the child's cheeks. Manon feels a small stirring of concern.

She swiftly moves into Cheerful Mother role. It is well documented how negativity affects children's development, she thinks.

'Quick bath for you. Then bye-byes,' she says. Gwenllian gives a hiccup.

Manon sweeps the supper bowl away from the child and keeps up a stream of small talk as she puts items into the sink and runs the hot water. She dries the dishes and then turns to pick the child up. Gwenllian has fallen asleep in a slumped position. The overall vision sends a feeling of dread through Manon.

'Ups-a-daisy!' she says cheerfully as she lifts the child up on to her hip, 'Maybe no bath for you tonight. We'll be smelly instead and have a nice bath in the morning!'

She thinks of the News Conference she could not bear to watch. Losing a child was the worst thing she could think of; whichever way you lost the child, it was a thought she could hardly bear. Please don't be ill, she pleads mentally to Gwenllian, please stay healthy...

As she puts Gwenllian in her bed and feels the heat coming off her skin, Manon shivers. The thought of how many babies she has lost enters her mind. After weighing up the options, she wheels the buggy into the bedroom and parks it next to the bed. If the child has a fever, then Manon does not want to share her bed and body heat with her in case it makes her worse.

Maybe I'm jinxed, a voice in her head suggests. She shuts it up; thinks instead of what clearing up and cleaning she needs to do now that Gwenllian is asleep. Keeping a clean house will help fight any germs she may have picked up. With the vision of herself as the Ideal Mother playing repeatedly in her head, she partly closes the bedroom door.

37. Manon.

The crying cuts through Manon's sleep. In a second, she is awake with no doubt about who is crying or where the sound is coming from. Her instantly-awake self recognises this as the way *real* mothers react.

She lurches in the direction of the baby; driven as much by instinct as the injured wildlife she has seen on television when they try to escape their predators. There is a *warm* smell coming from the baby – she registers this fact before she can even start to work out what the problem is.

In another step, she can see that the baby has been sick and that her blanket bears the result. Manon feels an instant panic. This is not 'milk-burp' that all babies do at regular intervals. The child is ill – just as she knew she would be. Her mother's radar had warned her of this very thing before she put the child to bed.

Her mind runs through a list of possibilities – what could have upset her digestion? What had *that woman* given her? Manon thinks back to twelve hours previously – the thought that someone has given her baby something that would make her ill, creates a feeling of hatred in her mind. She should have watched more closely. She should have stayed at home... This last thought brings a fresh helping of guilt. This is my fault, she thinks. If she dies, it will be my fault. She begins to cry as she lifts the soiled blanket off the child and tries to make soothing sounds.

'I'm so sorry, I'm so sorry,' she sobs while she picks the baby up.

The child continues to cry. The sound is torture to Manon. I deserve this, she acknowledges.

She puts the blanket to one side, ready for its journey to the washing machine. She fits the child on to her hip and rocks her side to side but the crying continues. The lateness of the hour and the darkness seem to add an extra desperation to Manon's predicament. She begins to think about help; who could she ask? Do I really need help, she thinks?

She thinks it all through. What is likely to be wrong with the child? She tries not think about what she may have been given by *that stupid woman!* Babies were sick all the time, weren't they? It didn't mean anything serious... did it? And tummy bugs always affected little ones first... And they got over it quicker. She remembers Sadie missing a day from work because her baby had had a vomiting bug. And then it was all over and Sadie was back in work.

Gwenllian yells a bit louder, as if to remind Manon that the problem is *here* and *now!*

Ok, she thinks, a bug is nothing to worry about. Keep her hydrated – a spoonful of cooled, boiled water every half hour; no food and everything cleaned with Milton. She feels a relief wash over her – what a panic over nothing! It's what mothers have to cope with! Another sleepless night – she half smiles to herself – what a challenge motherhood is!

Gwenllian seems to be feeling better – the crying is easing and she is looking sleepy again. Manon half rocks her while she changes the blankets. She notes that her nappy also bears the evidence of a tummy bug but is relieved that the fierce heat she had felt earlier on the child's skin has waned somewhat.

She waits until the baby is more settled then puts her back in her buggy. The child's face is still pink but her general appearance is more normal. Manon goes to the kitchen to boil the kettle – she needs to have cooled water ready for later on. She listens for any sounds that come from Gwenllian. She has ten minutes of peace before the crying starts once more.

She rushes to her and sees that she has been sick again. This time, Manon's anxiety levels reach a new height. She automatically changes the blanket and puts it in the washing machine with the other one, grateful that she has not yet switched it on.

Once Gwenllian is settled, Manon switches on her laptop and Googles '*Meningitis*'. The results frighten her. She goes back in to look at Gwenllian and tries to see her skin. She remembers seeing a mild rash on the child's bottom when she changed her nappy. Gwenllian is too restless to accept another examination and Manon cannot see enough to give her peace of mind. She goes back to the laptop and eventually gives in and Googles '*Sudden Infant Death Syndrome*'. The results are even more frightening. She begins to cry. There is only one more person she can contact, but she is afraid to do it.

But she hovers over the phone anyway – if Gwenllian gets any worse, she will have to do it.

38. Manon.

It has been a long night. Manon understands that she has been panicking unnecessarily. Gwenllian is now over her upset tummy and is catching up with her sleep.

Manon almost wants to laugh at the way she has over-reacted to a tummy bug. The bungalow reeks of Milton bleach solution and every surface gleams with cleanliness. The laundered blankets are on the washing line and waiting to dry fully. Manon put them out there at the crack of dawn and feels in control of the situation. She has also washed the toys and wiped down the hard surfaces of the playpen and door frames in an attempt to kill any germs. She tries to think of any significant areas that she may have missed. She has a bright torch which she switches on to examine parts of the kitchen that may still bear the traces of germs. She wishes she had an ultra-violet light – like the ones she has seen on television crime shows – that would show up any nasty bugs, she thinks.

She goes over the hard surfaces once more – a quick wipe over with water so hot that it hurts her skin. The bleach solution stings her knuckles where she has a graze – the pain makes her feel happy that she is killing the germs that had the *audacity* to infect her little girl. She stops and checks herself – does she feel sick? No, she answers herself. She worries that she will be ill herself. How will she care for Gwenllian then? Just before her heart rate zooms up again, she remembers Sadie – she had coped. Manon remembers her coming back to work, her face white and drawn.

I'm better now, she had said. It was a challenge trying to look after the little one when all I wanted to do was stick my head down the loo, but you cope...

Manon keeps a mental note of all Sadie had said – she has been waiting to compare her own experiences with Sadie's. In reality, Manon has secretly believed that she can do better than Sadie – it is just a question of priorities.

Once more, she wanders from room to room, trying to ascertain if she has missed anything that should be cleaned. What about inside cupboards? Would the germs have got in there? She goes back to the kitchen and opens the cupboard doors. Everything in there is so clean that it looks new - nevertheless, perhaps she should do it again...

When she finishes there, she checks the sleeping child before opening drawers and wardrobes in the bedroom. This is where most of the germs have been released into the air, she realises – she wants to kick herself for not having started in here. She gets another bowl of scalding hot bleachy water and a new cloth. She empties all the clothes out of the drawers and puts them in the washing machine. She cleans inside each drawer, paying particular attention to the corners and joins – she knows this is where child-hating germs love to hide.

Gwenllian wakes briefly and Manon gives her some cooled, boiled water before letting her go back to sleep again. While waiting for the washing machine to complete its task, she begins on the wardrobe contents. She pulls most of the clothes out on to the bed – some of them are 'Dry Clean Only' – she considers whether she should throw them out? Inspiration strikes as she remembers the golden rule about heat killing germs. She takes the items outside on their hangers and lets the heat of the day do its best. Gwenllian starts to cry while she is outside so she rushes back indoors in alarm.

The child is looking much better but has a grumpy, dissatisfied look. Maybe she is hungry, Manon considers... Perhaps a small amount of food?

She scrubs her hands and prepares a tiny portion of creamed rice for her. Gwenllian takes it greedily, opening her mouth wide for the next spoonful.

'It's all gone, bach,' she says, 'no more for you for now. Just in case it makes you sick.'

Gwenllian protests – a loud yell which is not quite crying – then stops and checks to see if it has had the desired result. Manon hesitates – would it be terrible if she gave her a *little* more rice? While she ponders, Gwenllian ups the ante and adds an ear-piercing squeal to the previous demand. Manon feels her breasts itching. She rubs at them absent-mindedly. She knows that this is the sound that babies are programmed to make when they demand attention – a sound that almost *guarantees* a result.

She scratches at her breast again – if only she was able to breast feed – that was one way of providing sterile nourishment. She wonders, with a sudden bloom of happiness, if she *is* coming into milk. That would be wonderful! Though maybe Gwenllian would be too old to take it...

She picks the child up and rocks her soothingly. Gwenllian is feeling sleepy again and Manon lies her down gently in her buggy. Better for her to rest until she is completely free of her virus.

She turns her attention to the wardrobes again. She pulls out everything until all that is left is a carved wood jewellery box. It is one her grandmother gave her when she was thirteen. She feels a fullness in her throat and pressure building behind her eyes. Manon never kept much jewellery in it. As a teenager, she wore most of her jewellery and, like many of her age, did not have anything of great monetary value.

The chipped corner stands out by its lighter colouring – it is enough to provoke a sob from her. She reaches out and carefully picks it up. It is large for a jewellery box – quite flat and wide. The carving on the front is of a group of trees. She traces the branches with her index finger. She wipes her hands on her T shirt – she fears smearing bleach or baby food on this most precious item. She touches the pale coloured chip – it is only a small piece that is missing. It gives the box character, she thinks; being shaped by its misfortune – like me, she tells herself.

Matthew damaged me and it – we both bear the scars in some way.

The metal clasp fits neatly to its attachment. She caresses it rather than trying to prise it free. Finally she puts her fingernail under the metal loop and flicks it open to release her painful memories.

39. Manon.

Manon sits on the side of the bed, the jewellery box in her lap. Tears run down her face and drip on to her collar bone. She battles with herself not to cry out loud in case she wakes and frightens Gwenllian.

The smell of the wooden box brings back too many memories of a past that can never be regarded as anything but sad.

It feels like yesterday. Sitting on the sofa in the other house; crying and crying until Matthew came home.

***

He had been all concern when he had seen her; convinced that she had been given news of a terrible nature. For ten minutes he had held her and tried to get her to tell him what was wrong. Even though their marriage had, by then, been on rocky ground, he did not want to see her upset or unhappy.

Eventually, the words had formed themselves through her mucus-clogged airways.

'I'm not pregnant.'

Matthew's response was to wait for the rest of it. Correct, she was not pregnant. And...?

Before he said anything unwise, his brain had provided another solution.

'I know, I know, but we said we'd wait a bit longer...' He hugged her and rubbed his arm up and down her back. His face was on her shoulder and his ear was near her mouth. When she next spoke, it was a screech of anguish that had left a ringing in Matthew's ear for several minutes.

'I've lost the baby!'

Matthew sat back.

'I didn't... You never... When...?' This last question had been an attempt at establishing if she was still talking about the miscarriage the previous year.

'Just after I came home from shopping. The pain... and then it happened...'

She had continued to cry while her whole body shook with the force of it.

Matthew had veered halfway between anger and sympathy. Why hadn't she told him? He had a right to know these things... He had waited a few seconds to ensure he said the right thing.

'Are you ok? Shall I take to hospital? Are you... bleeding a lot?' He had been on shaky ground. Women's internal workings were not part of his repertoire of knowledge!

'Of course I'm bleeding!' she had spat at him, 'I've lost my baby!'

He had continued to try to hug her but she had retreated into her own cocoon of devastation. Matthew had done the only thing a man could do in the circumstances – he went to make a cup of tea. While he had been waiting for the kettle to boil, he had let his mind wander – something had struck him as not being right, though he was not able to pinpoint what it was. Perhaps it was time to accept that Manon had a mental problem, he had thought, before guiltily reminding himself how upsetting it must be for a woman to have a miscarriage. All women must react in the same way, he had thought. He would have to try to be more understanding.

He had turned his attention to the present. He would have to ring some friends to tell them that they would not be able to make it that evening for their birthday celebration. He had not minded much. Only the previous month, they had been to an anniversary dinner at the same restaurant and Matthew had not been hugely impressed with the meal they had been served. He had tried to push his food around the plate to give it the impression of being eaten, but it had been overcooked and devoid of flavour. He had been saved from embarrassment by Manon doing the same, though she had later told him that she'd had stomach cramps and had not been able to face eating.

The kettle had switched itself off and the steam had continued to rise from its spout like an appearing genie, but Matthew had stood there, his mouth slightly open and a bewildered look on his face. That had been... a month ago? Surely no more...? It had been a Wednesday. He remembered as his friends had also got married on a Wednesday and there were some dreadful pun-based jokes about the word 'Weds'. He had thought back. What else had happened to identify the date? Wasn't it the same week that the computerised accounts system had failed in work? He had remembered talk about that, too – no-one had received their pay. He had pulled his mobile phone from his pocket and checked the calendar on it. The date had been thirty-one days previously. What had Manon meant? Had she been pregnant then? Is that why she'd had stomach cramps? He didn't think so. A pregnant woman with stomach cramps (especially one who so desperately *wanted* to be pregnant) would have done more than simply mention it in passing. He remembered when she had had the original miscarriages. He was certain that she would have been on alert to the possibility of it happening again. He had glanced at the kettle as if surprised at the fact that was standing in his own kitchen. His heart had started to beat more rapidly and he had recognised the beginnings of anger. He had taken a few deep breaths and continued to make the tea. He had picked up the cup with shaky hands and taken it through to her. He had waited until she had swallowed a few sips before he attempted the first question.

'So, how long have you known you were pregnant?' he had asked (trying hard not to sound as inquisitorial as he felt).

Manon had shrugged.

He had decided not to give in that easily.

'How long?' he had detected a rising of his voice and he attempted to lower his tone quickly.

She had cried once more; her face in her hands and shoulders shaking. The cup of tea rested precariously nearby.

'How many times have you missed?'

The shaking shoulders stopped. Matthew had been reminded of a small dog his parents had owned when he had been a child. When it had a bone, it would growl a warning while it gnawed away with its head bobbing back and forth as it worked at the marrow. But if Matthew had gone too close, the movement and growling would stop and its head would freeze into stillness. As an inquisitive child, he had gone closer to the motionless dog – daring himself to touch its head. Suddenly, it would snap at him and return to its guarding posture. It had even bitten him on more than one occasion – earning him a telling off from his mother.

'Manon? How many times?'

He had felt the stirrings of fear but could not have explained why. The head-down, motionless pose his wife maintained made him wary.

She had snapped her head up suddenly. Matthew had jumped slightly.

'Once,' she said.

'How late were you?'

'What's with all these questions?' she screamed at him, 'I missed one period! Ok!'

Matthew had let it rest and sat down opposite her.

His brain had been whirring with possibilities – he had felt out of his depth.

'I'm going to have to ring Mike and Michelle,' he had said eventually, 'We can't go out tonight.'

She had looked sideways at him – a picture of misery. Matthew had felt his insides clench with pity. Had she lost another baby? *His* baby too, he reminded himself. Manon had leaned forward to rest her face in her hands again.

'I don't mind. The food was awful there...' he had tried to find a way to say it, 'Remember? You didn't enjoy it either.'

Manon had gone still again.

'Or was that because you'd come on that you didn't feel like eating?' this last question had come out as a snarl. He had not been able to help himself.

'I wasn't pregnant then!' she had screamed at him, 'But now I've lost another baby. You just don't *care*...'

But Matthew had got into his stride.

'It's not that I don't care,' he had said, his tone similar to a cross-examining barrister, 'I just don't understand the maths. Thirty-one days ago, you weren't pregnant – you said so – and today you say you've had a miscarriage. According to my calculations, that would make you about...oh... *almost three days* pregnant?'

He wished he had not voiced those inaccurate words – he knew enough about pregnancy from Manon's obsession to know that it didn't work exactly to those calculations.

Manon had taken in a deep breath in preparation for a protest, but Matthew had not finished.

'Now I think back on it, these miscarriages came quite regularly – about every other month, I would say...' Once again the words were out before he could halt the exaggerated claim.

'You don't care that I've lost my baby!' she had snarled at him once more.

Matthew had stood up – the light behind him turned him into a dark and threatening silhouette.

'There was no baby!' he had said, 'You imagined it!'

She had screamed more loudly – her shrieks forming words or parts of words that Matthew could not understand. She had jumped to her feet and attacked him with her hands – her clawed fingers had struck his face before he had grabbed her wrists and forced her down into the chair. He had been aware of the cup of tea falling on to the floor, creating a large brown stain on the spotless carpet.

When he had judged it was safe to do so, he had let her go. She had jumped to her feet again and ran out of the room – to fetch a cloth, Matthew had supposed at the time. But that was before he had heard footsteps on the stairs and then the door of the spare bedroom slamming back against the wall as it was opened in a hurry. Maybe she was leaving him, had been Matthew's next thought. He had recognised the relief that this idea brought him. He had gone to the kitchen to get a cloth to wipe up the spilt tea and returned to the living room and began mopping at the floor. A feral instinct told him that he was not alone and he had turned around to see Manon standing behind him. She had been holding a wooden jewellery box – he recognised it as one she had owned for a long time. His mind had suggested that she certainly would want to take this sentimental item with her if she was leaving him.

'Leave that!' she had said, gesturing with her head towards the spilt tea.

She had sat down in an armchair, holding the jewellery box carefully. Matthew had wondered if she intended to take his wedding ring from him, but Manon had second guessed him.

'I don't want your jewellery,' she had said, scorn turning her face into a mask of ugliness, 'I have far more precious things than jewellery in here.'

Matthew had begun to feel a coldness seep through him.

She had moved to the sofa and patted the seat next to her. Matthew had cautiously obeyed, sitting at the edge of the cushion, his legs tensed for a quick getaway.

'My memories are in here,' she had said. Matthew had noticed a softness to her tone.

'You just don't understand what I've been through. But you will,' she had run her hand gently over the surface of the jewel box.

She had slowly opened the lid and Matthew found himself straining his eyes to see the contents. All he had been able to see reminded him of a precious stone collection he had once seen on the Antiques Roadshow. Inside the jewel box had been lined with some sort of fluffy blanket on which were placed tufts of what looked like cotton wool. The centre of each one had a dark object nestled on top.

Manon had let her index finger caress the tuft nearest to Matthew.

'This was the first one,' she had said, 'You can't tell what sex they are at this stage, but I thought Cerys or Cerwyn would have been nice names.'

Matthew had noticed another feature next to the white tuft – a piece of white card embossed with a curly gold design. He had started to feel very uneasy. Manon had taken the card out and handed it to him – he had felt a reluctance to touch it, but clamped it between his finger and thumb. He had seen a date on it – 14th April. Underneath, in Manon's handwriting, he had read 'Safe in the arms of Jesus'.

His mind had suggested that he was having a very bad dream. He had not been able to make sense of it. Manon had handed him another card – this time with 13th May and a different caption. One after the other, she had handed him the cards – taking the previous one back and placing it next to the cotton wool tuft. In a sub-conscious part of his brain, Matthew had taken note that most of the dates were only a month apart – in some cases a day or two more. There had been a voice inside him that had clearly stated his wife was insane. He had suddenly realised that Manon had asked him a question and he had not heard or responded.

'Do you?' she asked. She had been looking directly into his eyes – he noted the beautiful amber brown flecks that he had originally been attracted to and had wondered when they had lost their appeal for him? When they had developed a psychotic look maybe...?

'Do you want to hold them?' she had asked in the tone of someone who was not getting answers.

'Huh?' he had said – the question had not been making sense.

She appeared to have taken his response as an affirmative answer and she lovingly picked up one of the tufts – cradled between both her cupped hands. Matthew had not even begun to understand when the small tuft was handed to him. He had held his palm open until it was placed on his skin. He had seen, with horror, that the dark shape he had seen was some kind of dried *blood clot!*

His reaction had been to bat it away with a gasp of distaste. Manon shrieked and leapt down to pick it up.

'Careful, Matthew!' she had shouted.

Matthew had peered over into the box and had seen each tuft of cotton wool contained a shrivelled blood clot of various shapes. He had felt his stomach clench.

He had suddenly understood. He had jumped to his feet with something that had been close to a scream.

'You're a fucking nutter!' he shouted, 'You put...' (He could hardly bear to say it) '...clots of blood in there. There was no fucking baby. You're a nutter!'

Manon had screeched and held her cotton wool tuft close.

Matthew had felt himself getting very close to the edge. He had wanted to *hurt* her. Instead, he had turned his attention to the jewel box. He had slammed it shut and picked it up. The thought of what was inside had made him gag. Manon continued to scream and ran after him but he had sprinted out through the back door and hurled the jewel box and its gory contents into the garden. The box had bounced once, then flipped open. White tufts of cotton wool and small rectangular cards had flown in all directions.

Manon had shrieked even louder and tried to capture each one before the wind blew them completely away. She had stayed out in the garden for hours, searching for the ones that had disappeared. When she had eventually come back into the house, her hair had been stuck to her face by the evening drizzle and her skin had been white from cold.

But Matthew had not seen this. He had long left the house with his belongings in a rucksack.

40. Pablo.

Police Interview of Pablo Abadjiev in the presence of an appropriate adult (Mira Daskalov).

Yes, I am understanding what you say. It is Pablo Abadjiev. I am sixteen years old since March. I live with Mira Daskalov at the Lucky Strike Fair.

She is my father's girlfriend.

No, he is not living with us. He leave the fair more than one year ago. I have not hear where he is.

My mother is living in Bulgaria all the time.

Yes, I know you want to ask about yesterday. It was not my fault. I tell Striker how to use gun. I tell him correct way to hold gun. He cannot understand why it not working. I tell him and tell him... I try to help him... he is my friend. I have tried to save him.

Yes, I can tell you from the start.

We come every year. We go to shoot the rabbits when the fair is not busy. The dancing is in the tent and there is no-one at the fair.

We go to shoot the rabbits with my father before he leave us. Last year we go with Lazer Boswell – he has also gone from the fair before we come back to this place.

The guns were in the vans where we live. One of them was my father's gun. The other one, Striker bring. He say we can go shooting rabbits without Lazer. I say, is ok and I will go too.

No, not me. It was Striker who have the idea.

Yes, he is more young than me, but his father is the man who own the fair.

Ok, we go first to some farms but we see no rabbits. It is too much daylight. We walk until we get to the horse farm. We have been there before. It has woods and many rabbits.

We go to the house to ask if we can shoot the rabbits there, but there is no-one in the house.

We knock the door many times but no person came.

Striker say we have walked a long way and we can make less work if we can go in a car.

No, we have no car. We are too young to have a driver's licence. Striker say we can borrow car from the horse farm – he know where is key. I say, *Striker, you are stupid, we cannot take car.* He say we can bring it back after and they will not know. He say we can take it on the fields only – that is allowed, he say. Then, when is dark, we can put lights on and drive across field and see the rabbits and foxes and they don't move when the light is strong in their eyes.

Yes, Striker have this idea.

No, I cannot make him change his mind.

Yes, a little more young than me but I cannot change his mind.

We go to the stable and see the car by the side. The key is hanging on a metal hook on the wall. Striker take the key and we go inside the car. He is sitting at the driver seat. No, only him driving. I say still, *This bad idea, Striker.* He is not listening to me. No, I have not drive at all.

No, I have not drive!

Fingerprints?

I remember – one time I try to drive when we are stuck in the field. Then I will have my fingerprints on driving wheel.

Why we are stuck?

Because we drive into field to find good place to stay and watch the rabbits, but Striker drive into ditch and we are stuck. He try and try but the wheels are going around and the car is not moving. Then I try to drive it also, but is still not moving.

We have to leave it there. Stuck.

I tell Striker we must go back to the house. We are in big trouble but we must go back and find someone.

I know there is no-one there but maybe they come back...

We go back and the door is open but we still cannot find anyone. Striker is hungry so he look in the fridge and give me some chocolate. I am hungry too. I eat it – just a little. Striker is thirsty also and he take some bottles out to have a drink. I tell him he should put them back but he say he is looking. We can take some food and drink to the stable and eat there he say. We cannot decide what to take so we put it all in our bags. We can bring back what is left afterwards... Then we can hear someone in the house and I am scared because we have the food and bottles. I call, *Hello* but no-one calls back. We are trying to go out when I hear a voice say, *Come in*. We are standing in the kitchen when a girl comes into the room. She is looking shocked. I say, I am sorry but I heard someone say *Come in*.

I tell her we are coming to shoot the rabbits and foxes like we do every year. She say it is ok and that she is looking after the children in the house. I say that we will not disturb her or the horses and that we will go. I cannot give the chocolate and bottles back to her in case it make her angry... I think maybe we can leave it outside when we go...

First we go to the stable and eat the chocolate and have some drink from the bottles.

It was wine. It was not nice but we were very thirsty. We only drank a small amount. Then we go to look for rabbits.

No, we did not tell her about the car stuck in the field. I was scared of making her angry. She was only looking after the children. She could not have helped with car...

Then we go to shoot some rabbits, but we did not hit any. We had a lamp but it was not much light.

279

I say to Striker, we must take the bottles back to the house. He say, ok.

We go back and it is dark but there are some lights in the window and we can see the girl walking upstairs. Striker say we can have a small joke and give her a fright. He say he can climb up the wall and put his face against the glass. It was a little fun and we did not want to hurt her. We had a little more wine because the night was hot, then Striker tried to climb up the wall, but he was sliding down and laughing. I was laughing too and I was trying to help him. Then I say, watch me – I can do it. I climb up and just looked in through the window. Something was breaking under my foot and I knock my face against the window and I yell. There was a child in the bed and she jump up and scream. Then another child jump up and ran over to the other bed. My foot was stuck but then I could make it not stuck and I climbed down quickly. I did not mean to scare the children. It was only a small joke to scare the girl who was looking after them.

We ran into the room by the kitchen so that she would not see us outside. Everything was quiet and we had some more chocolate and wine. We decide to stay there until we could explain to the girl that it was just a joke.

No, she did not come into that room just then.

I don't know, but it was after we fell asleep. She was trying to close the door I think and we woke up. I tell her I am sorry to fall asleep there and say we must go. She ask what we did to the children and I say, we do nothing, just play a joke on her.

Yes, she was a little angry, but when we have a talk, she is ok and say we must go. So then we go.

We go to look for foxes again. This time is much later and there are more foxes and rabbits on the ground. We shoot at them many times, but Striker was getting a problem with the gun. He had problem before. He hurt his hand and his arm. The gun was not good and it was hard to open it. I think it was not used for a long time. I try to show Striker how to do it but he is saying he can do it himself.

No, we are not drunk. We have not had so much wine. We spill some by accident.

Striker was trying to make the gun work. I help him. I show him how to hold it to make it open but he was not doing it right.

No we are not fighting. I am just telling him how to do it. No there was no fight.

I don't know about his face. I have not hit him. He is my friend. I have not hit him.

I don't know how it happen but Striker try to open the gun but he turn it round. I tell him, that is wrong way and I try to turn it the right way. Then the gun go bang and Striker fall down. I am so scared and I shout at him.

No, I don't think he is really hurt then.

I say, don't be a pussy. I think he is having a joke with me. But he is lying on the floor and crying. I try to make him get up and my hand is wet and Striker is yelling. I put the lamp on and I see there is blood all over. I tell him to get up but he is still yelling and lying on the floor.

I don't know what to do. I am afraid he will die.

I think of the girl in the house and think maybe she can help to phone for help.

No, I have no phone. We have no phone with us because there is no signal in this place.

I run to the house and call the girl. I go into the room where the plants are growing. The girl speak to me through the door. She will not open the door. I tell her to phone for help but she says she will not. I tell her that Striker has had accident with much blood, but she say it is not true. She tell me that I have her phone! I do not understand her. I tell her that Striker can die if she does not help but she will not open the door. I am angry with her but I have no phone and Striker is bleeding.

I am very scared and I run back to Striker. He is more quiet. He can make noise of pain but not very loud. I try to speak to him but he does not answer.

I think I must take him to the house to show the girl and then she can phone for help.

No, the car was still stuck and too far away in another field.

I try to lift Striker but he is heavy and making pain noise.

Yes, I can carry him sometime but I also pull him. His face is on the floor – I have not hit him. I take him to the house and he is sounding like a bull with noise inside his throat. It takes a long time to get him to the house.

I take him in and put him on the floor. I make his body sit by the wall and I feel all the blood on me. I think then, it is too late. I think he is dead.

No, I did not call the girl. It was her fault that she did not call for help. I was very scared and I need to go from that place. I am crying because my friend is dead. I go from the house and I not know where. I walk much and I am afraid to go back to the fair.

I know it was stupid but I believe he was dead but I am not sure. He was quiet and there was much blood.

I try to hide somewhere but then the police have found me.

No, I did not hit him.

No, I did not shoot him. I try to save him.

I did not take the car or the food and drink. Striker say we can do all that.

We did not make any harm to the girl or the children. We are only playing a joke on her.

I don't know why I hide… I am scared… Striker is son of Lucky Strike Fair owner and I will be in trouble…

It not my fault he is dead. It is the girl who did not call for help. I cannot do anything else to help him.

41. Manon.

Manon sits with Gwenllian in her lap. They are watching *Shrek* on TV. Manon is delighted that the little girl is back to normal and now has a healthy appetite.

She glances at the clock; the day is wearing on. She feels sadness – another day going by. Every hour with her is one hour closer to losing her. Her thoughts are lifted by a squeal from Gwenllian as one of the film characters leaps into action.

'He's a silly donkey, isn't he?' Manon says.

Gwenllian turns her head towards her and smiles until it turns into a giggle. Manon laughs back and hugs her – only releasing her grip when the child struggles against the pressurc.

Manon can see through the living room window; there are three elderly neighbours talking across the road. She stiffens. Are they talking about her? She sees one of them incline her head in Manon's direction. Another one waves her hand in the opposite direction. They appear to be having a very animated discussion.

Shrek reminds her of her duties; she turns her attention away from the window. Gwenllian has her fist in her mouth. There is saliva running down her chin.

'Let me see,' she says to the child.

She puts her finger in Gwenllian's mouth while the child fights against her.

'You've got another *toof!*' Manon says in delight. Suddenly it all becomes clear to her. Gwenllian has been ill because she is teething! She breathes out in relief. Motherhood is emotionally draining! She continues to sit with Gwenllian in her lap; she offers a running commentary on the film. Her previous depression has been replaced by euphoria.

The film ends and Manon flicks through the channels to find another entertaining programme that can be left on while she prepares a meal and generally cleans up. She is reluctant to let Gwenllian go from her lap but she knows that she must attend to her responsibilities.

She puts her in the playpen and again notes with relief that Gwenllian is chewing at her own fingers.

She talks from the kitchen while she prepares food. Occasionally, a loud sound from the television interrupts her monologue and she rushes back into the living room to see what is being shown on the screen. She does not want the child to see anything that will scare her.

Just before she brings the food in, she sets up the high-chair and puts Gwenllian in it; then goes back to get the food. She looks at the bowl with some doubt; is it too hot to have mashed potato with gravy and vegetables? Gwenllian, however, has other opinions – she stretches her hands out with fingers spread open. Manon feels a ball of happiness inside her – there is nothing quite as gratifying as seeing a child with a healthy appetite.

They finish their lunch and Manon begins to clear away the dishes. As she returns to the living room to give the high-chair a final wipe down with her Milton-saturated cloth, she sees a large, silver coloured Mercedes pulling up outside her front gate. Her insides clench as the smartly dressed woman driver gets out. Manon turns around in a complete circle – her mind cannot accept the inevitable consequences. She lets a small anguished cry escape her, then curtails it as she notices Gwenllian glancing at her. She rushes to the child and picks her up, holding her tightly against her. Gwenllian is too full of mashed potato to accept this embrace and she wriggles – following it up with a loud yell. Manon releases her grip slightly. She glances towards the kitchen – an irrational vision of the two of them leaving the house and running across the parkland beyond has lodged itself in her mind.

There is a knock on the front door – Manon jumps slightly at the sound, though she has been expecting it. She walks slowly towards the door with Gwenllian on her hip. She feels as if her insides are being drained of happiness and refilled with some misery-creating element. The shape of the woman through the frosted glass turns slightly to one side and Manon can see her foot tapping impatiently. She tries to delay her hand as it goes to the catch – wouldn't it be wonderful if the door had jammed and she was not able to open it – ever!

The woman's hand comes up to knock a second time, but she must have seen Manon's outline as her arm drops back down to her side.

Manon opens the door. The woman wears an expression of dissatisfaction. She steps into the hallway and looks at Manon.

'Well?' she says, 'Everything been ok?'

Manon nods her head. She cannot trust herself to speak. Gwenllian makes a loud squealing noise and Manon uses this as a chance to gather her thoughts. She rocks her side to side on her hip, making reassuring 'Sssh' sounds at her.

Before anyone can say anything else, the sound of a car alerts them both – a dark coloured car that pulls up behind the Mercedes. Immediately afterwards, a police car pulls up behind that. A tall man gets out of the front car while two uniformed officers exit the vehicle behind. Manon looks at them in horror.

'You just couldn't help yourself, could you?' Manon's visitor snarls at her, 'You promised to keep this quiet. Why did I ever trust you?'

Manon's eyes fill with tears as the three men walk up the path towards them.

42. Manon.

The police officers and the two women stare at each other for a few moments before someone speaks.

'You!' exclaims Sergeant Dai Morris, staring at the women.

Tegwyn looks at him. His question remains unasked but it is clear that he is waiting for an explanation.

'What do you want?' Manon's visitor says with undisguised loathing.

Tegwyn steps into the conversation.

'We had an anonymous call,' he says smoothly, 'that there was a baby at this address. You've probably seen the news... We're just checking any reports we get...'

The woman barely glances at Tegwyn before directing her remarks at Dai Morris.

'And I'm not allowed to have my baby here, am I?'

Tegwyn holds up his hand.

'You understand how worrying it must be to the mother of the missing baby. We have to check.' He glances and smiles at the baby.

'And what's your name, then?' he says while half-tickling the baby's foot – his experienced mind telling him that winning over the child is the first step.

'Gwenllian!'

'Taylor!'

Both women speak together.

'It's a *boy?*' Dai Morris says.

'*It's* a girl! She's called Taylor. Not that it's any business of yours what her name is. You blew it as a father. You're not getting the chance to mess it up as a grandfather. Though as far I'm concerned, she's not your grand-daughter in any way other than simple biology...'

Tegwyn turns to Dai and murmurs, 'Perhaps you could wait in the car for a minute...'

Dai takes another glance at the baby and walks away from them.

'Shall we finish our chat indoors?' Tegwyn asks.

Both women turn further into the hallway. Manon is still holding the baby. Tegwyn and the other police officer follow until they are all in the living room.

'So you are Sergeant Morris's daughters?' Tegwyn asks.

Manon shrugs, 'We don't have anything to do with him. Beth didn't want him to see the baby.'

'Why did you let him come here, then?' Beth replies, 'That was the condition. Only Mam could see her. You promised.'

'I'm slightly confused here,' Tegwyn says, 'How did all this come about?'

Beth takes a deep breath; it appears to calm her.

'My husband and I run a financial company – in Abergavenny – we had arranged to take some of the top producing Managers to York for the weekend. One of these corporate events - bit of team building and a jolly – all expenses paid... that kind of thing. My nanny lives-in normally, but she had appendicitis, so Manon came up to look after Taylor. Our mother stays in touch with us – though *he* doesn't know - and Manon asked if she could bring Taylor back here so that Mam could see her just the once. But I insisted that she was not to let my... that... *pig*... have anything to do with her.'

She turns towards Manon.

'So much for that deal!' she says bitterly.

Manon begins to cry, 'I didn't. I never let him see her or anything. We only saw Mam – we met up with her in the park - she gave her some ice-cream. He didn't even know I was back living here. There was an anonymous call! You heard him,' she nods her head towards Tegwyn as she says this.

Tegwyn and the other officer exchange discreet glances – their thoughts are clear – enough is going on in Llanefa at the moment; every officer is working extra time due to the shooting incident. They do not want to become involved in a domestic dispute unless it is absolutely necessary.

The officer takes out a notebook to jot down some details so that they can leave the house as soon as possible.

43. Manon.

Manon sits on the sofa and stares into space. Everything is quiet.

Beth has taken Gwenllian (Manon still cannot think of her as 'Taylor') home with her; the police have satisfied themselves as to whom the child belongs. Manon has a flash of positive thinking when she remembers that Beth has not questioned her about why she re-named the baby. She assumes that Beth considers it to have been an attempt to keep the child's identity secret from their father – she decides to tell her that if she asks at a later date.

She looks around the room; so many traces of Gwenllian remain here. Manon can smell the clean baby odour that has dominated the house since Saturday morning. She inhales deeply – it is like Chanel to her. Her breasts itch again. I'm missing my baby already, she thinks. She acknowledges that this episode of 'missing her baby' is far more real and poignant than the 'miscarriages' she has had.

She can see the future more clearly. Beth and her husband lead busy lives; Manon cannot see how Gwenllian will fit well into that timetable. The live-in nanny is expensive (not that Beth is short of money) and the cost of child care is a topic that her sister often talks about. Manon needs to think about how to plan the next move. She does not work at all now. How much simpler it would be if she moved in with Beth instead of the live-in nanny. She would gladly do it for free, she tells herself. She is good at keeping house; she is (in her opinion) even better at childcare.

What better solution than for her to care for Gwenllian while Beth runs her successful business. Unlike the live-in nanny, Manon is happy to forgo days off (unless she takes the baby with her) and she has never been one to take holidays.

Beth often has to spend a day or two in London or Belfast while she untangles work problems or presents a training day for other companies. She could do this with confidence, knowing that Manon would care for the child.

Manon can see further ahead – taking Gwenllian to school for the first time, school concerts, swimming lessons, birthday treats – even stopping at McDonald's on the way home from school occasionally; maybe Gwenllian would have friends who would come with her. Manon smiles to herself as she imagines being surrounded by four or five little girls as they decide what to order from the menu. What fun they would have!

Of course, she would have to be careful not to call her Gwenllian in front of Beth – or to the child herself when she gets older – that would be asking for trouble.

But, as Beth's busy work life excludes her from Gwenllian's activities, it would be her – Manon – who cared for her, solved her problems, dealt with tantrums and, much later, gave advice about boyfriends and clothes.

Yes, she was still Taylor now, but over the years to come, she would be Gwenllian eventually.

44. Anna.

Natalie sat in silence. The kettle had boiled and switched itself off. She felt unable to move from the kitchen table or take her eyes away from Anna's face as she sat opposite her. When she had received the text message from her, asking if she was alone and if it was ok to call by, she hadn't expected this outpouring of words. The more she spoke, the paler her skin seemed to get; it was obvious that Anna needed to tell the whole story and to someone who would not judge her. Natalie was not convinced that she was the right person to hear it. Her overwhelming disbelief loomed over her as Anna spoke.

'...and even though my... wounds... were healing, I was still sick. Every time I thought about eating, my stomach churned and I either couldn't eat anything at all or I would eat it and then be sick.

My mother said that I must have caught a virus and she phoned The Poacher's to say that I couldn't work there until I was better. She cancelled all the people who were booked to bring their dogs for clipping and bathing and told them I would do it at a discount when I was over it.

I just went along with what she said. It was easier that way. I just couldn't seem to make a decision for myself.

She definitely didn't know that anything had happened to me and I was desperate for her not to find out. I was just... so ashamed. By the second week, I started to get better but I was afraid to go out – I thought he would be waiting for me again. College had started but I was too scared to go. After about a month, I was able to eat normally and I asked Dad to take me to college and pick me up. He said I could take his car but I was just too scared to be anywhere on my own. I didn't think I would ever be able to go anywhere without my parents ever again. I went to the bus stop once, but when it stopped and the people inside looked out of the window at me... there were only four or five of them... I just couldn't get on.

Then something awful happened. One of the girls in college was killed in a car accident – coming home from clubbing in Swansea with her friends. She wasn't from Llanefa but you probably heard it on the local news. It was like some sort of switch and I couldn't do anything except cry all the time. My mother told me that I was depressed and that I should go to the doctor. We had a row about it. But then, when I thought about what had happened to me, it wasn't as bad as Marcella being killed; all those people who loved her and missed her. It really made me think – what my mother would call 'Count my blessings'.

We all went to the funeral – the girls from college – there were hundreds of people there. Everyone was crying but I had sort of got rid of all my tears. Some of the people were saying things like we would see her again, she would send signs and that we would all be reunited eventually. It all sounded like crap to me. Some kind of coping mechanism for those left behind – Marcella was dead and it was just too awful to take in. I just sort of faded into myself. That was the first time I thought there might be something else wrong. I was sitting in the church and everyone around me was crying. I felt myself floating away – like looking at it all through a narrow tube – I could see all the people and hear the organ music, but it was as if I was looking at a photograph of it and everything looked small and unreal. The feeling got more intense and then I felt so sick that I had to run outside... I managed to get out of the church and then I felt better. Everyone said that shock can do that to you, but, by then, I had accepted the obvious. I was pregnant.

I looked it up on the internet. Even if you are on the Pill, having a stomach upset can stop it working. I had had about two weeks of throwing up, so that was why the Pill had not worked.

The thought that I had his disgusting genes inside me, made me feel even sicker. I told my mother that the virus had come back and that she was right – I was a little depressed and that I would go to the doctor – although that was just an excuse. Obviously, the doctor confirmed that I was pregnant. I didn't tell him any details but I said that I wanted an abortion as quickly as possible and I didn't want my parents to find out. He said I was an adult and that any medical history was confidential between him and me. I was terrified in case he wasn't telling me the truth - my mother goes to WI with his wife and if she found out... I just couldn't bear it. All the talk and...'

Anna covered her face with her hands. The sound of two coughing sobs broke through before she regained control.

'I knew had to deal with it on my own and I planned to leave Llancfa anyway. That made me feel... stronger somehow... able to cope. I had saved some money ready so that I could go away so I used that to get a private abortion. I told my mother that I had been given some tablets and that I was feeling much better. I had to make sure she didn't suspect anything – she's really old fashioned and I was so afraid she would just look at me and know I was pregnant. I worked out what to tell her – that I was going with a friend from college to an interview in Cardiff and staying two nights. She was a bit unhappy about that but I didn't back down. Once the time came, I was very scared and I nearly told her the truth. I wanted to hug her before I left. I didn't though. We don't do that sort of thing at home and that would have made her really suspicious... but I needed to hug her so badly... needed to be her little girl and she could make things better... how stupid is...'

Anna broke down again. When the tears stopped, she blew her nose loudly.

'They were so kind at the clinic and I half told the doctor what had happened to me. Said that I hadn't really wanted... you know, but I didn't tell her all of it. She said that I could get counselling and that she could arrange it. I really panicked then; told her I was ok and that it hadn't been quite as dramatic as it sounded. I just couldn't bear the thought of all the people being involved and I just knew it would get back to Llanefa and I couldn't cope with that. They would all say that it was my own fault. Sometimes I think it was my own fault...'

Her face distorted once more as the tears came again. Eventually, she became calm. She looked at Natalie, her face bloated and greasy with tears.

'Have you ever watched *The Accused?* With Jodie Foster? She gets interviewed about the rape... She'd slept with a lot of blokes.... And, anyway, she says, *'I'm just some slut who got passed around.'* when they question her about her past and it's obvious that they think she brought it on herself. These films... you know... they're well researched. That kind of attitude really does exist... I just couldn't think of... especially as so many people would be on his side.'

Anna bowed her head and cried some more while Natalie shuffled uncomfortably on her chair.

'I felt very painful after the procedure but I had to get back home the next day. I was... bleeding a bit and they gave me a large sanitary towel type thing to wear. I just felt as if everyone could see it and would know what I'd done. On the train on the way home, a woman came into the same carriage as me and she had a young baby with her. I had been half asleep and the baby's crying woke me up. It was awful – like an omen. I started to think about what I had done. I had killed a real person...the wrong one. I thought about that again after...

I cried so much on the way home that an old lady and her husband asked me if I was all right. I told them I had split up with my boyfriend and she said that she was certain he wasn't worth crying over. I thought about what had happened to me and told her she was right and that I was being silly. What I wanted to say was that he wasn't even worth *spitting* over but that would have been stupid and would have attracted attention.

Deep inside I had already decided that the only thing I could do to make it all go away was to... I thought about getting off the train, waiting till it started again and... I couldn't see any way I would ever feel better. And then something saved me – a crowd of people – about eight or nine of them – got on the train. I recognised one of them from somewhere. They sat down near me and I could hear them talking. They were actors. Not big names, but recognisable. I listened to them joking and teasing each other about one of them having to eat hedgehog or something for a survival type programme. It just felt like fate – that I'd done the right thing. It made me determined to put all this behind me and aim for what I had planned all along. It was the first time I'd felt so positive since it happened.

When I got back home, I told my parents that we'd had a good time window shopping after the interview and that I had slipped and pulled a muscle in my back and that I would have to take it easy for a day or two. That gave my mother a chance to moan at me but at least she didn't suspect the truth.

I went back to see our family doctor later for a check up and he said that I was fine. I decided to start doing normal things again – sometimes it scared me but I had to do them if I wanted to plan my future again. I worked a lot and I didn't have time to think too much about what happened. When I did spend time thinking I either felt really better or so bad that I wished I had jumped under the train...The busier I was, the less time I thought about it.

I told myself that every day was a little bit better. In time, I thought things were going to work out for me, but that was a mistake...'

45. Anna and Natalie.

Natalie put the mug of tea down on the table and added a plate with her mother's home made cherry cake cut into slices. She sat down at the kitchen table; her foot hit against something underneath. It gave her an excuse to look away from Anna's distressed face for a second. She pushed the object away with her foot before looking up again.

'Sorry, didn't mean to stop you in mid-sentence,' Natalie said.

Anna gave a weak smile before taking up the story again.

'...and I was feeling ok about it - ish. It had all been arranged anyway. It pays well on Show days and I didn't want to miss it. It was on Cwm Isaf Farm fields again, but you know that...

It felt a bit weird, but I felt that I had to get on with my life – if I didn't, then he would have won. My parents always go away for August Bank Holiday and I had the house to myself – I didn't mind that – they can be a bit clingy sometimes.'

Anna stopped and stared at her cup of tea. She looked up; Natalie thought she looked as if she was on the verge of tears again.

'You know, I really, really thought I could deal with it. I thought I was a strong person.'

'You don't have to tell me if you don't want...' Natalie began.

'No, that's ok – I want to tell you everything. I owe you that after sort of involving you. You probably saw me at the show? It was a regular sort of day for me – the usual stuff – people getting drunk. Some of them were the ones who had been to the funeral. Owen was checking up on me all the time and I felt as if I was giving off some kind of signal to him – not in a bad way. Just...oh, I don't know what I felt. Like it was some kind of test...

Anyway, the day passed and then it was time to go home. I wanted to walk. To be honest, I didn't want to go in a car with anyone – too many people full of booze and... I couldn't bear it if one of them tried... And I wanted to make everything *normal* again... it was the first time I'd felt like that...'

Anna began to cry quietly. She bowed her head over her mug of tea. Natalie saw a tear plop into the cup.

'Look, you really don't have to say...' Natalie said again.

'I'm ok. Really. It's just, sometimes it all floods back, you know? It was so awful. I thought it would be ok until I went back up the path towards home again, I could hear footsteps behind me. Or I thought it was behind me, but the faster I went, I realised that the footsteps were in front. I slowed down and I was trying to work out how close they were but when I stopped, the footsteps stopped too. Then I could hear him calling me "Anna darlin", that's what he was saying – not really loud, not shouting or anything but I didn't know where he was. I couldn't see him and I didn't know if he was watching me. I was terrified. I started to run, but I didn't know in which direction to run. I knew he was playing games with me. I was afraid to put on the torch on my mobile because he would see it. Then the horses started to walk up to the fence again – I couldn't hear him, because of the sound of their feet on the earth. Then I stood still and listened – all I could hear was the thump of horses' feet. That made me more scared. I didn't know where he was and I just expected him to attack me again. I stood there for ages – I was crying and shaking. I almost felt like shouting to him to get it over with, but while I couldn't hear him I kept hoping that he had really gone away...

I don't know how long I stood there, but then I started to run up the path towards home. There was a bit of moonlight and I was watching out the whole time. By the time I got to the top of the path and on to the lane, I felt a bit better. I thought maybe he'd had his fun and was going to leave me alone. I ran all the way down the lane to my house. When I got there, I just stood in the garden for ages. The house was so dark because there was no-one there. We never lock the side door – it's sort of on the wrong side of the house – no-one knows there's a door there, you know? We lock the front door – isn't that stupid? I thought about phoning my brothers but I just couldn't think of how to tell them... But I did go into the house and switched on all the lights and went into every room. I was in the bathroom when I heard him again. Outside. On the drive. He was calling my name and laughing that horrible chuckle... It just made me want to die. I wanted to fall down with a heart attack or stroke or something. And...'

This time, Anna broke down into hysterical sobbing. Natalie reached across the table and held her hand. She stroked her arm in an attempt to comfort her.

'... and I was so scared that I... wet myself... all down my legs and on to the bathroom floor...' she managed those few words before breaking down again. Natalie felt her own eyes fill up in sympathy. She got up and went around to the other side of the table and hugged Anna. Anna clung to her like a child until Natalie felt the heat and wetness of her tears soaked through her T-shirt. The suggestion of the heart attack or stroke came back to Natalie's mind and she began to worry how much more Anna's body could take.

Eventually, the crying subsided into occasional sobs and bouts of shivering. Natalie got up and went to put the kettle on again. The un-drunk tea on the table had grown a thin film on its surface. Natalie glanced across at Anna – her face was so distorted with crying that she looked like a completely different person to the one who had turned up at the door after her unexpected text message.

'I was huddled on the bathroom floor for a while,' Anna continued, 'then I went to hide in the pantry. At some point, I realised that he had stopped calling me. I ran to my room, got my diaries and notebooks and just panicked. I don't know why I put so much stuff in the bag – I just grabbed everything. That's when I went to the police station. I was so stupid – running away from there – my mind was all over the place – nowhere felt safe. I really felt that the only way out of it was to... kill myself. I sat up on the quarry bank trying to pluck up courage to jump. That's where I wrote the note. Then, when I did jump, I didn't even do that right. Thank God your boyfriend found me and helped. He was great. He didn't try to force me to go to hospital or to the police or anything. Then, all that stuff happened with you and the little girls.'

Natalie flinched at the memory of it. They both sat in silence for a few minutes.

'I never even said thank you to him,' Anna continued, 'Will you tell him from me that I'm sorry? He's a good bloke, your boyfriend.'

'Well, actually, he's...' Natalie stopped, then grinned, 'Yes, he is, isn't he?'

'Anyway, the police had their statement from me in the end. It was a relief. I don't think they believed me completely, but...'

'What's going to happen now?' Natalie asked, hoping Anna would not ask if she believed her.

Anna shrugged.

'Will you... see someone... counselling and stuff in the meantime?' Natalie asked.

'I don't think I'm ready for all that yet,' Anna said, 'Too much unfinished business.'

Natalie looked up in surprise.

'What's unfinished?' she asked.

Anna stared down at her hands; 'There's something I haven't told the police. How I found out it was him. Not all of it. I haven't even told you about that... What I've done... They'll probably think I deserve to suffer after that. I don't deserve counselling.'

Natalie understood instantly.

'I know all about that,' she said, 'It's not your fault. I read about it in your diary.'

'You read them all...?'

Natalie nodded and looked away; she felt guilty.

'You know what I did...?'

'You didn't do anything wrong!'

Anna looked at her hands. 'All the time, it was like... whaddycallums... earworms – when a song sticks in your head and goes around and around – *we're going to have to get a bigger boat* – it just didn't make sense. And then, when I saw him again... and that smell of his soap... it was awful. I just wanted to die. It all came back to me then – one time in the Poacher's – there was some do on. That friend of Dai the Fish's – he's a bit slow. The others take the piss out of him; he said he'd caught a salmon *this big!'* She held her hands apart to demonstrate, 'He never catches anything much – he's hopeless, they all say. But he – *that fucking pervert* was there. And he was trying to be sarcastic and said, *you'll have to get a bigger net* – and that sort of got mixed up in my mind. Because of *Jaws* I suppose... Once I remembered that...but I didn't remember it until after – well, you know if you read the diaries...'

Anna leaned forward on the table and let out a sob, though no more tears came.

'All the time I didn't know who it was and then I knew and it was even more disgusting to picture him doing all those filthy... things to me... And then I knew that I wasn't afraid of him any more... And then... well, you know what happened...'

Natalie reached down under the table and lifted the bag that contained the notebooks. It landed with a thud on the tabletop.

Much later, Anna stood at the door, her bag slung over her shoulder.

'Thank you,' she said, 'You've been so kind to me. I don't deserve it...'

'Of course you do!' said Natalie, 'Listen, let's keep in touch – you know, as friends. Not because we have to go to the inquest and court and all that stuff...'

Anna looked at her. A small look of hope had appeared on her face.

'And if you still want to try the Newport thing, I'll come with you for an interview or whatever...'

'You would?'

'I'd enjoy that! Different to what I'm used to! Let's go for it!'

'Thank you. I think I might...'

Natalie reached forward and gave her a quick hug, 'Take care of yourself'.

Anna's eyes filled with tears again.

'Don't worry about having to go the police again,' Natalie said, 'It wasn't your fault. You'll feel better after you've told them the full story.'

Anna looked doubtful.

'Do you want me to come with you?' Natalie asked.

'No, no. You've done enough already... I'll let you know how it goes...'

Natalie nodded.

'What are you going to do now?' Anna asked.

Natalie knew she meant it as a general question in relation to all that had happened, but she chose to ignore it. She put a wicked grin on her face.

'What I'm going to do now is eat all those pieces of cherry cake. I'm starving!'

As she shut the door, she realised that she actually meant it.

I'm like Anna, she thought. I was trying to kill myself too.

She stepped purposefully and without guilt towards the kitchen table. After one and a half slices, she felt full. She put down the half eaten slice. Did she feel guilty, she asked herself? The memory of the skeletal image on the hospital's CCTV camera flashed into her mind.

No, she answered herself. One and a half slices were fine. The image of the bathroom scales also presented itself in her mind. There was no need to weigh herself just yet, she thought...

46. Anna

Addition to Recorded Interview of Anna Evans.

'...and I now want to add to the statement I made on that date.

I said in the last statement that I remembered who raped me because of the smell of his soap. That was only half true – but it wasn't just that memory that did it.

About a week before Llanefa YFC Show, I had clipped a Spaniel dog for Mrs Oates who lives in Llwyncelyn Road. I've clipped that dog a few times before and I always walk him back to her house because she says it will save her having to walk him again once he's come home. I charge her a bit extra for doing that. The only time I don't walk him back is if it's raining heavily – then I take my father's car.

I walked along the roadway into Llanefa and then took the cycle path around the little park to get to Llwyncelyn Road. I dropped the dog off and started to walk back the same way – I like walking, it gives me time to think about things, plan things out. It looked a bit overcast and thundery so there were no children that I could see in the park or on the cycle path. It was about teatime or a bit later.

As I was walking along, I could see a man walking towards me. As he got closer I could see that it was Tommy Elfyn, the ex-councillor. He stopped in the middle of the path.

'Where's the dog, then?' he asked me, 'Lost him?'

'Taken him back,' I said.

No, I hadn't seen him on the way to Mrs Oates's house. Afterwards, I wondered if he had been watching me.

He asked me if the dog grooming business was going well and I said that it was ok.

Then he asked me if I'd seen someone – I can't remember what name he said, but it was obviously someone I didn't know by name so I said I'd hardly seen anyone and didn't know who he meant. He just shrugged and left it at that. He started asking about how my parents were and had my oldest brother moved house yet. I just gave him some polite answers. Then he asked me if I was ready to apply to the Council for planning permission for the dog grooming parlour. I said, I didn't know. I was hoping to move away and get another job but I didn't tell him that. I hadn't even told my parents.

He said I should hurry up and apply to the Council before they changed their guidelines. I didn't know what he meant so I just agreed with him.

'Do it soon, now;' he said, 'I can help you. Got a bit of pull with the committee.'

He stepped closer to me and lowered his voice as he said this.

'I like to see people helping each other,' he said.

Then he put his hand up and touched my arm, winked and said, 'Darlin'.

Yes, it was the same voice!

I felt as though I had stopped breathing. It was like being nineteen and going through it all over again. As his hand moved, the smell of his soap wafted up and I suddenly realised who he was. I wasn't really lying when I said I'd recognised the smell of his soap when he came to the pub. So many times I thought I could smell it, that sickly sweet perfume. It just made me gag. And then it would be gone before I could work out where it was coming from... I couldn't even be certain that the smell was there at all... just thought I was being... oh God... I didn't want to smell it... and I did want to... it was so...

It's ok. I'll be ok. In a minute, I'll be ok...

Sorry, sorry, I just... sometimes it... I'm ok now.

Yes, I'll try to remember. I was just standing there. I didn't think I could move. It felt like, I don't know... ages, hours... it must have been seconds because he was putting his arm back down...

'We've got a good arrangement, darlin,' he said.

I just wanted to turn and run but my legs were shaking so much that I don't think I could have taken two steps without falling over. My heart was thumping so hard -- I could hardly breathe. I felt so scared. And then, suddenly, I felt very angry.

'You!' I shouted at him, 'It was you!' That's all I could say. Over and over. 'It was you!'

He tried to look confused as if he thought I should have known all along.

'You raped me, you fucking pig! You raped me!'

I was screaming this out and he was glancing around and making calming gestures with his hands.

'Don't be silly, now,' he said, 'just a bit of fun between us...'

Fun!

'You almost killed me!' I shouted at him, 'I wanted to kill myself because of you...'

And then I started crying and he was still trying to make me keep quiet and looking around.

'Look, now, there's no need...' he started to say something but I wouldn't stop yelling at him – I don't know what I was shouting – just swearing I think...

He must have been desperate for me to shut up because he grabbed both my arms and shook me.

Yes, shaking me and my head was going up and down. I was really scared again. His face was... awful... the eyes.

He started shouting. Something like, 'Stop it, you silly bitch! I didn't rape you. You wanted it! Stop your nonsense! Stop it!' Something like that...

And his eyes started to look scared and then I started to feel so angry. I broke away from him and stepped back.

'I didn't want anything, you scumbag!' I shouted at him, 'I'm going to report this. Then, let's see how much *fun* you'll have...'

I don't know if I meant that or just said it because I wanted to see *him* terrified – make him realise what it felt like. I don't think I would have reported it because I didn't want anyone to find out.

He just stopped and stared at me. His eyes were huge and his mouth was open. His face went really red, then white. He rubbed his stomach a few times. I thought he probably felt sick. I felt sick too.

'You've made me ill, now,' he said, 'Ulcer. All your fault if I end up in hospital.'

He stood up really straight, though he still looked pale.

'Go ahead,' he said, 'we'll see who believes your stupid fairy-tale. We both know I didn't give you anything you didn't want.'

I just turned and ran down the path – I couldn't run far; my legs were still shaky. And then I panicked that maybe he was running after me. I stopped and turned around really quickly. I was ready to... I don't know... kick him or... or something.

But when I looked I could see he was bent over slightly. I thought he was probably in pain if what he said about the ulcer was true. I didn't even consider going back to him. I felt that an upset stomach was the least he deserved.

I started to feel... safer... stronger somehow.

So I shouted at him instead.

What?

Well it was, you know... I was really upset. Do you have to know...? It was just, you know, spur of the moment... I didn't...

Ok, ok. I shouted, *Fuck you. Fuck your ulcer! I hope it kills you!*

I didn't mean... well, I did, but... I was feeling... Oh, I can't do this... I'm sorry, I just can't...

No, it's ok thank you... I'll be ok in a minute.

The he shouted at me and I heard him say something like 'My heart!' but I carried on walking away. I didn't think he would be able to shout if he had a bad heart. And anyway, I didn't care... I felt shaky but relieved. I realised then that I wouldn't report it. It felt as if I had got rid of my fear by shouting at him and seeing him scared. He couldn't frighten me anymore. He was just a perv. I felt stronger than I had ever been since that awful night. I heard him shout my name once, but I ignored it and carried on walking. I felt that the roles had been reversed and now that he was afraid of me instead of me being afraid and not knowing who to be afraid of.

It was the next day I heard that he had died and that a jogger had found him on the path. I felt... nothing... maybe a bit... but I kept thinking about what he had put me through. Should I have gone back when he called me? Did that make me as bad as him?

You're not really answering that question, are you? I wish you would tell me one way or the other... That's been going around in my mind - wondering if it was my fault that he died. And the memory of what I had shouted at him... And then I think he should have lived and been punished. I wanted to see him suffer, but I don't know if I would have had the courage to report it... I just don't know what to think anymore...

Oh God! It's just so... I can't... No, I'm ok... I think I've still got some tissue here...

I couldn't say anything to anyone and then I heard that the YFC Show was having a late start and a wake for him. It was too late for me to back out of it. I felt as if a huge weight had been taken off me. Almost as if things were back to normal. I hadn't walked through the Devil Tree path at night for three years. I hadn't walked anywhere at night for three years – I was too scared.

But I went to the show all day and I managed to keep it all together. But as the day went on, so many things were the same as they were three years before. The heatwave, the same venue, the walk home felt the same and I could hear his voice calling me and his steps following me, even though I knew he was dead. When I thought about it I knew it wasn't possible for him haunt me but... that voice... I don't know how that happened. Was someone else trying to freak me out? But it was *his* voice...I'll never forget that voice...I keep waking at night and listening. Sort of expecting to hear him again. I know that can't really happen, but...

Yes, I'm ok... really.

Yes, everything else I put in my first statement was correct.

I just want to say that I didn't deliberately kill him, but I'm not sorry he's dead.

47. Tegwyn.

One week later.
Most of Llanefa police officers seemed to be crammed into the CID office. The chatter continued in clusters; discussions about rugby, new cars and holiday destinations.

The door opened; Tegwyn and Alun James came through. The chatter stopped immediately.

Tegwyn sat on the edge of Alun's desk. He held a few computer print-out sheets in his hand.

He addressed the men.

'Just to de-brief you all, this investigation has been scaled down now. Most of you can revert to normal duties. We've got a few more statements to take and we're waiting to see if any more allegations come in. Those of you who have more statements to take, try to get them in as soon as. I want this all tidied up and ready for court. I've got a list here of who else needs to be spoken to, but all that will be done by CID officers. Everything else will be on the Bulletin wall so check it to see if your name is on and what you need to do. Any questions?'

There was a murmur before someone said, 'At least they can't close CID down now, Sir! With all this...'

Tegwyn pulled a face.

'Optimism is a fine quality,' he said, half grinning, 'but it wasn't exactly Crime Central here!'

Mike Connors gasped, 'If a rape, burglary, stolen car, a shooting and baby abduction doesn't rate as a reason for keeping CID, what does?'

Alun responded immediately, 'Not quite as dramatic as that, Mike. You missed it all while you were sunning yourself in Florida! Some of us were slogging our guts out here!'

'But, still...' Mike said.

Tegwyn added, 'At the end of the day, this was a shooting – probably manslaughter. There seems to be no evidence that the boys had been fighting - so not a murder. The burglary was petty – they took some wine and stuff from the fridge. The theft of the car was also linked to it. The rape, we now know, didn't happen that weekend, but three years earlier. Admittedly, we are going to have to go through all the historical allegations and any unsolved sexual crimes that he may have been involved with throughout the county. That will drag on for a while, but obviously there will be no prosecution involved...

And the baby abduction... well, that didn't involve us at all. The only action we took involved a simple...' (Tegwyn looked around the room to check that Dai Morris was not there), '... domestic dispute.'

'How's the child now?' someone asked, 'The vet's child...'

Alun's face took on a concerned look (he had recently become a grandfather), 'She's doing ok apparently. The twin was ok too...'

'What happened to them?' asked Mike – this was even fresher news to him having only that morning returned from Annual Leave.

'She became unconscious,' Tegwyn said, 'The doctor confirmed that she had something called Long QT Syndrome. A heart defect. Seems the mother had been giving her an over-the-counter allergy medicine after a cold or cough. It contains something that builds up in the body and can cause problems with the electrical activity of the heart or, more accurately, those with a particular heart defect. It's often genetic, which was why the hospital kept both children in for a while.'

'So the fairground boys didn't harm them...?' someone else asked.

'Not really,' Alun said, 'but anything like over-excitement, a fright, that kind of thing can set it off and cause collapse in extreme cases. Could even have been the heatwave...' It was clear that he had looked into the condition in detail – the actions of a neurotic grandfather. 'The babysitter didn't do anything wrong. Whether or not it was caused by the fairground boys, we'll never know...She was lucky that her boyfriend turned up with the car, though. Could have been nasty otherwise. The child will need medication from now on. And she'll be checked regularly. I doubt that the mother will ever go away without them again...'

'Ok, going back to the shooting incident,' said Tegwyn, 'We've got some property that needs returning. A bread knife, bloodstained clothing – that kind of thing – speak to Arwel; he's got the list of items that are not needed as evidence...'

'Like bottles of wine that need drinking!' some comedian remarked at the back of the room. Some laughter broke out before the remark triggered a question from someone.

'Had the babysitter been drinking as well? She couldn't even find her phone! And it was only lying underneath the bathroom scales, the Scenes of Crime boys said! And then she said that she was talking to this Striker boy through the door...impossible! The coroner's report kicks that statement into touch!'

Tegwyn sighed. It was a point that had occurred to him and been thought through many times.

'Well,' he said, 'going by the evidence, it's unlikely he that he was capable of speaking when Pablo dragged him back into the utility room, so it's highly improbable that Natalie had any kind of conversation with him just before she found the unconscious child. But, these boys had been pestering her throughout the late evening – she'd had many conversations with them. It would seem likely that the stress she went through just jumbled up the sequence of events in her mind. I think we can dismiss that part as confusion on her part. We're happy that she was not involved in Striker's death in any way. Hopefully, it won't come up at the inquest. That's all we need is for the media to start any *'beyond the grave stories!'* We'll have enough of that if this rape thing makes the headlines. And, before you ask, that's another case of stress causing mental confusion! She was obviously terrified – understandably. Her imagination did the rest...'

'Good for tourism!' Alun added, 'we'll have the world and his wife coming to see the Devil Tree!'

Tegwyn rolled his eyes.

The door opened and Dai Morris came in wearing a disgruntled expression.

'Someone has left boxes of stuff in the Sergeant's Office. Property to be returned or something...? I appreciate it's got to go somewhere but I don't want to be banging my bollocks against them every time I turn around!'

'I'll move them now,' Jamie said,' I'll put them in the charge room.'

'Good, good,' Dai said, 'Anywhere, as long as it's out of my way. You know the truth about eggs.'

Jamie stopped. Tegwyn and Alun drew in their breath.

'Actually, Sarge, I don't! What is the truth about eggs?'

Dai's face lit up in triumph. He slapped Jamie on the back.

'They come out of a chicken's arse!' he said. 'Fancy you not knowing that! No wonder you can't pass the Sergeant's exam!'

Dai forced a long chuckle and kept it up until he had left the room. Jamie's face had gone slightly pink. Alun covered his eyes with his hand.

'Well done, Jamie!' he said sarcastically, 'now we'll have some other stupid bloody phrase every bloody day! Go and move those sodding boxes!'

Jamie walked away. The back of his neck had gone red with the effect of the blush.

Tegwyn watched him go and was suddenly reminded of the minister who spoke at Tommy Elfyn's funeral. *'Salt of the earth; a good egg'* is what he had called him. It put a different slant on Dai Morris's now redundant catchphrase, he thought.

48. Manon.

November. The wind throws hard darts of rain at the window of Manon's bungalow. She sits and watches CBeebies on the television. A mug of tea and plate of chocolate digestives rest on the coffee table beside her. This is how she spends her spare time – watching CBeebies and snacking.

She feels let down by Beth. It would have been so simple to have moved in with her. She does not understand why Beth is so against the idea, but Manon refuses to give up trying.

She looks away from the television screen; the room still bears the presence of the child. The playpen is still set up and the high-chair is folded nearby. The plastic container filled with toys rests against the sofa. Manon likes to have these reminders in every room. Her bedroom has a stack of baby towels placed neatly on a wooden chest at the bottom of the bed. She washes them regularly even though they are not used.

The kitchen has a cupboard dedicated to baby items – feeding bottles, cheerfully patterned bowls, plastic spoons and a blender that she does not use for her own food.

The rain lashes the window with a stronger force. Typical Llanefa weather, she thinks. She remembers it from her childhood – it makes her feel miserable; it reminds her of her father.

Thankfully, he has stayed away since the day he came to investigate the anonymous call about the baby. She does not think she could have stayed here any longer if he had tried to make contact. She glances around again – strange how this bungalow has become 'home' to her when she never intended staying long. The thought of moving in with Beth has kept her here – she is certain that her sister will see sense in time. Meanwhile, there is nothing to be gained by moving – this place was difficult enough to find – she does not need the stress of finding somewhere cheap in another town. She doubts that she will find anywhere else at the same price – Llanefa is known for its cheap housing.

She checks the computer regularly to see if there is anything nearer to Abergavenny but rarely finds a small house that she can afford to rent.

It was just as well that Tommy Elfyn had helped her to find this place – it had been a life-saver for her. People said that he had been a problem-solver and they were right – although Manon remembers that he did not do anything for free.

He had bumped into her in Carmarthen when she was first looking for somewhere to stay. He had been the perfect uncle figure.

'Let me see if I can sort something out for you in Llanefa,' he had said, 'Your father and I used to be pals before that little nonsense with the cricket club. It wouldn't be right if I couldn't help you out. I know you don't see eye to eye with him now, but there's no need for him to know. I've still got some contacts at the council.'

And so she had ended up at this little bungalow – which was meant to be for elderly people only. Manon had not asked questions – she had been too relieved to dig too deeply.

After she had moved in, he had kindly called around to see if there was anything she needed – though she soon found out that he had an ulterior motive. The visits became regular and the payments she made were done gratefully. It was the only means of gratitude she had.

After he had died, she wondered how long she would be allowed to stay here, but so far, no-one has contacted her from the council. She hopes it will remain so until she has talked Beth round. She has become attached to this little place. It is probably due to the happy memories of Gwenllian. The thought of her makes her breasts itch again.

She rubs her knuckles against her chest to relieve the itchiness.

She gets up and runs her hand over the rail of the playpen – she imagines that she can still smell Gwenllian – the good smells of her, clean after a bath and even the bad smells of her soiled nappy and the time she was sick. Manon is suddenly overwhelmed by an urge to take the bleachy cloth around the hard surfaces. She battles with herself not to do it – she does not want to eradicate the olfactory remains of Gwenllian.

But the urge stays with her. She bends down to sniff at the playpen – it smells clean. Her fattened waist bumps the bar as she does so. Too many chocolate digestives!

She has never been fat before. She smiles knowingly. What a wonderful way to get fat! She strokes her hand over her growing tummy. How had she taken so long to notice it? When the reality had dawned on her, she had almost fallen down with the sheer joy of it.

After Gwenllian had gone, she had been so self-absorbed with feeling bereft that she had put all thoughts of normal female workings out of her mind. She had considered herself to be in mourning once again. It had not been until she had missed a second period that the overwhelming joy had taken the place of her misery. She had even bought a pregnancy testing kit on-line. She is going to keep the testing stick forever. She does not intend to have scans or hospital appointments. This pregnancy is hers alone.

Her breasts itch again. A wide grin spreads across her face as she thinks ahead to the due date that Gwenllian's baby brother or sister will be born.

A few miles away from Manon's cosy home, the stormy wind is bending all the trees along the Devil Tree path. The graceful willows give in to the pressure, their branches sweeping the top of the hedgerows in places.

The Devil Tree itself is fighting back – a rigid, quivering shape that refuses to be moulded by the storm. It shakes its arm-like branches and tail. The ivy clump at the top of the tree shivers as the wind tries to tear it from the bark. Beneath the ivy, the diseased tree bark shows through as a whitish colour. And, had anyone been walking by at the time and seen it, the whiteness would have borne an uncanny resemblance to teeth.

The End